A Yes or No Question

Lauren Monica

Book Cover Illustration: Kate Lozovska

Book Cover Design: Angelee Van Allman

Copy Edit: Kristin Campbell & Brittani DiMare

ISBN 979-8-9887867-2-6

ISBN 979-8-9887867-3-3 (ebook)

Visit the author's website at laurenmonicawrites.com

For my mom,
all I have and all I am is because of you.

CHAPTER 1

GRAHAM HOLDS OPEN THE door to the diner, allowing the rest of us to walk through.

I'm immediately hit with the sweet smell of syrup mixed with pungent fry oil. Stepping over a crack in the checkered linoleum tile, I inch past several boxes overflowing with things like sugar and flour. Although cluttered, the space has a warmth to it, like what I'd imagine a real home would feel like. Somehow perfect in its disarray.

We're greeted by a sign that reads, *"Seat Yourself,"* so we all file into an empty corner booth.

Avery looks around with that scrunched face she makes, probably noticing how different the diner is from the places we usually go. We're only here because it's close to the food bank that the two of us have been volunteering at for our high school senior project.

I watch her eyes drift over to the table closest to ours and land on a group of college-aged girls. They look as if they're wearing their clothes from last night, mascara smudged, and hair out of place. They're talking a bit too loudly, like they forgot it's nine in the morning.

I follow her gaze as it settles on another table that's occupied by two older men; one who's too skinny and the other who's far from skinny at all. They have enough food for six people spread out in front of them, with hardly any space left on the table. The skinny man is talking with his hands, seemingly trying to explain something important. He's becoming increasingly exasperated when he's interrupted by a girl, who gives a smile like she knows him and refills his cup of coffee.

"Damn, she's hot." Logan whistles, eyeing the same table.

I crane my head to get a better look at her. She really is pretty. Well, I don't know if *pretty* is the right word.

Her long brown hair is so dark it almost looks black, the color contrasting with the light pink uniform she has on. She looks like she barely put any effort in, yet she's still striking.

Avery shoots Logan a look that she tries to disguise as disgust. "If you want to slum it," she mutters.

"Still hot, though," Logan says.

Graham throws his arm over my shoulders, and I shrug it off, a reminder that I'm not his anymore.

I'm pulled from pretending to read the menu when someone says, "I'm Maria, and I'll be your server this morning. Can I get some drinks started for you?"

I look up to find a woman who's maybe in her forties. She has blonde hair with overgrown roots and is wearing too much eyeshadow. She taps her pen against her pad as she waits for our response.

We all order coffee.

"Cream and sugar?" she prompts.

"Do you have oat milk?" Avery asks.

"Sorry, hon. We only have milk milk."

Avery sighs. "Oh, um ... okay, I guess that's fine then."

I try to focus on my menu again, but my attention catches on the younger waitress walking past us. She stops at a table where a man is sitting by himself. He looks worn, his shoulders hunched in a way that comes from days of driving without rest. Based on his salt-and-pepper beard and leathery skin, he's probably pushing his mid-fifties. That, or life has been a little too hard on him.

They're close enough that I hear the routine words leave her lips. "I'm Sam, and I'll be your server. Can I get you started with something to drink?"

He looks up from the menu and freezes. His head moves back slightly, like he wasn't expecting to see her there, and then his entire posture suddenly changes. He rolls his shoulders back and puffs out his chest. "Well, hello. Aren't you a pretty little thing?"

"Can I get you something to drink?" she repeats with a slight edge to her voice.

"Coffee. Get me some cream and sugar, too." He pauses for a beat before adding with a wink, "I bet you know how to give some good sugar, don't you?"

Gross.

She drops her gaze to the floor before heading back to the kitchen without giving him a response.

I see how his eyes follow her all the way there. Well, more like they follow her *ass* all the way there.

"Don't you think, Susan?" Avery asks.

"What?"

She rolls her eyes and repeats herself, "Tell Graham that Red Window is so much better than Francisco's for dinner before prom. It's way nicer, isn't it?"

I really don't care where we go, but Avery will be a lot more annoying than Graham if she doesn't get her way.

"Uh, yeah. Red Window is definitely better."

Avery gives Graham a satisfied look. "See?"

Logan drops his elbows to the table. "We're still meeting at Graham's for pictures, right?"

They all look at me, waiting for an answer. Even though Graham and I broke up a month ago, I told him I'd still be his date to prom. I guess they're trying to see if I've changed my mind.

I paste on a fake smile. "Works for me."

Graham shifts closer to me, like my answer was an invitation, and I fight the urge to move further away. "My dad said we can use the Rolls-Royce."

"All right, man! Sick!" Logan says as Avery's face lights up.

Graham's dad is a big record producer, and he's never been shy about flaunting the perks.

They start talking about who's going to prom together, but I tune them out as Sam moves past our table again. She sets down the creepy guy's coffee, cream, and sugar. He orders and drops his menu down in front of him. As she leans over to grab it, I see his hand trail up her bare leg and begin to move under the skirt of her uniform. She quickly steps to the side and slaps it away.

"Don't even think about it," she hisses.

"Oh, come on. I saw how you shook that ass when you walked away. You were practically beggin' me to watch."

She scoffs, and he doesn't like that.

"Yeah, not a chance," she tells him coldly.

I look over at my friends to see if they're hearing all of this, but they're lost in their own conversation, completely oblivious to what's happening around them.

My attention shifts back to Sam as she moves to pick up the menu, but before she can grab it, the man snatches her wrist.

"Why don't you watch that tone of yours, huh? You sound like a bitch."

She pulls her hand back. "Then you clearly don't know what I sound like when I'm being a bitch. Don't fucking touch me again, or you won't like what happens."

He laughs. "You've got a mouth on you, don't you? I kind of like that. Makes me want to find out what else you can do with it."

Is this guy for real?

She gives him a pitying look and walks away without another word.

Our food has arrived, and we're all quietly eating when the sound of the front door crashing open makes me jump.

Every eye in the place shifts to the guy walking through it.

The first thing I notice are his tattoos. I've never seen someone with so many, especially someone my age. They litter his arms, down to the knuckles of his hands. He's tall, with scruffy brown hair and a look on his face that no one would want to be on the receiving end of.

He takes in the diner, like he's looking for something, or *someone.*

One of the girls at the table next to us leans over, propping her cleavage up, trying to catch his attention, but he sweeps right past her like he doesn't even see her there until his eyes lock on our waitress. He tips his head up in acknowledgment. "Where is she?"

Just as he asks, Sam rounds the corner, and he instantly moves toward her.

"Which one?" he questions, towering over her small frame.

She points. "The guy in the back booth, sitting—"

He's already heading toward the creepy guy's table, moving with such speed it seems like he's covering three strides in one.

"Oh, here we go," our waitress says under her breath.

What's happening?

Without a word, he grabs the creep by the back of the neck and slams his head into the table.

My fork clatters against my plate as I let out a gasp.

The creep begins thrashing, trying to get out of the guy's hold, but when he realizes that his efforts are useless, he stills. The creep's eyes are wide, expression utterly stunned, like he has no idea what just hit him.

Sam stays rooted in place, not looking surprised, until the guy turns back to look at her. He motions for her to join them while keeping his other hand firmly planted on the back of the creep's neck.

As I watch her walk toward him, I notice that everyone in the restaurant is purposely not looking their way. It's like they're pretending nothing out of the ordinary is even happening.

Weird.

The girl reaches the table and positions herself next to him. He glances between her and the creep and grits out through his teeth, "Apologize."

The creep hesitates before speaking, which results in his head getting picked up and slammed against the table again. The mug beside him tips from the force of the blow, and coffee pools around his head, dripping down the table.

"Now. I'm losing my patience," the guy says, each of his words clipped.

"I'm sorry, okay?" the creep spits out.

"What are you sorry for?"

"What?"

"What. Are. You. Sorry. For?" he asks slowly, enunciating every word.

The creep scoffs. "You've got to be kidding me."

"Do I look like I'm fucking kidding?"

The girl fidgets as the men stare each other down.

"I don't know what you want me to say, man."

Just as the guy begins to pick up the creep's head again, a woman who must be the manager rushes into the room.

"Jameson!" she scolds. "That's enough."

Jameson looks over at her and lets go of the creep's head, putting his hands up in mock-defense.

The man scooches back further into the booth, touching his head to check for damage. When he realizes he's fine, his expression turns hard, fear replaced with anger.

"This piece of shit was trying to get his hands up her skirt. You expect me just to let that go?" Jameson says, attempting to reason with the manager.

"You've clearly handled it. People are trying to eat here," the manager responds, surveying the room.

I follow her gaze around the space. Everybody's heads are down, their attention on anything but Jameson.

"Yeah, all right," Jameson says, looking over at the man. "I'll leave when he does."

The creep crosses his arms over his chest. "I'm not leaving. My food hasn't come yet."

Jameson lets out something that sounds faintly like a laugh, and when the man makes no attempt to get up, Jameson narrows his eyes. "This is the last time I'll ask you nicely."

"If that's what you consider asking nicely, I think someone needs to teach you some manners," the man snorts, motioning to the spilled coffee on the table.

Jameson juts his chin forward. "That someone gonna be you?"

A nauseating smile spreads across the creep's face. "Oh, it'd be my pleasure."

Jameson watches the man as he starts to slide out of the booth, turning to Sam just long enough to ensure she's out of the way. The man only gets one foot on the ground before Jameson lunges for him.

He grabs the creep by the front of his shirt, twisting it to secure his grip. The man swings at him, but Jameson dodges it with ease, and when he returns a punch, he doesn't miss. His fist connects with the man's jaw, wiping away that arrogant smile.

"Oh my God," Avery whispers.

The creep's head falls back from the blow, but Jameson snatches the man up by his hair to yank his head forward again. He leans in so only the man can hear him, and the color drains from the creep's face at whatever words Jameson gives him.

He mutters something else, and the man nods in return before he's shoved in front of Sam. His eyes are on the floor, his jaw already turning an angry shade of purple.

"I'm—"

"Look her in the eye when you're talking to her," Jameson interrupts.

The man's gaze jerks up in response. "I'm sorry for how I talked to you." Jameson takes a step forward. "And that I"—he swallows—"that I touched you like that."

Sam nods.

The man looks from her to Jameson before starting toward the door.

"Where are you going?" Jameson demands.

"W-what?" the man stutters. "You told me to leave."

"You didn't leave a tip."

"A tip? I didn't even get my food," he complains.

"And whose fault is that?" Jameson snaps. "It sure as shit isn't hers."

The man relents, walking over to the table and pulling his wallet from his back pocket, dropping a five onto the table. He starts to pocket his wallet when Jameson cuts in.

"Since you enjoyed the service so much, I think she deserves a little more than that, don't you?"

Letting go of a breath, he pulls out another five.

Jameson tsks. "Come on; you can do better than that."

"Jameson ..." the manager warns.

He holds up his hands. "I'm just making sure he pays for all he took."

Stepping forward, Jameson flicks his eyes from the man's wallet to the table, waiting until he sets down a twenty. "Now you're getting it," he says, dropping a heavy hand onto the man's shoulder, making it clear just how much bigger Jameson is. His hand tightens until the man sets down another bill. "Good. Now get out of my fucking sight."

The man doesn't need to be told twice. He practically sprints toward the door, looking nowhere near as smug as he did when Jameson walked in here.

Jameson shifts toward Sam. "You okay?"

"I'm fine," she assures him.

He watches her for a moment before he turns to the manager. "She's taking her break."

The woman nods as he takes Sam's hand and leads her toward the door. They pass our table on the way out, and Sam's eyes catch mine. Her head subtly shifts from side to side, as if she's trying to shake off the situation. Still, her steps don't falter as she follows Jameson outside.

I look back at my friends just as Graham says, "I know that guy."

CHAPTER 2

I STRAIGHTEN. "WHAT DO you mean, you know him?"

"I bought weed from him a couple weeks ago," Graham answers.

"That guy looks like a drug dealer," Logan mutters, mopping up syrup with a forkful of French toast. "What, were you just walking down a dark alley and you found him there?"

"No, I got the hookup through my friend, Dylan."

"Who's Dylan?" I ask. "I can't imagine you guys having a mutual friend."

"He's the guitarist for the band Lights Out. You know that local group my dad just started working with?"

We all nod.

"They've been hanging around the studio, recording their first album. They were all smoking and invited me to join. I asked him who he was buying from, and he told me about Jameson." He pauses. "He definitely has a reputation, but that was insane."

Avery scoffs. "Uh, yeah. I wouldn't want to be on his bad side."

"When Dylan took me to meet him, he told me to watch myself around Jameson's girl," Graham says. "I wasn't really sure what he meant then, but it makes sense now."

"I bet he gets into a lot of fights over that one," Logan mumbles through a mouthful of food.

Avery swats his arm. "What's that supposed to mean?"

"Oh, come on. She's sex on legs. I bet she's never met a guy who didn't want to sleep with her."

Avery rolls her eyes.

"She seems like a real handful," Graham says.

"I'd take a handful or two of her any day," Logan cuts in. "Crazy chicks are always the most fun, especially when they look like that."

Avery pushes her plate away. "Really, Logan? Are you ever going to stop?" She slips out of the booth, and he throws his head back with a groan before following after her, nearly running over our waitress in the process before she steps back to let him by.

She releases a sigh. "It's not even lunch, and I can already tell it's going to be one of those days." Rummaging through her apron, she sorts through a stack of checks before setting ours on the table. "Bring this up front to pay," she says, motioning to the woman behind the counter. "Lucy will get you settled."

"Thank you," I respond with a smile.

We go to pay, and I tell Graham that I've got it. He asks me if I'm sure, and I wave him off. I run the credit card my parents gave me and leave our waitress a hundred-dollar tip, hoping it helps her bad day turn into a good one.

Graham leans his hip against the counter. "What time do you have to start your shift?"

"Eleven. What time is it?"

"Five till," he answers.

I start for the door. "How is it already that late? I'm barely going to make it."

"It's not like they can fire you. Who cares if you're late?"

"I care," I say, stepping outside and scanning the street for Avery and Logan.

Pulling out my phone, I dial Avery's number. It rings three times before she picks up. "Where are you?"

"I'm at the food bank," she replies. "You should hurry up. I think you're the last one."

"I'm coming," I say before hanging up.

She doesn't sound upset anymore, so she must have settled things with Logan. I don't know how she deals with the constant ups and downs.

They're more than friends but have never dated. Instead, they throw their flings in each other's faces, attempting to make the other jealous. As if by doing so, they'll finally admit what they really are. It's exhausting.

"She's already there," I tell Graham. "I'm the last one, so I've got to hurry."

"Okay, I'll see you later," he says, leaning toward me.

I take a step back. "I really have to go."

He nods stiffly. "Yeah, all right. Text me later. Maybe we can do something."

"Sure," I call over my shoulder, already heading down the street.

Maybe I shouldn't be so quick to judge Avery and Logan. Things with me and Graham aren't much better.

He's trying to win me back after I broke up with him last month because I walked in on him kissing Ava Thompson at a party.

The thing is, when I saw him wrapped around her, his lips moving over hers, I felt nothing. If anything, I felt a sense of relief. We'd been going out for about seven months before I broke it off.

At first, things had been good. He was romantic. He planned dates, got me little gifts. He really tried. My parents loved him, and we became a sort of "it couple" at school. Everybody said how great we were together, so I believed them. Or, at least I tried to.

He made sense on paper, and he did things that made me feel special, but I never felt all the way in. I thought it would become easier with time, but it only became more difficult.

I began to feel like a thing he possessed rather than a person. After a few months, it was like the shine had worn off. I wasn't a thing for him to chase anymore. It was as if he'd gotten bored of me.

I thought about ending it a few times and wondered if maybe he would, too, but I think he loved the image of us together too much.

We were the perfect couple, and it was hard to give that up. The pressure from the outside, our parents, our friends, it was like a third person in our relationship. So, we both stayed and pretended like we were as perfect behind closed doors as we were in the minds of everyone around us.

Until I caught him cheating and couldn't pretend anymore.

The only people who know what happened are Avery and Logan. Well, and I guess Ava Thompson. I don't want everyone to know my business, but I think Graham is holding out hope that we'll get back together since nobody knows he cheated.

What he doesn't know is that his cheating was just my excuse. It was the out I had been looking for.

I don't regret breaking up with him, but I didn't expect it to be so hard to have him around all the time. He's Logan's best friend, and the four of us are always together. It's like a package deal—if I want to have my friends, I have to have Graham, too.

They've been trying to get me to give him a second chance. They swear he was drunk. That it was just a meaningless kiss.

Sometimes, I think it would be easier to get back together. It would be less awkward, and things could go back to how they used to be. But when I think about how things were, I wonder if they were really that good to begin with.

So, now we exist in this weird in-between. The lines are still blurred, since he's in my friend group and I know he wants me back. I've told him that will never happen. I've said it to Avery and Logan, too. I just don't think any of them actually believe me.

I rush into the stockroom, finding Leah already in the middle of her announcements. Avery waves me over to where she's standing at the front of the room, and I'm relieved when Leah sends me a warm smile, not seeming bothered that I'm late.

I tune in to what she's saying, trying to make myself focus.

"… have a new member joining our team." She gestures toward a girl standing in the corner by herself. "This is Samantha Barlowe."

Avery taps my arm. "Susan, it's—"

I suck in a breath. "The girl from the diner." *What's she doing here?*

She takes a step forward, crossing her arms over her chest. "It's Sam," she bites back.

She's changed out of her work uniform, the old-fashioned dress replaced with ripped jean cutoffs and a black muscle tee that dips down, revealing a small tattoo and a black lace bralette.

Leah rocks on her feet nervously. "I'm sorry. This is *Sam* Barlowe. Since all of you have been here for several months now, please be available to help her with any questions she may have."

"Where's her partner?" the guy in front of me asks.

Leah appears uneasy again, like she isn't sure how to answer the question. She quickly looks to Sam as if she's asking her what to say, but Sam only stares back blankly, giving no indication that she's going to acknowledge the boy's question.

"Um, Samantha ..." Leah starts but corrects herself when Sam shoots her a glare. "Sorry, I mean Sam." She clears her throat. "Sam doesn't go to Crestview, so she's not participating in your senior project."

I could have guessed that. There's clearly something she's leaving out, though.

"Then why is she here?" someone whispers.

"She's probably doing community service," the girl beside me responds quietly.

"What do you mean *community service?*"

"Like because she was arrested," the girl answers, turning toward Sam. "I mean, look at her. Why else would she be here?"

I follow their gazes, landing on Sam, and find her face expressionless. Her features are so void of emotion that it must be practiced. It's as if she's carefully crafted this guard she can put up whenever she feels she needs its protection. *Like after the morning she just had.*

Leah shifts the conversation and starts giving out the assignments for the day. Since Sam has no partner, Leah tells us she'll be paired up with one of our groups. Everyone drops their eyes, trying to avoid that uncomfortable moment when groups are assigned and nobody wants that last person standing.

Has she actually been arrested? And if she was, what did she do? It must not have been too bad if she isn't in jail, right?

Distracted by my thoughts, I look up, and just as I do, I catch Leah's attention.

Nodding toward us, she says, "Sam, why don't you pair up with Susan and Avery?"

CHAPTER 3

I OFFER SAM A small smile as she walks over to us, but I don't get one in return.

Does she know I was at the diner earlier? She looked right at me, but maybe she was too caught up in everything to remember.

She stares back at me with that same mask of indifference tightly in place, and I let go of the idea that she remembers me.

Our group's task for the day is to organize the batch of canned donations that came in this week, so we all head back to that section of the stockroom and begin working.

An uneasy silence consumes the first few minutes. It would feel weird for Avery and me to talk amongst ourselves and exclude Sam, but it's clear that neither of us knows what to say to her, and we definitely aren't planning on mentioning what we saw at the diner.

Sam doesn't seem to mind the quiet at all. It's almost like she's forgotten we're here.

What must be ten minutes go by before I decide to be the one to start a conversation. I tell myself that I'm just trying to be nice, but really, it's because I'm curious. I want to see what she'll say, what she's like.

"Hey. It's nice to meet you," I start then question my choice of words the minute they leave my lips. It only makes me feel more unsure when all she does is stare back at me with that same blank look on her face. "Um, I'm Susan, and this is Avery," I try again. "We both go to Crestview."

Avery leans around me to say hello, but I can tell it's forced.

Still, Sam just stands there.

"Where do you go?" I ask, looking at Avery for help, but she only gapes back at me, wide-eyed, like she's trying to tell me to stop talking.

"Lincoln," Sam responds.

"Oh, cool," I say lamely, trying to think of something else to ask. "Are you a senior?"

She nods, just as Leah comes over, and I'm thankful for the distraction.

"Hey, girls." She beams. "This all looks great. I'll have Aiden carry in the last batch of boxes, and once you get those unloaded, you're free to go. Oh, and don't forget to come get your sheets signed when you're done."

She starts to walk away then turns back. "Actually, Avery, I have some filing I need help with in my office. Do you think I can steal you away?" She looks between me and Sam. "You've got this covered, right?"

Avery's shoulders drop, clearly relieved to get away from Sam.

"Of course," I answer.

"I'll text you later," Avery calls over her shoulder.

Aiden drops off the final boxes, adding to our existing stack, and we start unloading them without a word to each other. I decide I'm not going to say anything unless she does, so I'm left with only the sound of cans clanking together to keep me company until she finally breaks the silence.

"I don't need to tell you to forget about what you saw, right?" she says without looking at me. There's an edge to her voice mixed with something else. Fear, maybe?

My stomach sinks. *She does remember me.*

"There was nothing wrong with what I saw," I reply, surprising myself.

At that, she turns and catches my eye, clearly not expecting that response.

"I saw what that man did," I clarify.

She remains quiet for so long that I think she's done talking, but then she says almost to herself, "He just wouldn't stop." She shakes her head ever so slightly, just like she did when she walked past me in the diner, as if expecting the act to clear the memory away. "And your friends?"

"What about them?"

She raises an eyebrow.

"Oh, no, they're not going to say anything."

I leave out that Graham knows who Jameson is and the fact that after what we saw, we'd all be stupid to start anything with him.

Nodding, she leans over to grab another can when a phone starts ringing. She realizes it's hers and pulls it from her back pocket to answer. The other side of the line is muffled, so I can only make out her side of the conversation.

She fidgets, peeling away the label of the can she just set down as she listens. Then she nods in understanding, as if the person she's talking to can see her. "No, it's fine. I'll just catch the bus." Reaching for another can, she says, "Yeah, I will. Okay, see you tonight." She tucks the phone into her pocket and turns back to the box of cans.

A few minutes pass before I get up the courage to ask, "Do you need a ride home?"

She stills. "You want to give me a ride?"

"I mean, if you need one. I don't have anywhere I need to be."

Wow, that sounds pathetic.

Just when I think she's going to laugh at me for offering, she shrugs. "Yeah, that'd be cool."

We keep to ourselves as we finish stocking. Sam seems to be lost somewhere inside herself, so I don't attempt any small talk.

I empty my box before she does, so I help with the last of her cans. Once we've broken down the boxes, we head to Leah's office to get our sheets signed.

"All finished?" she asks when we reach her desk.

I hand her my sheet. "Yup. We set the broken-down boxes out by the dumpster."

"That's perfect," she says. "Thanks for all your help here. I probably won't see you again since your project hours are finished, so best of luck in college."

"Thank you. I had a great time."

Sam snorts, and it draws Leah's attention. She reaches her hand out. "Your sheet?" she asks, all the warmth in her voice gone.

Sam drops it on the desk, and Leah signs it before passing it back. "I'll see you on Monday."

Sam salutes her. "Can't wait." Then she turns and strides out of the room.

Leah sighs, muttering something under her breath.

I give her a small wave. "Bye."

She forces a smile. "Bye, honey."

I catch up with Sam, and once we're outside, she says, "Lead the way."

We walk to the back lot, but when we reach my car, she stops short. "This one's yours?"

"Uh, yeah," I answer, not quite sure how else to respond.

My parents bought me a BMW for my sixteenth birthday, which I hate. It's not that I don't appreciate them getting me a car—really, I do—it's just … I hate that they got me *this* car.

It feels obnoxious to drive something so nice, especially since I didn't earn the money to pay for it. To my friends, it's normal to drive this kind of car, but in situations like these, it makes me feel like I have to prove that I'm not some stuck-up brat.

"Nice," she says, and I can't tell if she's being genuine. She rounds the car before settling into the passenger seat. I follow, getting behind the wheel and watch as she shuts the door gently.

"Where do you want me to drop you off?"

She leans back. "Do you know where the old drive-in movie theater is?"

There are still drive-in movie theaters?

By the look on my face, she must realize that I have no idea what she's talking about, so she says, "I'll just direct you."

I nod and move to put on my seat belt as she starts rummaging through her purse and tossing things onto her lap. She has one of those purses that's like a magician's bag, the ones that somehow seem to hold an endless supply of random things. Piling on her lap are a tangled-up mess of necklaces, a half-eaten bar of Hershey's chocolate, a black lighter with dice on it, a book with a cover that's barely still attached, a tube of lipstick, and a pack of cigarettes that she soon realizes is empty.

"Fuck," she says to herself then begins digging through the bag again, shaking its contents almost manically until she finally pulls out a slightly bent single cigarette. She lights it and glances over at me expectantly. "Are you waiting for something?"

"Oh, no. Sorry." I shift the car into drive, trying not to think about the fact that she's smoking in my car.

She rolls down her window as we pull out of the parking lot. Flicking the ash off her cigarette, she says, "It's a left here."

She continues to give me directions as our surroundings become increasingly run-down. The buildings we pass are boarded up and tagged with graffiti. The grass around the shopping plazas is overgrown and lack the manicured plants and flowers I'm used to.

We get farther from the main road and start taking turns that bring us closer to a worn-out-looking neighborhood.

I might be imagining it, but it seems like she's continually glancing over at my speedometer.

Am I driving too slowly? We just passed a speed limit sign that said forty, and that's how fast I'm going.

Sam points up ahead to a place called Junior's Food and Liquor. "Can you swing by the corner store real quick?"

"Yeah, sure," I answer and signal to take a right into the parking lot of the small market.

Putting the car in park, I'm not sure if I'm supposed to go inside with her. Not wanting to ask, I decide to just follow her in.

We pass by three older men crouching next to one of those big ice freezers, except this one is missing its doors and there are no bags of ice inside. One of them takes a swig from a bottle covered in a brown paper bag while the other two speak animatedly to each other, waving their hands around and pointing to the dice and bills between them. Hearing us approach, they look up and stop their conversation.

"Look who it is," one of them says, jerking his chin up at Sam.

"How're you doing, Joe?"

"Better now that you're here, hon."

She lets out a small laugh. "Yeah, I'm sure you are."

One of the other guys shifts his gaze to me, and I find myself instinctively moving a step behind Sam. "Who's this doll you've got yourself with? Looks like she'd get eaten right up hanging around with you."

"What's that supposed to mean, Al?" she replies, faking offense.

He gives her a devious smile. "You know exactly what I mean, sweetheart."

When she doesn't answer, the third man says, "Well, aren't you gonna introduce us?"

"This is Susan," she tells him with no further explanation.

"Susan," he echoes, enunciating each syllable like he's testing the name out. The look he's giving me makes my stomach curl.

Sam doesn't show it, but I think she feels it, too, because she says, "Yeah, all right. We've got places we've gotta be."

We don't. Well, at least I don't.

"See you around," she calls out as she begins walking toward the front door.

They all grunt their goodbyes as they watch us walk away.

Stepping inside, I'm met with an overwhelming smell of floor cleaner and coffee. I've never been in a store like this before, but it just looks like a little grocery store.

I follow Sam up to the front, and we wait behind a woman who's clearly too old to be wearing a skirt as short as the one she has on. She's smacking her gum loudly as she impatiently taps her dirty flip flop.

Once it's our turn, we walk up to the counter and are greeted by a guy who looks maybe twenty.

"Sam," he says in greeting as he moves to grab a pack of the same kind of cigarettes she pulled out of her bag earlier.

Does she know everyone?

"Eight thirty-five," he tells her as she searches through her bag, pulling out crumpled dollar bills and laying them on the counter in a messy stack.

As she continues to search, he says, "I've been trying to get a hold of Jameson."

She looks up briefly. "He's been busy, but I'll let him know."

He rubs his hand nervously up and down his arm. "Yeah, of course. No biggie. Are you still stopping by Dougie's tonight?"

"We'll see how it goes, but we'll probably swing by."

He nods and just then seems to realize that I'm here. "Who's this?"

She must not hang out with a lot of people if everybody's this curious about who I am. Or maybe it's because nobody's seen me before. Everybody seems to know everybody somehow.

"This is Susan," she replies again, leaving it at that.

"She coming tonight?" he asks her, but his eyes are still on me.

"Oh, uh, probably not," she says, still shuffling through her purse for stray money. Blowing out a breath, she looks up at him. "I've only got seven dollars and like"—she counts out the coins on the table—"sixteen cents."

"Don't worry about it." He winks, sweeping the money off the counter.

She grabs the pack. "Thanks."

The register dings as the bottom drawer slides open. "Hope to see you tonight."

When Sam doesn't answer, I glance up and realize he's talking to me.

"Oh, um ..." I start, fumbling over my words.

"We've gotta go. Come on," Sam says, angling her head toward the door.

I follow behind her, thankful that she cut in again.

Once we're back in the car, she turns toward me. "He's not for you."

"What?"

"If you see him again, just stay away, okay?"

What's wrong with him? He seemed nice.

She's staring at me, and I realize she's waiting for an answer.

"Okay," I assure her.

I don't know why it matters. It's not like he's someone I'll ever run into again.

CHAPTER 4

I PULL BACK OUT onto the main road, lost in thought, when the sound of Sam hitting the pack of cigarettes against her hand brings me back into the moment. She rolls down the window again as she lights one.

Wow, she smokes a lot.

Pointing, she says, "Take this left."

Her phone begins to ring as I'm turning, and she shifts onto her side so she can pull it out of her back pocket. Something must have happened when she moved, because she starts cursing, which makes me look over in her direction.

She's frantically trying to grab something off the ground before stomping her foot on it. It's then that I smell burning and realize she's dropped her cigarette.

She seems to have successfully put it out, but it's too late. A horrible crunching noise rings though the car as my head slams back against the seat. My body locks up, my fingers curling around the steering wheel, when I realize I've just driven over a median.

Both of our eyes drop to the cigarette burn that now mars the mat under her feet, knowing that it's the cause of the accident.

She picks it up and brushes her foot back and forth over the mark, as if that'll make it go away. Without saying anything, I put the car in reverse and try to back off over the median, but nothing happens.

"The car's stuck," I say, voicing the obvious.

She opens her door. "I'll go look."

I watch her walk around to the front, squatting down by the wheel. She checks the other side before sliding back into her seat. Huffing out a breath, she says, "It's not going anywhere."

"Okay, thanks for checking," I tell her before grabbing my phone and searching for the number of my car insurance provider to see if they can come tow the car.

"What are you doing?" she asks.

I explain, and she stares back at me as if the concept is completely foreign to her.

"I'll just call Billy. Hold on," she says, like it's obvious.

"Who's Billy?"

"My boyfriend's cousin. His dad owns a mechanic shop."

Well, that's convenient.

She calls a number and lets it ring a few times before muttering, "Shit," and telling me to "Hold on." The next number she calls continues to ring, and just when I think they won't pick up, she says, "Billy there?"

She waits for the phone to be handed over, and then responds, "I'm fine, but I need a tow." A few seconds pass before she explains, "We drove over a median and got stuck." She pauses. "This girl from the food bank." A laugh springs from her at his response. "Fuck off, you perv, and just come get me."

Why is he a perv?

"Across from Matty's."

I look out the rearview mirror and see an old-looking little shack called Matty's Burgers. Well, actually, the sign says "*atty's Burgers*" since the *M* fell off.

She hangs up the phone and turns to me. "He'll be here in like thirty minutes."

"Okay, thanks."

"Sorry about the floor," she offers, nervously twisting one of her rings.

"It's not a big deal."

"Billy will take care of all the labor, and if he needs to buy any parts—"

"Seriously, it's not a big deal," I interrupt, trying to reassure her, but she just keeps fidgeting with the ring. "It was an accident. You have nothing to be sorry for."

"Aren't your parents gonna say something? You know, when you get home?"

I slowly shake my head, and she must read the truth on my face.

"Oh," she says, watching me with newfound interest.

"And don't worry about any parts. I've got their credit card, and they rarely ask questions."

"It's so weird that people like you actually exist."

I blink at her words.

"Not that there's anything wrong with you," she corrects. "You actually seem pretty cool for a rich kid. I just mean I can't imagine having a magical money card that no one checks." She looks at me so intently that I want to curl into myself. "But I guess money doesn't solve all your problems, does it?"

"No, it doesn't," I whisper.

"Well, either way, I'm sorry. I hope you don't have anywhere you need to be."

"I don't," I answer, remembering I told Graham I would text him about plans for tonight. I shoot him a quick text saying that something came up as Sam leans forward and switches on the radio. She fiddles with the stations until she finds one she likes before sinking back into her seat. I check if Avery messaged me, but she didn't, so I relax back into my seat and wait.

We don't say much else to each other, and the time passes by slowly as I anticipate Billy's arrival. I wonder what he'll be like. After Jameson's outburst this morning, I'm not sure what to expect from his cousin.

The sun is just beginning to set when Billy pulls up in a tow truck with the words *"Baxston and Sons"* written across the side.

From the moment he steps out of the truck, I can see the resemblance to Jameson. They have a similar build, although Billy's a bit taller and has a lightness to him that Jameson doesn't.

As he walks toward us, I can't stop myself from staring. His hair is thick and dark, pulling up in a few places, like he's just run his fingers through it, and his black T-shirt clings to his full chest and toned arms. A body that can only be built through physical labor, evidenced by the grease stains that cover his hands and jeans.

He reaches the car, and Sam gets out to meet him, so I follow.

He tilts his head up to her in greeting. "You good?"
She nods.

He walks to the front of the car to inspect the damage, crouching down to look at the tire. "Yeah, this is more than just stuck. The tire is fucked. He glances up at her. "What're you doing driving around in a Beamer?"

Sam's gaze drifts in my direction by way of explanation, and he follows it. He lazily drags his eyes down my body before moving them slowly back up to meet mine.

My heart speeds up. I've never been looked at like that before. Like I was being devoured.

"What's someone like you doing serving hours?"

I try to get out the words, but they just won't come. So, Sam answers for me.

"She's not. She was there for some school project. Goes to Crestview."

"Ah." He smirks, and it somehow makes him even more good-looking. "Richie rich. Explains the ride." He nods toward the pickup truck. "Well, hop in, and I'll give her a tow."

Sam moves for the front, and I gladly take the back. Being around Billy makes me uncomfortable, not because he scares me like Jameson, but because of how it made me feel to have his eyes on me.

Because I liked it.

CHAPTER 5

AFTER HOOKING UP THE car to the tow thing, or whatever it is you do to tow a car, Billy throws the truck into drive.

He peers over at Sam. "Heard some shit went down at the diner today."

"Yeah," she mumbles quickly, clearly trying to brush it off. Turning to look out the window, she asks, "Have you seen him?"

"He stopped by for a bit around lunch, but he's been out for a while. Something with Marcus."

She nods, but her body tenses as if his words imply something more.

Billy glances back at me through the rearview mirror. We lock eyes, but I immediately drop mine.

"So, what's your name, Richie?"

I clear my throat because it suddenly feels like it's full of cement. "Susan."

He snorts. "Yeah, that makes sense."

"What do you mean *that makes sense*?" I ask before I can take it back.

"You just look like a Susan. Bet it's a family name, isn't it?"

"My grandmother's." I blush as we slow at a red light.

"So, what's she doing driving you around in her fancy car?" he asks Sam.

"Jameson couldn't make it, so she offered."

He finds my eyes in the rearview mirror again, but this time I don't lower them. "Surprised you wanted to slum it any longer than you needed to." There's a challenge in his expression, like this is some sort of test. "But maybe you want to feel a little rush, hmm?" he purrs. He's still holding my eyes captive, and my skin begins to prickle. I'm itching to break contact, but I don't want him to win this game that he's started.

I don't want to prove that I'm exactly who he thinks I am.

"Is that what you want?"

The question bounces around in my mind, trying to dodge the truth.

Billy watches me, waiting for an answer. He attempts to keep his face impassive, but his teeth sinking into his bottom lip to hide a smile is his tell.

He knows he's won.

The spell breaks when the truck jerks forward, and his attention snaps back to the road.

I exhale a breath and unclench my fingers, realizing my nails have been digging into my palms.

We pull into a mechanic shop with a name that matches the one on the side of his truck. They must have already closed for the night because the parking lot is empty.

Billy takes us in through a side door that leads to an equally empty break room. It has one of those foldable card tables and a few mismatched chairs in the middle. Pushed up against the far wall is a makeshift kitchen with an old fridge, microwave, and coffeepot.

"Chill here for a bit while I take a look at it. I already know the alignment's fucked up, but if I can't patch the tire, you'll need a new one."

"Thank you," I murmur as I move to take a seat at the table, watching as Sam heads for the coffeepot. Wordlessly, she walks out of the room before returning with the pot filled with water.

I've never used one of these old coffeepots before. We have a built-in espresso machine at home, but I usually just grab a coffee on my way to school.

She moves through the steps like she's done this a thousand times, removing the old coffee filter and dumping the grounds before returning it to the machine, then popping open an unlabeled silver canister and scooping fresh grounds into the reused filter. She then pours the water that was in the pot into the back of the machine before she begins pacing impatiently while she waits for it to brew.

The rhythmic drip of the coffee hitting the pot is soothing, and the small room is soon filled with its rich smell.

"You want some?" she asks as she pours herself a cup.

I don't like to drink any caffeine past two in the afternoon, and I know if I drink coffee this late, I definitely won't be able to sleep tonight.

"I'm good. Thanks, though," I answer.

It was nice of her to offer. I'm kind of surprised she did.

She sits down at the table across from me, opens a carton of milk she pulled out of the fridge, and smells it before pouring some into her cup. Then she reaches for the container of sugar sitting between us and dumps in a shocking amount. Each time I think she's finished pouring, she keeps adding more. Finally, she sets the sugar back on the table and takes a sip of her scalding hot drink like she's too impatient to wait for it to cool down.

I try to think of something I can ask her, some way to start a conversation. After spending most of the day with her, it's pretty apparent she isn't one to start small talk.

There are a million things I want to ask her, most of them suddenly revolving around Billy, but I don't want to ask something too personal and have her shut down before we even start. Every time I think of a question, I immediately come up with a reason not to ask it.

As my thoughts continue to spiral, my anxiety gets worse and worse until I begin to wonder how I've even gotten myself into this situation. What am I doing on a Saturday night in a part of town I was told to avoid, with people I don't even know?

The sound of Sam's chair dragging across the tile floor pulls my attention. She pours herself another cup of coffee before sitting down across from me again and pulling a book from her purse.

"You like to read?" I blurt out.

She flicks her eyes up from the page she's just opened to. "I guess."

Judging by the worn state of the book, it's either borrowed from someone who loves reading, or she's playing down how much she actually enjoys it.

I try to see what book it is, but can't make out the title.

This is something we have in common. This is something I can talk to her about.

"What are you reading?"

She flashes me the front of the book as she says, "*The Picture of Dorian Gray.*"

That is so not what I was expecting. Then again, I wouldn't have pictured her as a reader to begin with.

"I love that book."

Her head jerks up, and she looks at me like she wasn't expecting that at all, like she was bracing for judgment and is caught off guard that it never came.

She closes the book and takes another sip of coffee before saying, "It's one of my favorites."

"Mine, too. I love the opening line."

Her lips pull into an almost smile just as we're interrupted by a deep voice calling, "Sam."

"Back here," she shouts in response.

Heavy footsteps sound until Jameson appears in the doorway.

CHAPTER 6

HE ASSESSES SAM THEN turns his gaze to me before dragging it back to her with a questioning look.

"Have you talked to Billy?" she asks.

He shakes his head.

"I didn't want to call and bother you since you were"—she glances at me briefly—"busy."

He's leaning against the doorway with his arms crossed over his chest. He says nothing, so she continues to explain.

"This is Susan," she starts, tipping her head in my direction. "She offered to drive me home, but we, uh, we hit a curb and got stuck. I guess the front tire is messed up. I called Billy, and he came and gave us a tow."

I look back over at Jameson and notice him clenching and unclenching his left hand, his cracked knuckles caked with dried blood. A reminder that this isn't the first time I've seen him today.

He locks eyes with me, a question written on his face, but he breaks his stare when Sam asks, "Coffee, Jamie?"

Next thing I know, he's sitting in the seat next to Sam. That must translate to a yes because she promptly brings over a mug and pours him a cup before setting the pot in the middle of the table.

He skips the milk and sugar, taking a sip of the black coffee. His tattooed hand looks funny gripping the white mug, like the two don't belong in the same space.

I try to make out the words painted across his knuckles, but I don't want to get caught staring for too long and look away.

Suddenly aware that nobody is talking, I glance up at them. I understand Sam not being talkative with me, but I thought it was because she doesn't know me. Now I'm wondering, if they're always this quiet. Jameson hasn't said a single thing since he walked in here. But then I notice they seem to be communicating without words, looking at each other with changing expressions that they both appear to understand.

The sound of Billy's hand coming down loudly on Jameson's shoulder makes me jump. I must have been so consumed by my thoughts that I hadn't even heard him come in.

My movement catches everyone's attention. Jameson shoots me a disapproving look, while Billy appears amused.

"What're you guys having a little coffee date or something? How come you didn't invite me?" he says, pulling back the chair next to mine. He drops down and folds himself over the table, grabbing the pot of coffee.

Sam gets up and brings him back a mug.

I shift in my seat as I again think about how odd it is that I'm here, sitting around a table with three strangers while they drink coffee and I watch.

Billy motions to me with the pot. "You're not having any?"

"Um, no. I'm good. Thank you, though."

"You don't drink coffee?" he questions.

I don't want to tell him that I don't like to drink caffeine this late. I'm trying to think of something else to say that doesn't make me seem as uptight when he says, "It's just a yes or no question, baby."

I flush at the word *baby*. "No, I do."

"But you don't want any right now?"

It starts again, trying to think of an excuse, how to answer.

"Yes. Or. No," he says slowly.

"No."

"See? That wasn't so hard, was it?"

"No," I tell him, rolling my lips to keep from smiling.

He grins back at me. "Good."

Then he just moves on without asking for any explanation, like me saying yes or no is enough of a reason in itself. That somehow never occurred to me as an option before, that it could be that simple. I'm so used to being what others want me to be that I often cover up my actual needs and feelings with stories and explanations. This is the first time I've felt like maybe I don't need to do that.

Billy continues, unaware of the sudden epiphany that I'm working through in my head. "The tire couldn't be patched, so I'll need to put on a new one. I don't have a match for the rest of your tires, so I'll have to order it. Should be here by Monday."

"Oh, okay," I answer as I pull out my phone and think about who I can call to come and get me. My parents are still out of town. I guess I can call Graham or Avery, but I really don't want to. I'm not sure how I'll explain this whole situation. How am I supposed to tell them that I offered Sam a ride home after everything we saw at the diner and the story Graham just told us about them?

Noticing my hesitation, Jameson says, "If you need a ride, Sam and I can take you. Return the favor."

"What about Dougie's?" Billy cuts in. "I told him we'd stop by."

I reach for my phone again. "I can call someone to come get me. I don't want to make you change your plans."

"It's fine," Jameson states matter-of-factly. "If you need a ride, we'll give you one." He sends Billy a pointed look. "It's still early."

"Wait," Billy interjects, seeming oblivious to Jameson's warning tone, or maybe he's just immune. "Why don't we bring her with us? You wanna come hang, Richie?"

My stomach flutters at the idea that he wants me to come.

I look around the table to gauge how to respond. Jameson looks like he's trying to communicate something to Billy, and Sam looks ... well, she kind of looks happy at the idea, but maybe I'm just delusional from the high of Billy inviting me.

I shrug shyly. "Sure, I'll come."

He smacks his hands against the table as he pushes his chair back. "Well then, let's fucking go!"

CHAPTER 7

EVERYONE GETS UP, AND I follow them outside. Jameson has his arm draped around Sam, her body pulled into his, and I can feel Billy's presence one step behind me.

We stop in front of one of those cool classic cars that no one really drives anymore. The paint is a shiny black, the parking lot lights bouncing off it like it was just waxed.

Jameson moves for the driver's seat, and Sam breaks away from him, walking over to the passenger side, which means I'll be in the back seat with Billy.

It feels like my body is vibrating, and I can't tell if it's from nerves or excitement. Probably a little bit of both.

The car only has two doors, so Billy has to drop the passenger seat forward to allow us to climb in. After lowering it, he bows forward dramatically, sweeping his hand in the direction of the back seat. "After you, Richie."

I hold back a laugh at how ridiculous he looks as I begin to fold myself into the back seat. My face heats with the realization that, in the process, he's getting a good look at me from behind.

He follows me in, and Sam rights the seat before sitting and closing the door carefully.

The back seat is small and only feels smaller as Billy tries to fold his long legs behind the seat in front of him. His knee brushes against my thigh, and I try to ignore the rush it sends through me by looking around for a seat belt, but come up empty.

Noticing my confusion, Billy says, "It's a lap belt."

"Huh?" I respond, looking down and shifting my body, trying to find it.

He leans over me and feels along my sides, pulling up the two halves of a seat belt and clicking them together over my lap. Then he slouches back in his seat, never bothering to secure his own.

Jameson turns the key, and the car roars to life. A rock song blasts through the speakers as he aggressively pulls left onto the main road. The speed he takes the corner makes me lose my balance and hit my elbow against the side door.

"Whoa." Billy chuckles as he pulls me back toward him. "Drives a little different than the Beamer, doesn't it?" I look over at him as he reassuringly adds, "You're good." And the way he says it makes me believe him.

His knee is bobbing up and down to the beat of the song while he drums his hands against the back of Sam's seat. She doesn't seem to mind, or maybe she's just too distracted by Jameson's hand that's alternating between the gearshift and her thigh. As we idle at the first light, he mindlessly moves it up and down her leg, inching higher and higher with each pass.

Sam lights a cigarette, which catches Billy's attention.

"Let me bum one," he tells her.

She hands the pack back to him, and he tilts it in my direction. "You don't seem like someone who smokes."

"You make a lot of assumptions about me."

He arches an eyebrow. "Well, do you?"

I drop my eyes. "No."

"It looks like I'm two for two, so it seems like I'm pretty good at making assumptions about you."

"What do you ...? Oh, that Susan is my grandmother's name."

I guess every assumption he's had about me has been correct.

He flips open a silver lighter, and with the sound of a clink, his face is illuminated by the soft glow of a flame. He lights the cigarette before handing the pack back to Sam, who has just passed hers to Jameson.

The whole experience is a sensory overload. The music continues to play loudly. Smoke stings my eyes and tickles my nose. The car jerks as Jameson shifts gears and weaves between lanes.

My body is still vibrating from the closeness of Billy. But the adrenaline of it all feels good. Like instead of just being alive, I'm actually living.

The car slows in front of an old house with chipped paint and a cluttered lawn.

What would my friends say if they saw me here?

Sam lowers her seat, allowing Billy to climb out. I almost lose my balance trying to get out behind him, but he grabs my arm to steady me. Once I'm safely standing, he drags his hand down and links it in mine before leading me toward the house.

Halfway up the yard, I turn back when I realize Sam and Jameson aren't following us. They're still sitting in the car.

Billy sees me looking and says, "They'll come in soon."

I wonder what they're doing in there.

We make our way up the porch steps that creak under our feet. He pushes through the door without knocking, and as we walk in, it feels like all eyes are on us.

Everybody looks at me questioningly, like they aren't sure what I'm doing here. But once they see my hand in Billy's, the guys drop their gazes, and the girls' expressions pinch with jealousy.

We continue through the living room and into a narrow kitchen that's connected to a small dining area with an opened screen door leading to the backyard. There's a group gathered around the kitchen island that's littered with bottles of liquor and red Solo cups.

One of the guys drunkenly yells, "Ah, there he is!"

How long have they already been drinking?

Billy lets go of my hand but not before everyone noticed he was holding it and embraces the guy with a loud slap on the back. "Dougie! How're you doin', man?"

I watch him as everyone watches me, getting the same reactions I did when we first walked through the door.

"And who's this?" Dougie asks, glancing in my direction.

"Susan," Billy responds in my place.

"And who is Susan?" he says, assessing me. "I've never seen her around before."

"That's 'cause she's from Crestview."

Dougie looks amused and says to me with a short laugh, "So, what the fuck are you doing here with him, then?"

I hesitate, not sure what to say to that.

"She volunteers at the food bank with Sam and gave her a ride home, but on the way, they got into a little accident. Her tire needs to be replaced, so I'm helping her out."

Dougie scoffs. "Yeah, I'm sure you're *helping her out* just fine."

The energy in the room shifts, and so does everyone's attention. I glance over my shoulder to see Sam and Jameson walking in.

Dougie tips his head up to Jameson in greeting before letting his eyes quickly sweep over to Sam.

"Shots?" he asks, turning to Jameson.

There's a moment of uncomfortable silence before Billy cuts in with a, "Hell yeah!"

Dougie pours clear liquid into Solo cups for everyone gathered in the kitchen, which means I also get one. I usually only drink wine coolers or mixed drinks, if anything at all. I've never had straight liquor before.

I look around, and everyone seems completely in their element, unlike how I'm starting to feel. It's not like it should be a big deal. I'm eighteen, and it's Saturday night. This is what I'm supposed to be doing, isn't it?

I watch as Sam throws the shot back easily. Jameson follows suit, and with that, so does everybody else. I mimic what they do and try not to cough from the burn, clearing my throat as quietly as I can. The noise still catches Billy's attention, and he grins over at me as he pours himself another.

"Are you gonna get mad at me if I make another assumption?" he asks. When I don't answer, he continues, anyway. "That's the first time you've ever done a shot, isn't it?"

Not wanting to confirm his assumption, I just look back at him. I don't want to seem lame or give him the satisfaction of being right again.

He searches my face for an answer then says, "That's cute."

"Why is it cute?" I respond without thinking.

He pauses for a moment before saying, "Your innocence is refreshing."

Before I can analyze the meaning behind his words, we're interrupted by Jameson calling Billy's name. They communicate without words as Jameson nods his head toward the guy standing beside him and then to the front door.

Billy nods in understanding before walking over to them. He only makes it a few steps before he turns around and says, "Come on."

I follow, and as we get closer, I realize the guy they're standing with is the clerk from earlier today.

When he sees me, his face lights up. "Susan, you made it."

There's a question and a hint of something else in Billy's stare when he asks, "You two know each other?"

I flick my eyes up to the store clerk, whose name I still don't know, and notice him fidgeting from foot to foot.

Sam jumps in, explaining, "We swung by Junior's earlier."

"You must have made quite the impression, then," Billy says, inching closer to me.

The clerk zeros in on the subtle movement and snaps his head up. "I didn't know she was your girl, Billy."

What's happening?

Before Billy can clarify that I'm not, Jameson grunts, "All right, let's move this along."

Billy tells me to stay with Sam before giving her a look I don't understand. Then he follows behind Jameson, who's leading them toward the front door.

Once they're gone, Sam grabs one of the bottles from the kitchen island and cocks her head toward the open screen door, telling me, "I need a smoke."

I trail closely behind her as we step out onto the crowded back porch. It's unusually warm for the middle of May, and the slickness of humidity sticks to my skin. The sun has long ago set, and the only light is coming from the warm glow of the house behind us and the flames of a small bonfire down on the lawn.

Rather than stand with the other smokers on the deck, she continues down the stairs into the small square backyard. She also avoids sitting with everyone around the fire and instead drops down to sit with her back against the chain-link fence that encloses the space. I mirror her, trying not to think about what I might be sitting on.

She takes a pull from the liquor bottle before offering it to me. I wave my hand to pass, and she takes another drink before leaning it against the fence in the space between us.

After lighting her cigarette, she takes a drawn-out drag, closing her eyes as she inhales. When she turns away from me to exhale, I ask, "Where'd they go?"

She waits a moment, as if deciding how to respond. "Jameson has something Dean needs," she answers vaguely.

So that's the clerk's name, Dean.

I don't know what makes me say it. Maybe it's sitting out here together in the dark that makes it seem like nothing is off limits. Or maybe it's the strangeness of today. Or that it just feels like I have nothing to lose, knowing that tonight is likely the last time I'll see her. But whatever the reason is, I surprise myself by confessing, "I know Jameson sells drugs."

She looks up at me slowly. "And how would you know that?"

"My ex-boyfriend buys weed from him."

"I didn't realize you've met Jameson before," she says, flicking the ash off her cigarette.

"I haven't."

She looks confused, so I clarify, "I mean, we saw him at the diner today, when he ... well, you know," I say, lowering my eyes. "Um, Graham—that's my ex—he recognized Jameson this morning."

She stubs out her cigarette. "Why were you at breakfast with your ex-boyfriend?"

That's what she's going to focus on? And how do I explain me and Graham?

"It's ..." I hesitate. "It's complicated. My friend, Avery, has a thing with Graham's best friend, Logan. He's always around, and sometimes it's—"

"Sometimes it's what?" she asks.

I grab the bottle between us and take a sip. "Easier."

She reaches for the bottle, and I hand it back to her.

"Why'd you break up?"

"I walked in on him kissing another girl," I mutter.

"And your friends still hang around him?"

I stiffen. "It's not like he cheated on them."

She shakes her head. "That's not the point. They—"

The sound of dead grass crunching under footsteps cuts her off, and I tilt my head up to find Billy and Jameson standing over us.

"Your phone dead?" Billy asks Sam as he drops down next to me.

She looks around like she forgot she has one, while Jameson sits down beside her. In one swift motion, he pulls her closer to him, draping her legs over his.

"We've been looking all over for you two. I guess we should have known we'd find you tucked away in a corner," Billy teases.

"Everything all good?" Sam says, turning her attention to Jameson.

He nods as she hands him the bottle, and he takes a quick drink before passing it to Billy, who takes a longer one.

Watching them, I remember that Jameson drove us here, and that he's supposed to be my ride.

I lean into Billy. "Will Jameson still be okay to drive me home?"

"What?" he responds then follows my gaze down to the bottle in his hand and realizes what I was referring to. "Oh, yeah, he never gets out of control with alcohol."

I don't miss how he specifically clarifies that it's *alcohol* that Jameson doesn't get out of control with. I've already seen how he let his control slip earlier today.

I slide my eyes over to his scabbed hand resting protectively on Sam's leg.

She gestures to Billy to hand her the bottle, the contents getting lower and lower.

As she finishes pulling it from her lips, Jameson asks, "How much have you had?"

She waves him off. "I'm fine."

"That's enough for tonight," he says with finality as he takes the bottle from her and hands it back to Billy.

"How come he gets it?" she whines.

"Because he hasn't been sitting out here, drinking half the bottle."

"I said I'm fine," she tells him again, sounding more agitated this time.

"Watch yourself," he warns, his tone harsh before he softens it. "Just be here with me, yeah?" He grips her face gently and turns it so her eyes meet his. Something passes between them, and she nods.

"Good, you're good," he says.

I'm not sure who he's trying to reassure.

Her or himself.

CHAPTER 8

SAM MOVES TO REST against Jameson, and he wraps his hands around her waist, bringing her to his chest. Billy and I sit across from them, close but not touching, as we lean back and look up at the sky.

The quiet is comfortable, like we're all existing solely in this moment, a temporary reprieve from the complexities of our lives. But it's soon shattered when someone yells, "Yo, Baxston!"

Both Jameson and Billy look over in unison, turning toward the voice coming from over by the bonfire.

"Come join the party!" the guy says, holding a Solo cup over his head and waving it back and forth excitedly. He's definitely one step away from being fully hammered.

Billy jumps into a standing position and reaches out his hand to pull me up beside him.

Rather than disentangling Sam from his body, Jameson stands with her still wrapped around him before setting her down.

Billy lazily drapes his arm around my shoulders when I hear Sam squeal behind us. I turn around to see what caused it but only catch the tail end of whatever it was, watching her swat Jameson's hand away as he wears a satisfied grin.

As we get closer to the bonfire, I realize that the guy who called us over was Dougie. He's refilling his beer from the keg, laughing loudly at something another guy just said.

Billy leads us to the three remaining chairs around the fire. Jameson takes one and pulls Sam down with him while Billy and I take the other two.

Dougie's eyes drift in our direction, and he groans. "Why's everyone sitting? Come on. We need music! We need vibes! Where are the vibes!" He looks around, waiting for a response, and when he doesn't get one, he throws his hands up and says, "Fuck, I'll find one," then walks back toward the house.

I'm not exactly sure what that means or what he went off to go find, but as he walks away, a group of girls starts toward us. Two fade into the background as one of them steals all the attention. My eyes flick from her to Billy then back to her again as I notice she's walking right toward him.

A flicker of jealousy hits me, although I know I have no right to feel it. It's just that this girl is gorgeous, and she knows it, too. She has dark hair that's tousled just right and full lips that seem to be set in a permanent pout. Her jeans are so tight they look painted on, and her little silky cami leaves just enough up to the imagination.

It's instantly obvious that she's the girl all the guys want—well, other than Sam. If Jameson wasn't wrapped around her possessively, I'm sure all the attention would be on her instead.

The mystery girl stalks toward Billy like he's her prey and she can't wait to play with him. He notices her approaching, and I swear I hear him mutter, "Fuck me," under his breath.

Oblivious to his annoyance, her lips flick up just slightly into a knowing smile.

She's completely unaware that I'm here, and again, it bothers me when it shouldn't. Billy and I are nothing to each other. Just because he invited me along doesn't mean anything. I just didn't realize how much I've been enjoying his attention until it might shift to someone else.

She stops in front of him and leans over the chair he's sitting in, brushing her hand up his arm as she breathes, "I've been looking for you."

"Well, you found me," he replies, his tone suddenly distant. He sounds completely different than he did when he was teasing me earlier.

She doesn't seem to notice as she moves in closer and whispers something in his ear.

"I'm busy tonight," he responds just as coldly as before.

Rejection flashes across her face before she sets her lips back into a puffed-out pout. Trying to up her game, she rubs her hand up his neck and into his hair, her touch making it clear that this isn't the first time she's had her hands on his body.

She whispers something again, in hopes of convincing him to make himself available. I guess it doesn't work because he leans away from her touch and says, "I told you I'm busy tonight, and that hasn't changed in the last thirty seconds."

She stares back at him, confusion lining her face, before she notices me sitting in the chair beside him.

She scoffs. "Fuck you, Billy."

Locking eyes with me, she sneers. "Enjoy it while it lasts, sweetheart. He'll grow tired of you soon. He always does."

I'm about to tell her that we aren't together when she shifts back to Billy and says bitterly, "I haven't seen this one before. Who even is she?"

He doesn't answer her, and her lips purse, clearly irritated that she can't get him to respond. I guess any attention is better to her than none because she adds, "I'm so done with your shit. I could get anyone, Billy. Anyone."

When he still doesn't answer, surprisingly, it's Sam who says, "Apparently not, if you keep crawling back."

The girl snaps her eyes to Sam, and she suddenly isn't so talkative anymore.

Sam leans forward, as if inviting her to say something else.

"Whatever," the girl huffs before turning to me. "Have fun being his latest flavor of the week."

She waits for a beat, giving Billy time to change his mind, before spinning and walking toward a group of guys on the other side of the fire. She struts away with just as much confidence as she did when she first approached him, clearly not wanting anyone to know that she's just been rejected.

Billy clears his throat and glances over at me sheepishly. "Uh, sorry about her. She's a ..."

"Bitch," Sam finishes for him.

"You've gotta stop going back to that, man. No pussy can be worth that much crazy," Jameson adds.

Billy narrows his eyes at them then turns back to me. "She's ..." He pauses, opening and closing his mouth, as if trying to find the right words and failing before settling on, "It's complicated." I'm not sure how to respond, and sensing my discomfort, he continues, "That's not why I asked you to come. I didn't invite you here so I could sleep with you."

Sam laughs a bit too loudly then quickly covers her mouth, like she didn't mean for the sound to escape.

I'm starting to see why Jameson cut her off.

Billy shoots her an agitated look. "What?"

She shakes her head. "Nothing."

"There must be something you find so funny."

"It's just, who are you right now? All 'I didn't invite you here so I could sleep with you,'" she says, lowering her voice to mimic his. "As if you hang out with girls for any other reason."

Jameson lets out a low laugh.

"I'd cut your losses with this one, though," Sam begins, jutting her chin in my direction. "I don't think you're her type."

Billy's lips pull into a cocky grin. "I'm everyone's type."

"She's got an ex who's still hanging around," Sam says, shifting back against Jameson's chest. "Bet he's rich, too."

Wow, alcohol really makes her filter disappear.

I look up and find Billy watching me.

"That true?"

"He's around, but I'm never getting back with him," I answer defensively.

"But he's rich?"

I shrug. "Yeah, so?"

He tilts his head to the side. "What would happen if you brought me home?"

I go still. "What?"

He leans forward. "You heard me. What would your parents do if you brought me around?" When I don't answer, he says, "You couldn't, could you?"

"Sure I could," I tell him, crossing my arms over my chest.

He clicks his tongue. "Mmhmm." His elbows drop to his knees, and he stares back at me like he's trying to figure me out. "You know, Richie, it's not fun to always do what's expected of you. Think of all you're missing out on."

My body feels warm from what he might be insinuating, and I drop my eyes, willing my mind to steady.

Maybe he just meant that it's a shame I always do what's expected of me because it's clear that he doesn't. That none of them do.

But as I peer back up at him, the expression on his face tells me it's more than that.

CHAPTER 9

DOUGIE RETURNS WITH A speaker, the hypnotic sound of low bass pouring out of it.

A small group begins to form, mostly made up of girls, but also a few couples, dancing to the music. I notice the girl who came up to Billy grinding against another guy, glancing over at him every so often to see if he's watching her.

He isn't. Instead, he's talking to Jameson about a car that was brought into the shop earlier today. I guess it's some really cool model or something. Honestly, I have no idea what anything they're saying means, but I still like listening.

Sam, on the other hand, seems like she's getting antsy, swaying to herself as she sits on Jameson's lap. Eventually, she shifts her body so she's facing him and takes out the pack of cigarettes that's in the front pocket of his flannel. She pulls one out then stands.

Jameson briefly pauses the conversation to grab his lighter and holds it up to light the cigarette dangling between her lips.

She turns away to exhale then leans over him, holding up her weight on the arms of the chair, and feathers her lips over his.

They're so in sync with each other. It's like their interactions are choreographed.

"I'm gonna go dance," she tells him.

He nods, and she disappears into the crowd.

Billy turns to me. "You're not gonna go, too?"

"I don't really like to dance."

He smirks. "Course you don't."

Their conversation starts up again, and I let my eyes drift back to everyone dancing.

I've always felt self-conscious dancing in front of other people. I can never get out of my head and just get lost in the music. I'm always thinking about what I look like to those who might be watching. How people must think I look out of place. I notice the same discomfort in most of the people out there, like they, too, are dancing for the eyes of others, looking a bit out of place themselves.

I watch the girls grinding against guys, attempting to try to look sexy, but they only come off as desperate. The girls who don't have a guy to dance against move with their friends, clearly trying to catch the eye of someone who might want to pair off with them. They're all dancing for someone else.

But not Sam. She's in the middle of everyone, yet she doesn't dance against anybody or position herself as part of a group.

People seem to move around her little bubble as if she owns the space. She looks like she's in a trance, eyes closed and hips moving as if completely taken over by the music. Sometimes her head will roll back, or her hands will slide up her body and into the air. It's like she isn't even in control of her own movements. I've never seen someone dance like her. She's completely uninhibited.

The song ends, and she's pulled back into reality in the slight beat before the next one starts. She opens her eyes and looks around until she finds a guy holding a bottle. She briefly glances over at Jameson and, after seeing he's not watching, makes her way toward the guy who's more than happy to give it to her.

She takes a much longer pull than seems normal then hands it back to him. As she starts to walk back to where she was originally dancing, he grabs her arm and bends down so she can hear him over the music. She responds, and his eyes drift over to Jameson. One look at him, and the guy promptly steps away.

Back in her spot, her dancing is getting sloppier. I'm not sure if I should say something to Billy or Jameson. He's been keeping an eye on her, looking over every so often, but he missed the few minutes it took her to find the guy who shared his bottle.

She's becoming more and more out of it, and I begin to worry that, at some point, she might actually need someone to go help her.

I lean forward to tap Billy's arm, and Jameson tracks the movement. As if he somehow already knows what I'm about to say, his eyes dart to Sam. The moment he spots her, it's clear that he sees what I do.

He mutters something to Billy that I can't hear, causing Billy to look in Sam's direction. Once he finds her, understanding washes over him, prompting him to turn to me and say, "Time to go."

I watch Jameson stalk over to her, his body growing more rigid with each step. She startles from her haze when he grasps her shoulders, and her eyes pop open. She looks disoriented, as if she forgot where she was for a minute.

He moves closer to her and says something against her ear. She responds by dramatically throwing her head back like a little kid throwing a tantrum. From the looks of it, she's telling him she doesn't want to leave, but he's not having it.

Billy and I wait for them at the perimeter of people dancing as Jameson ushers her out of the crowd. He's walking behind her with both of his hands on her hips, using them to both steady and guide her.

When she sees us, her face lights up, and she lunges forward, throwing her arms around Billy's neck. "Billyyyy!" she draws out his name. "Tell Jamie I don't want to go home."

He tenses and flicks his gaze up to meet Jameson's.

"I don't want to go home," she says again, more to herself this time. "He's gonna be mad."

I'm not sure who she's referring to when she says "he." Is she talking about Jameson, since he told her to stop drinking and she didn't?

I glance over at him. He definitely looks mad.

She spins around to face Jameson, stumbling in the process. He reaches out to catch her as she pleads, "Just take me home with you."

"You know that'll only make it worse, baby," he answers in a low voice as he tucks a strand of hair behind her ear. "You told me to tell you no when you asked, remember?"

Okay, so the "he" isn't Jameson.

"He's probably not even there," Billy tells her. "It's Saturday night; I'm sure he's at the bar."

She doesn't look convinced, so Billy takes out his phone and says, "Want me to check with Al?"

She nods, but it looks funny, each movement just a little too slow.

Billy holds the phone up to his ear as he waits for it to ring. Plugging his other ear with two fingers, he makes his voice loud enough to hear over the noise. "Al, it's Billy. Is Wes in?" He waits for a beat before shouting, "Yeah, man. You, too." Pocketing his phone, he says, "He's there and too shitfaced to be coming home anytime soon."

"Okay," she says, barely above a whisper. Her shoulders drop as she begins to stagger toward the house.

She only gets a few steps before she whips around, almost losing her balance again. "What about Carson?"

"There's no way he'll be home on a Saturday night," Jameson answers.

"But what if he is?" She's becoming panicked again. "He'll tell him. You know he'll tell him." She fidgets with the ring on her finger, and Jameson notices, swiping a hand through his hair. "I don't want him to come after you."

I still don't understand what she's talking about. Tell him what? And why would someone she knows come after Jameson?

He tips her chin so she's looking at him and runs his thumb along her jaw. "I'm not going to let that happen. No one is gonna come after me. You're safe. I'm safe." He palms her cheek. "If his car is there, we'll leave, okay?"

"Okay," she says.

Carefully, he asks, "Can we go now?"

She nods, turning back toward the house.

There are so many questions I want to ask, but based on the tension coming off of both Jameson and Billy, I decide to keep them to myself.

We're almost to the stairs when I hear a curse, seeing Sam trip over herself and land on the ground.

"Shit," Jameson breathes before kneeling down next to her.

She looks up at him, her eyes wide and glassy, filled with tears that she's refusing to let fall. "I didn't mean to. I always fuck it up. Why do I always fuck it up?"

Jameson shushes her. "You didn't fuck anything up."

"You promise?" she asks in a voice that doesn't sound like her own.

"Would I lie to you?"

She shakes her head.

He stands up, taking her with him, and crouches down so she can drape her arms around his neck then hoists her up so she's fully wrapped around him.

Once again, we start toward the house, this time finally making it all the way out to the car.

Billy and I climb in the back, and then Jameson carefully sets Sam into the passenger seat.

This time, the car ride is quiet. There's no music playing and no teasing from Billy. The silence feels charged with something, like it's holding some sort of secret.

Sam falls asleep not long into the drive, and I try to work through the meaning behind her words as I watch headlights pass by. I know there's something they aren't telling me. Not that they have any reason to, but it just feels like I'm in this foreign world and everyone but me knows what's going on.

Before I can even begin to process the last hour, or really the entire day, the car slows in front of a house.

Jameson cranes his neck to look at the partially hidden driveway, where there's a single car parked.

I remember his words to Sam. *If his car is there, we'll leave, okay?*

The leather of his seat creaks as Jameson shifts back, catching my eye in the rearview mirror. "I'm gonna need you to do me a favor."

Chapter 10

It takes me a minute to realize that Jameson is talking to me.

I feel the heaviness of both his and Billy's attention as they wait for me to respond.

Swallowing, I hear myself say, "Sure, what do you need?" I know it's my voice, but it's like somebody else is talking, as if the words just came out on their own.

All at once, scenarios begin to play through my mind as I wonder what Jameson could possibly need from me. He doesn't seem like someone you want to be blindly promising favors to but, for some reason, it doesn't feel like he would ask me to do anything bad. Well, maybe that's the wrong way to put it. I don't think he would ask me to do something without a good reason.

I wait for him to explain, but instead of answering, he takes the keys out of the ignition, effectively hiding the car under the shadow of night. The low rumble of the car disappears, and there's nothing but the moon illuminating our faces. The only thing I'm left with is the sound of my heartbeat thumping loudly in my ears.

Sam is still asleep, so he turns to her and lightly runs the tips of his fingers up her arm, but she doesn't stir.

After glancing over his shoulder at Billy, he tries again.

Still nothing.

He looks reluctant but shakes her gently, and that does it. Her eyes snap open as she jerks away from the contact, bringing her arms up to shield her face. She looks around, confused, before Jameson slowly brings his hands up to hers and lowers them.

"It's me," he says softly.

The worry melts from her body but returns just as quickly when she realizes we're sitting outside her house.

"His car is here," Jameson tells her. Before she can respond, he continues, "I think you should have Susan go in with you. If he thinks you were out with her, it shouldn't be as big of a deal."

Me? Go in with her? We don't even know each other.

So many questions race through my mind. I want to know what I might be walking into and why she can't just go inside herself or with Jameson. They have to tell me something before sending me in there, right?

Sam blows out a breath, not looking so sure. "What are we supposed to say? He'll ask who she is and what we were doing."

She begins to fidget, bouncing her knee manically, so lost in thought that she doesn't even seem to notice. "I should have just gone home or not had so much to drink. I could've just told him that I was at work," she says to herself.

I turn to Billy for an explanation, but his eyes are on Sam.

"Fuck," she mutters, and Jameson's hand comes down on her knee, stopping the movement. "Why do I always have to make things so difficult?" she adds, but the words are louder this time, like she's fishing for a response. It's like she wants someone to confirm that she's just as screwed up as she thinks she is.

As if reading her thoughts, Billy says, "You're not the one who's messed up. You know that."

Jameson opens his mouth like he's about to say something, but then he closes it, as if he thought better of it. Instead, he reasons, "Tell him that she just started at the diner and invited you over to hang out after your shift."

She thinks about it for a minute before conceding, "Yeah, okay. That makes sense."

"He might not even be awake," Jameson says, trying to reassure her, but she only gives him a disbelieving look in response.

He shifts in his seat until he's facing me and says, "Don't talk to him unless you have to. Or, unless he directly asks you a question."

"Okay," I respond but realize that if I'm ever going to ask for answers, this is the time to do it. "Um, who are you talking about, and uh, w-why…?" I stutter. "Why is it such a secret that we were out?"

Sam still looks out of it, so Jameson answers for her, "Carson is Sam's older brother. He's a total prick who likes to rat her out to her dad, who's an even bigger prick." He spares Sam a quick glance before continuing, "Her dad doesn't like it when she goes out, especially if she comes home trashed or if she was out with me."

"But you're her boyfriend."

"I've had my issues with her brother and her old man, but after our last chat …" He runs a hand through his hair. "After our last chat, I'm not allowed in their house anymore."

That must have been quite the chat.

"What about Billy?" I ask. "Why can't he go in with her?" I don't expect him to answer any of my questions, and now that he is, I can't seem to stop.

"People usually see me and Billy as the same thing. If I'm banned, so is he. That's why it would help for you to go in there with her. It'll only create more problems if Carson tells her dad that I dropped her off drunk. They won't care as much if they think she was with you."

"Why?"

"'Cause you're a girl," Billy explains.

"Why does that matter?"

"It just does," Jameson snaps.

Apparently, he's done playing twenty questions.

Jameson sweeps his gaze over Sam, landing on her eyes. She looks back at him, but it's unfocused. He brushes his hand against her cheek, rubbing away her smudged mascara with a swipe of his thumb. "Text me when you get into bed."

Her eyes clear, and she dips her chin.

"Tell me you will, so I know you heard me," he says as he slowly drops his hand away from her.

"I will."

He nods to himself then gets out of the car just as she opens the door. She lowers her seat to allow Billy and I to get out, and then walks over to Jameson, who's leaning against the trunk of the car.

I slide out of the back seat and try not to look over at them, but it's hard not to. She's standing between his legs as he drapes himself around her.

Jameson's lips are moving as he speaks to her quietly, his words meant just for her. She nods back at him before he lightly presses his lips against hers.

Just as Billy and I come up beside them, Jameson pulls away and turns toward us. "You good to go?"

"Yeah," I answer.

Sam whispers to Jameson before she starts toward the house. I glance over at him before following, feeling like I need his permission for some reason. He watches me for a second before tucking his chin in answer.

I turn to leave, but Billy grabs my wrist. "Don't stay any longer than you need to, okay? Just get in and get out."

"Got it," I breathe, his warning making me even more nervous.

Before I change my mind, I hustle up Sam's lawn, trying to catch up to her. She slows once I'm next to her.

"Thanks for coming in," she says without looking at me.

"No problem," I tell her, attempting to keep my voice light.

We reach the porch, and I fight back the urge to turn around. After all this build up, I have no idea what we'll be met with when we walk through her front door.

CHAPTER 11

THE DOOR SQUEAKS WHEN Sam pushes it open. The wood on the bottom is split like someone once kicked it, and it scrapes against the floor, keeping it from opening fully. She pulls the door forward then leans her hip against it, allowing it to finally push in all the way.

We walk into a dark living room that's only illuminated by the light of a TV and the amber glow of a lit cigarette between the fingers of a guy who I can only assume is her brother. He's sitting on a couch that looks too big for the room and too small for his body, his bulging arm draped across the back of it, and his long legs splayed out in front of him. It seems weird that he's related to Sam, given how small she is. The only way you can tell that the two of them are brother and sister is their nearly black hair.

He continues to stare at the TV as he says, "Where the hell have you been?"

A second passes before she responds, and his impatient eyes drift over to us, his gaze settling on me. He sits up slightly, his forearms coming to his knees.

She starts to answer, but he cuts her off, "Who's this?"

"A girl I work with—Susan."

He switches on a nearby lamp before he turns his attention back to Sam, his eyes burning a hole into her as he waits for an explanation.

"She just started at the diner, and we hung out after. She gave me a ride."

His jaw tenses. "You were supposed to be home."

"What? Since when?" she asks nervously.

"Cathleen got called in," he grits through his teeth. "I got stuck with Jace 'cause you weren't here. Fucked up my whole night."

"I didn't know. Why didn't you call me?"

"What's the point? You never answer."

"How can I answer if you don't even call me?"

His eyebrows jump up as he inches his head forward, daring her to continue.

She rocks back on her heels, as if subconsciously distancing herself from him. "I'll pick up next time."

"Wrong answer."

"I'll be home next time," she corrects. She then remains perfectly still as he holds her under his stare, drawing out each long second before he finally shifts his focus to me.

"Why is she here?"

"I told her I would let her borrow a book," she lies easily.

He doesn't look away from me as he says, "Go get me another beer first."

I stay stuck in place as she exits the room.

Her brother doesn't stop watching me the entire time she's gone, and I try not to squirm anxiously under the weight of his stare.

I distract myself by looking at random things around the room, letting my eyes drift to anything but him. There's a recliner next to the dated floral couch he's sitting on. It has a brown, cracked leather fabric that's turned faded, like it's seen too much sun. There aren't any photos or really anything personal. There isn't even anything hanging on the walls. The room's paint has become a sad beige, likely once white that's yellowed from the constant smoke in the air. And there's one of those little walker toys in the corner, the ones that toddlers hold and push around when they're learning how to walk. The colors look so bright in the room, a direct contrast to everything else.

The sound of glass sliding against wood pulls my attention to the coffee table. Her brother stubs out his cigarette in an ashtray that's overflowing before his hand comes up to grab the beer bottle being offered to him. He gestures with it to the ashtray. "This needs to be emptied."

"Can I just go get her the book first so she can leave?"

He leans back and pops the cap off the beer, tossing it onto the table. He's creating quite the collection.

"Hurry up," he tells her.

She's gone just as fast as she came, and I'm left alone again with her brother.

"Do I make you nervous?"

I startle at hearing his voice directed at me for the first time.

"What? No," I answer, wishing my voice didn't sound so shaky.

"Then why are you looking at everything in the room but me?"

I drag my eyes over to him, and his mouth turns up in a satisfied smile.

"You have beautiful eyes."

His words feel slimy as they slide over me, making my skin crawl.

He looks at me expectantly until I mutter, "Thank you."

"Why don't you come sit down by me?" he says, patting the seat next to him.

My stomach sinks.

"I have a boyfriend," I lie, not sure if it's the right thing to say.

"What does that matter?" he snaps just as Sam comes around the corner.

A look washes over him as she walks into the room, like he didn't want our conversation to be interrupted.

What would he have done if she hadn't walked in? Does someone like him listen if you say no? From the way he's watching me, it doesn't seem like it's something he's told often.

Sam glances between us, her face impassive, but I know she can sense my obvious discomfort and the anger building in her brother. She thrusts the book into my hands and ushers me to the front door.

I make it a step outside then turn and hold up the book. "I'll get it back to you."

"Sam!" her brother calls from inside the house.

She has one foot on the porch, gripping the door. Glancing over her shoulder, she says, "I've gotta go."

"Are you going to be okay? I mean, just with your brother and everything?"

"I'll be fine," she tells me, but it doesn't sound too convincing.

She plasters on a fake smile to reassure me and inches the door closed, signaling for me to leave, so I take a step back.

Halfway down the lawn, I look behind me, but she's already gone.

When I get to the car, Billy swings the door open and searches my face for something before lowering the seat so I can climb into the back.

Once I'm inside, Jameson turns to me and says, "Tell me what happened."

CHAPTER 12

I EXHALE A LONG breath I didn't even realize I was holding. I was so tense when I was in that house, under her brother's constant stare, that I didn't allow myself to feel or move, or let it show just how uneasy he really made me. He seems like someone who would feed off that, so I tried to feign indifference. But now that I'm in the car with Billy and Jameson, who both feel oddly safe and comforting after being around Sam's brother, the anxiety is starting to come to the surface.

I open my mouth to answer Jameson's question, but the words I want to say won't come. It's like they've dried up and become a tangled mess, one that I don't have the energy to sort through.

Without saying anything, Billy jumps out of the car, lowers his seat, and climbs into the back with me. His hand comes down around mine in an effort to calm me.

"He do something to you?" Billy asks, his voice low.

I shake my head. "He just wouldn't stop looking at me, watching me."

"Did he say anything to you? Ask who you were?" Jameson questions.

I shake my head again. "He asked Sam, not me."

"He buy the story?"

"I think so. She told him that I worked at the diner, like we planned, and that we hung out after." I pause before adding, "He was upset with her, though."

Jameson mutters something that I can't make out.

"He said she was supposed to be home because someone named Cathleen got called into work, so he had to watch Jace and that it ruined his night."

"Cathleen is her older sister, and Jace is Cathleen's kid," Billy says.

That explains the toy I saw in the living room.

"Did he do anything to her?" Jameson asks with a sharp edge to his voice.

Has he done something to her before?

"No. She told him that she would be home next time, and then he asked why I was there. She told him that she was going to let me borrow a book. He seemed to believe her and eventually let her go get it."

"*Eventually*?" Jameson presses, his tone giving away his slipping restraint.

"He asked her to get him a beer first. When she came back, he wanted her to clean out the ashtray he was using, but I think she could tell I was uncomfortable and didn't want things to escalate, so she asked if she could go get me the book."

Billy runs his thumb in small circles over my hand. "Did he talk to you when she wasn't in the room?"

"He asked if he made me nervous because I wouldn't look at him."

The circles Billy's tracing on my skin stop.

"I said no, but really, I was avoiding him. I felt like I had to look at him after he called me out, and when I did, he told me I have beautiful eyes then asked me to come sit by him. I wasn't sure what to say, so I told him that I have a boyfriend, and then Sam walked back in."

Billy looks out the window toward the house before bringing his focus back to the conversation.

"Sam walked me to the door, but he was calling for her. I asked her if she was going to be okay, and she said yes, but it kind of seemed like she was lying." The air in the car hangs heavy as I ask, my voice coming out just above a whisper, "Does he hurt her?"

Billy goes still as Jameson continues to look back at me. Something flashes across his face before his expression returns to his usual blank stare. "There's a lot of ways you can hurt someone."

I wince at his words, at the way he said them and the truth I know they hold.

"I know," I say, the vulnerability clear in my voice.

Jameson tilts his head. "Aw, honey, I'm sure you don't." The sweet name drips with condescension. "You come back from what you just described this shaken up, and I can promise that you have no idea what it is I'm talking about."

"Jameson," Billy warns. "Don't be a dick."

"I'm sorry," Jameson says, sliding his hands down his face. "This is just hard." He blows out a breath. "Sorry."

"It's okay," I tell him quietly.

Billy leans in closer to me as Jameson moves his eyes to Sam's house. "I'm giving her ten more minutes, and then I'm going in there."

And so, we wait.

The silence grows heavier with each minute that passes, all of us watching the clock tick closer to something that none of us want to happen.

Seven minutes pass.

Eight.

Then nine.

And finally, ten.

Still, there's nothing from Sam.

Jameson begins to open the door as Billy mutters, "Fuck," under his breath.

"Come on; think it through," Billy says, his voice close to pleading.

Jameson whips his head around. "I do think it through. Every fucking day, I think it through." He stills. "I close my eyes, and I see her in that house."

"I'm not saying you don't or that this is easy, but think about what happened after last time."

Jameson drops his head back against the seat and closes his eyes. He takes an audible inhale then roughly exhales, a clear attempt to gain back the control that's slipping.

After giving himself only that breath to reconsider, he turns for the door and says, "I've gotta go in there. I can't risk it. Not after last time."

Billy doesn't try to convince him again, knowing that Jameson's mind is made up, and starts to get out of the car to follow him in.

I realize that it doesn't matter if Billy thinks it's a good idea or not; Jameson is going in, so that means that Billy is going in, too. I've never seen such blind loyalty before.

He looks down at his hand in mine, like he forgot they were still connected. Pulling it away, he says, "Wait here."

Before I even have time to respond, Jameson drops back into his seat and slams the door closed. "She texted."

"And?" Billy asks, his voice tense.

"She's okay. She's in bed."

Relief washes over me.

I'm aware that I barely know them, but the look Sam gave me when I asked her if she was going to be okay flashes through my mind. Followed by the struggle Jameson clearly felt trying to make that choice and how Billy was willing to follow him into whatever might be waiting for them ...

I just don't want anything bad to happen to them. They seem like they've seen enough of it.

Jameson starts up the car. "Where do you live?"

I key my address into Google Maps and hand him my phone. I'm not sure how to get there from here and figure he doesn't either.

We keep to ourselves the whole ride to my house, the quiet only interrupted by my phone calling out directions.

The houses slowly get bigger and the neighborhoods better maintained until we eventually make it to my street.

I've always known that where I live is nice and have never taken it for granted. I know that I've grown up privileged, but so have all of my friends. It's never really seemed out of the ordinary before. But as we drive back tonight, I look at it all through Billy's eyes.

I watch the way he watches the houses. His expression is hard to read, like there's a war going on behind his eyes. A battle between hating that this is just handed to some people and wishing that it had been handed to him.

"It's the next one on the left," I say.

We pull up to the front gate, and Jameson looks back at me.

"The code is 4768," I tell him.

He slowly shakes his head before cranking down his window and punching in the code.

We drive through the gates and down the long driveway before finally stopping in front of my house.

Billy looks around. "Damn, Richie, you're really living up to the name," he says before pushing the front seat forward and climbing out, extending his hand to me.

"Thank you for the ride," I tell Jameson, sliding toward the open door.

He turns so he's facing me and holds my gaze for a moment too long before he blinks and the intensity of his stare breaks. He reaches down to grab my phone and hands it to me. "Thanks for earlier with Sam."

"It was no problem," I reply, trying to keep my voice even.

He faces forward again as I take Billy's outstretched hand and get out of the car.

Once I'm standing, Billy leans over me, caging me beneath his body, his arm resting against the roof of the car. "Guess I'll see you Monday, then."

"Monday?" I ask, the word coming out breathless.

His tongue juts out to wet his bottom lip. We're so close, his body hovering right over mine. "When you come to pick up your car," he says, and it sounds like a smile.

"Oh, yeah, my car. Thank you for fixing it. I mean, I guess you didn't fix it. But you know, for telling me what was wrong with it." I pause. "And for coming to get us." I can't make the words stop spilling out.

His eyes are light with amusement. "You're very welcome." He lingers on each word like there's another meaning hidden in each of them, his lazy drawl like a slow caress up my skin.

My mind begins to play through all the other things I could thank him for, and a warm flush spreads up my neck to my cheeks. I'm suddenly afraid that he can read my thoughts, worried that they're somehow written across my face.

"Well, I'll see you on Monday. I'll come by after school. Is that okay?"

He steps back, allowing me to slip out from underneath him. "Yeah, that works."

Unsure what else to say, I turn away from him, anxious to put some space between us, and start toward the front door.

I twist the key and look over my shoulder to find him still watching me. I wave shyly, before walking into the house.

Shutting the door, I hear their car peel out of the driveway and jump when my mother asks, "Who was that?"

CHAPTER 13

I ROUND THE CORNER and follow her voice into the dining room.

"I thought you were coming home on Monday," I say as I take in all the papers and files spread out on the table in front of her.

"The McNeal case got moved up. I wanted to get an early start," she answers, not taking her eyes off the document she's holding.

Of course she didn't come home early from her trip to see me, let alone bother to tell me about the change in plans.

I stand across from her awkwardly, not sure what to say. I never seem to know what to say when it comes to her. It's like we're strangers pretending we know each other, acting as if we care about what's going on in the other's life.

I don't know what I'm waiting for. I guess to be acknowledged or dismissed. I start counting in my head, seeing how high I can get before she says something.

I get to two hundred and fifty before I give up and turn to leave.

The squeak of my shoes twisting on the polished floor must remind her that I'm here because she looks up from the paper she's holding and states, "You never answered my question."

I turn back and look at her blankly.

"Who was that?" she repeats, glancing at the driveway that's clearly visible from the large window to her right. "And why on earth were you driving around in a car like that?"

"I drove over a curb, and my tire got messed up," I explain. "My friend's cousin is a mechanic, so we took it to the shop he works at, and they drove me home."

She tries to crinkle her face in judgment, but there isn't much movement; it's been frozen in time for as long as I can remember. "Who do you know who has a cousin that's a mechanic? And why are you getting home at"—she checks her phone—"after one in the morning?"

I wonder if she realizes what she sounds like, as if we're above associating with people who are related to mechanics? Like the idea of it is pure lunacy.

Billy's words from earlier play through my head. *What would your parents do if you brought me around?*

"Susan," she urges impatiently.

"A girl I met at the food bank."

The bracelets she's wearing clang against the wood of the table as she sets down the document. She has on a matching silk pajama set and her full collection of daily jewelry. She's always told me that, "Just because you're at home doesn't give you an excuse to look like a slob."

I can count on one hand the number of times I've seen my mother look anything less than perfectly put together.

"What were you doing at a food bank?" she questions.

Of course, she doesn't know.

"For my school project, remember? I've been going since January."

"So, does this girl go to Crestview? Is she doing the project with you?"

I could lie, but after how this conversation has been going, I want to see her squirm.

"No, she's there for community service."

"*Community service*?" She repeats the words as a question. "So what, you've been traipsing around with this hoodlum girl and some mechanic? What are you thinking? And you let them drive you home?" She's nearly hysterical.

I suppress the reply that's crawling up my throat. Who does she think she is, questioning me like this, trying to act like a concerned mother when she's never here? She has no idea what I do with my time and who I spend it with. It certainly isn't spent with her. She makes sure of that.

"They're nice. You don't even know them."

"I don't need to know them. Those are not the kind of people you want to surround yourself with, Susan."

"Why not?" I want to hear her say it.

She gives me a look like it's obvious. "You know why."

"I really don't. I like spending time with them."

She scoffs. "Please, what can you possibly have in common with kids like that?"

A lot more than I have in common with you.

"I don't want you seeing them again."

"That's not your decision to make."

Just like that, her lawyer face is on, and I know I'm about to get the speech she always gives. "Your father and I have worked hard to provide a certain kind of life for you, and we aren't just going to sit back and watch you throw it all away."

"I'm not throwing my life away by going to a party on a Saturday night. That's what normal people do."

"Is that what you want? To be normal? I thought we raised you wanting more than that. If you surround yourself with people going nowhere, pretty soon, you'll find that you're going nowhere, too."

"Again, you don't even know them, so how do you know they're going nowhere? God, you're so judgmental."

"I'm not judgmental. I'm honest."

Knowing that I'll never reason with her, that she'll always be stuck in her ways, I just stare back at her until she effectively changes the subject.

"We have lunch at the club tomorrow, and I expect you to be ready by noon." She opens the folder in front of her, dismissing me. "Wear the blue dress I just got you from Saks. I had Claudia hang it in your closet."

I begin to walk away before she calls, "And, Susan ..."

I look back over my shoulder.

"Wear your hair down straight tomorrow. It looks much better that way."

Whenever I think things might change with her, she always proves me wrong.

I leave the dining room, pulling my hair from the high ponytail I had it in.

Sunday moves by slowly. I revert back into the girl my parents want me to be. The box I'm used to living in. I wear the blue dress and my hair down straight. I sit through lunch with my parents and plaster on a smile as people come up to our table to say hello. I go to the tennis lesson I have every Sunday. I never asked to play and was never asked if I liked playing. I don't. But

I've never complained, so I guess whose fault is it that I have to go every week? Although, I don't think complaining would do me much good, anyway.

When we finally arrive back home, my parents and I go our separate ways. I trudge up the stairs, my body slick with sweat and my mind racing. Pushing open the door to my room, my eyes go right to the easel in the corner. The sight of it has my fingers dragging over my palm, my hand curling in on itself.

I walk over to my bed and pull the letter out from under the mattress, just to remind myself that it's still there. That it's real.

I read the first sentence, and then read it again.

Congratulations! You have been admitted to the School of the Art Institute of Chicago.

Shoving it back under the mattress, I slump down, resting my back against the bed and pulling my knees to my chest.

I applied, never thinking I would get in, so I didn't consider what I'd do if I was accepted. Nobody has ever seen my art as something worthy of pursuing, so when I got the acceptance letter, it validated what I've always been told was nothing more than a silly hobby.

But the letter came too late, not that it would have mattered even if it came first. I got my acceptance letter to Brown two days earlier.

It's always been the plan that I would go to my parents' alma mater, the place where they met. That I would follow in their footsteps and become a lawyer.

Once, a few years ago, I brought up going to art school, but that was dismissed before it even became a real conversation, which is why this letter is under my bed and why I've told nobody about it. There's been several times I've thought about telling my parents, but every time I attempt to bring it up, I can never follow through.

I haven't wanted to paint since getting the letter. What used to be a way to escape has only felt like a reminder of how trapped I am. But after last night, a part of me feels ready again.

I stand, stripping out of my tennis skirt and workout top before throwing on a big T-shirt. I don't bother with a shower since I know I'll soon be streaked with paint.

I get out all of my supplies and throw on my headphones, cranking up the music until it feels like I'm lost in it.

From the first brush stroke, my body begins to relax.

Why did I spend so long away from this?

The mask I've been wearing since I woke up fades, and I sink deeper and deeper into the art.

I'm not sure how long I've been at it when I feel a delicate hand tap my shoulder. My brush clatters to the floor as I startle, pulling off my headphones.

My mother is standing behind me, her arms crossed tightly over her chest.

I slide my hands down my face and let out a breath. "You scared me."

She sighs. "You have paint all over your face now."

I look down at my hands and see them smeared with wet blue paint.

"And I tried knocking, but you had that god-awful music blaring. Really, Susan, how many times do I need to tell you not to listen to music that loud?"

I ignore her. "Do you need something?"

Her eyes are fixed on my hands, paint dotting my skin and caked under my nails. "Your father and I would like to speak with you about your plans for the summer."

"Now?" I ask, looking down at myself.

She waves her hand in front of me. "Well, after you get cleaned up."

"Can I just finish this section?" I ask, picking my brush up off the floor.

"This is an important conversation about your future. You can paint later," she says, making it clear that she finds my art to be a complete waste of time.

"Fine," I tell her.

She waits at the door until I stand. "Good, we'll be in the library. Don't keep us waiting long."

After she leaves, I drag myself into the bathroom and step into a hot shower. I scrub the paint off my skin, watching the colors wash away down the drain, and try not to think about how my dreams for the future are going right down with them.

My father looks up from the newspaper he's reading as I walk into the library. He sets it down and checks his watch before his eyes drift over to my mother. She has a glass of wine in hand and a thick open file balanced on her lap.

I sit in the chair across from them as they turn their attention to me.

"I've set up an interview for an internship for you," my father starts. "It's with an associate of mine."

I shift in my seat, and he catches the movement. He reaches for his tumbler of whiskey. "This is an outstanding opportunity, one that isn't afforded to most people, especially those of your age. She has a stack of resumes on her desk, but yours is at the top, so long as you don't give her any reason not to select you for the position."

I force my shoulders to relax. "Thank you."

He brings the drink up to his lips, savoring what I'm sure is an expensive sip. "There's nothing more important than who you know, so don't keep to yourself and waste this experience. Of course, you'll have plenty of time for that while you're at Brown, but this will give you a head start."

I nod.

"You'll need to be dedicated. You can't let anything slip if you want to get to the next level. I've already talked to Mrs. Duncan about a recommendation letter for …"

His words begin to fade together, piling on top of each other until the weight of them squeezes my chest. I drag my nails along my palm just to feel something, digging them in until the pain makes me pull away.

"Are you even listening to your father?" My mother's words cut through the fog.

"Huh?"

She clicks her tongue. "What has gotten into you?"

"I …" Hesitating, I look between my parents. "Sorry, I guess I'm just a little overwhelmed."

"There's no need to be," my father says. "We've been preparing you for this for years. You just need to stay focused."

"That's right," my mother says. "All this time painting and reading, going out with your friends, you need to get your priorities straight, Susan. Maybe then you won't feel so overwhelmed."

"But I—"

"But nothing," my mother cuts in. "Do what needs to be done, yes? You're more than capable."

I stare back at her, wringing my hands.

Her gaze lands on the movement, and she drags her eyes up until they reach mine. "Susan," she prompts.

I drop my hands. "Yes, I understand."

Turning to my father, I add, "I appreciate you setting up the interview."

He picks up the newspaper again, signaling that he's said his piece.

"You should go get ready for bed," my mother says. "It's a school night, and it's getting late."

I'm glad for the dismissal and stand to leave, not bothering to wait for a goodnight from either of them.

CHAPTER 14

I WAKE UP WITHOUT the emptiness I usually feel. I'm actually looking forward to today because I have to go pick up my car, which also means I get to see Billy.

I take more time than usual getting ready then rush through the rest of my morning routine, making sure that I don't run late.

I asked my father yesterday if he could drive me to school since I'm without a car, and he agreed. But both my parents are going to be working late tonight, so they told me I'll have to get a ride to the garage this afternoon.

Coming downstairs, I find him with his cell phone pressed against his ear as he paces restlessly. I drop into a stool at the kitchen island, and he turns to me, holding up a finger. I nod in response before grabbing a set of flashcards I made for biology from my school bag.

I try to focus on flipping through them, but his clipped responses and dramatic sighs keep distracting me.

Is this what my life is going to be like? All those years of school for this?

I look at my father—I mean, *really* look at him—and it's then that I notice just how miserable he seems. His hand is clutching the phone tightly, like he wishes he could shatter it and then maybe he won't have to be on this call anymore. His red-rimmed eyes have bags under them, like even when he sleeps, he never rests. His shoulders are pulled up to his ears as he continues his pacing.

"That's not my problem, now is it, John?" he snaps into the phone. "I'll be at my desk in thirty, and it better be there waiting for me." He doesn't give the man time to respond before hanging up.

Tucking the phone into his pocket, he glances at me. "Let's go."

The short drive to school is as silent as most moments are when I'm alone with my father. He's never really known how to talk to me. We just don't have that kind of relationship, the kind where you share things or talk about your feelings.

I think that's why conversations with him are always so difficult. He doesn't know much about me or my life, so he wouldn't even know what questions to ask, let alone understand the backstory behind anything I might say.

Still, I wait for him to say something—anything.

He never does.

I lean forward to turn on the radio, needing something to fill the emptiness, but stop when he says, "Leave it. I don't like music in the morning."

I slump into my seat, sitting on my hands so I won't fidget, and stare out the window, watching the trees whip past us until we finally pull up in front of the school.

That ten-minute drive felt like it lasted an hour.

I grab my bag and get out of the car, moving to shut the door when I hear him call my name.

"Don't forget about the meeting I set up for you tomorrow with Mrs. Duncan about the internship."

"I won't," I answer.

"It's at five thirty. Don't be late."

"I'll be there."

He nods decisively before staring at me like he isn't sure what I'm still doing here.

Right.

I close the door with a mumbled goodbye and head into school.

The first half of the day goes by without much excitement. I anxiously wait for lunch, worried about how Avery will react when I ask her to bring me to pick up my car. Or more so how she'll react when I tell her that I drove Sam home.

But, by the time I walk into the cafeteria, I'm settled on my story. I figure that if I leave out the party and how the night ended, it will just sound like I was being nice by driving someone home who didn't have a ride.

I pull back my usual seat next to Avery, across from Graham and Logan, and take out the salad I packed.

I've just started pouring the dressing when Avery says, "Did you hear that Katie and Liam broke up?"

I shake the dressing around and answer, "No."

Her eyes light up at the fact that she knows gossip that I don't. "Apparently, he dumped her for some sophomore. I mean, that's so vile, right?"

"Um," I start, not sure how to respond to that. She makes everything so dramatic that, a lot of the time, I'm not sure what to say. She usually doesn't even notice, though. She's more than happy to hear herself talk. Sometimes, it feels like it doesn't even matter that I'm here as long as she has someone to listen to her.

"Talk about downgrading. Katie's on the dance team," she says, motioning to herself. "I mean, we're clearly at the top of the food chain."

She likes to remind me any chance she gets that she's on the team and I'm not.

"Oh, no offense, babe, you're obviously up at the top, too. Like, duh. It's just ... I don't get how he could be so stupid. Katie is way better than some rando sophomore."

Katie's also incredibly annoying, but I'm not going to say that. Instead, I tell her what she wants to hear. "Yeah, I don't know what he was thinking. I bet he'll realize what a mistake he made and they'll get back together by the end of the week."

That seems to satisfy her.

I glance between Graham and Logan, who are deep in their own conversation, completely tuning out Avery's latest gossip. I take the opportunity to ask her for a ride to the garage, not wanting to draw more attention to the situation than I need to.

"Are you free after school? My car is in the shop, and I need a ride to go get it."

"Sorry. Mom and I are getting our nails done," she responds as she holds her hand out in front of her, inspecting them. "Why don't you ask Graham?"

I shoot her a glare that she ignores, just like she seems to ignore the fact that Graham and I broke up.

Hearing his name, he looks over at me. "Ask me what?"

"I need a ride to go pick up my car. It's in the shop."

"What happened? Are you okay?"

"Yeah, I'm fine," I tell him. "It's just the tire. I accidentally drove over a curb. It was nothing major."

"I can drive you to go get it before everyone comes over tonight," he offers.

His dad is out of town again, which means he's having people over. I don't think he can stand being in that big house alone.

"Thanks," I answer before adding, "It's, um ... it's at a garage on the south side. It happened while I was driving home from the food bank."

Not a lie.

His brows furrow in confusion. "Why didn't you just ask the guy who towed it to bring it to the place you usually take your car?"

"I didn't call someone to come tow it."

He stares back at me. "Then how did you get it to a garage?"

I shrug as if it's no big deal. "I was driving Sam home from the food bank when it happened, and her boyfriend's cousin is a mechanic, so she just called him. It was easier that way."

Avery and Logan are staring at me now, too.

"You drove that weird girl home? She's probably a criminal, Susan," Avery says with a shocked expression on her face.

"Not to mention her boyfriend is psychotic," Logan adds. "You *were* sitting next to us when he fully assaulted a guy, right?"

"I was just trying to be nice," I respond, attempting to explain myself to them. "And they're not that bad."

"*They're not that bad*," he repeats like I'm insane.

"Wait, how did you get home?" Graham asks, as if it just occurred to him.

"They drove me home," I mutter.

"Who's *they*?" Logan jumps in before Graham can.

"Jameson and Billy."

"That scary guy drove you home?" Avery asks, gawking at me. "And who's Billy?"

"He's Jameson's cousin. He helped me with my car."

Avery's eyes go wide. "Oh my God. What were they like?"

"Why would you put yourself in a situation like that?" Graham cuts in.

"It wasn't that big of a deal. It just happened. I needed a ride, so they gave me one." I decide to stick with the plan and leave out that we went to a party and that they needed my help getting Sam home. If they're freaking out this much about the fact that I got a ride home with them, then I can't imagine what their reaction would be to that.

"You could have called me, you know?" Graham says, failing to hide his irritation.

I'm not your problem anymore, is what I want to say. He made that perfectly clear when I walked in on him and Ava Thompson kissing.

"I didn't want to bother you and make you come all the way over there," I tell him. "Really, it was nothing."

"You're lucky it was nothing. You saw how that guy's anger comes out of nowhere."

I scoff. "It hardly came out of nowhere. He was defending her."

They all gape at me.

"So you spend one night with these people, and you think that's an appropriate way to respond to things?"

"That's not what I mean."

That's not exactly true. I know Jameson definitely over-reacted, but it's not like he was completely unjustified. That creep had it coming after what he did to Sam.

"Then what did you mean?" Graham questions, his tone full of superiority.

"Can we just drop it? Honestly, you're all making this a bigger thing than it was. I'm not saying that he should have done that, and me getting a ride home from him wasn't me excusing his actions. I didn't think that deeply about it." I'm lying through my teeth. I just want the conversation to be over.

"Sure," he says, but it comes out clipped.

I'm relieved when Logan changes the subject, asking Graham, "A couple of the guys on the team want to know if they can come tonight, too. I also told Juliana she can come. That's cool, right?"

Juliana is one of the girls that Logan "hangs out" with.

Avery's face drops as Graham answers, "Yeah, that's fine."

But she's quick to add, "Brandon's coming, too."

I know she hasn't asked him to come yet and is just trying to even the score with Logan. It's what they do.

We spend the rest of lunch going over our plans for the night. Logan and Avery continue to throw the people they're bringing in each other's faces, but at least the attention isn't on me anymore. I'm happy to sit back and fade into the background.

Just like always.

We look glaringly out of place in Graham's Porsche as he parks in front of Baxston & Sons garage. It's some fancy model that he always likes to tell me about. All I know is that it's white.

The drive over was tense. I could feel everything unspoken pressurizing beneath the surface, hidden under the light conversation. Whatever is going on between us is beginning to feel like a rubber band that has been pulled so far that it can snap at any moment. It's getting harder for me to be around him, and I think he can tell.

Walking into the front room of the garage, my pulse picks up. It feels unnerving that I'm going to see Billy again after Saturday night, especially with Graham right beside me.

When I woke up on Sunday morning, it felt like the day before had been one long fever dream. It was so different from my regular life, how I would usually act, that it almost felt like it wasn't even real. That it didn't even happen.

But now, walking up to the front desk, about to see Billy again, the reality comes crashing down on me. The fluttering in my stomach that I felt that night wasn't just because of the crazy things that were happening. I know now, as I feel them again, that they were also because of Billy.

I'm a bit let down when I see an older man behind the counter instead of Billy. I skate my eyes over the patch sewn on his coveralls that reads, "*Luke*."

"What can I do for ya?" He has one of those voices that sounds weathered, like it belongs to someone who's seen too much of life.

"I'm here to pick up my car. It's under Susan Parker."

He tilts his head to the side as he slides his attention from me to Graham then back to me again. He lingers for a moment like he might say something but decides against it.

Does he know who I am? Did Billy tell him that I was com-ing?

Graham shifts beside me, and I push the questions out of my head as the man begins to slowly tap at the keyboard.

I distract myself by looking around. Billy led us in through a side door the other night, so I never saw this front room. Taking it in, I realize I've never brought my car to a garage like this. Whenever I've needed an oil change, I always bring it to the BMW service center, and my car is too new to have ever needed anything major done to it.

The service center I'm used to is huge and modern. It has pretty much every amenity you can think of to make your wait more comfortable. There are snacks, drinks, big TVs, and areas to work. Where I'm standing right now couldn't be any more different.

Instead of the many desks that line the service center, there's only the one desk that the man is currently standing behind. It's overflowing with papers and has three empty coffee cups just waiting to crash to the floor, next to a fourth mug that the man is periodically sipping from. The few chairs and single couch in the waiting area sit atop stained tile, and just like around the table in the break room, they're all mismatched.

An older woman is sitting in one chair, watching us wearily, and there's another younger woman a few seats down, who's eyeing Graham like he's an expensive steak.

I continue to scan the space, wondering if I'll eventually spot Billy. I keep flicking my gaze back to the door that leads out to the garage, as if he'll appear at any moment.

"You're all set to go," the man says, his gruff voice pulling back my attention.

After I pay, he tells me, "It's out front."

Wait, that's it?

I expected Billy to come out at some point. He told me I would see him here.

I begin to get this panicky feeling that I'll never see him again. I know that sounds completely unreasonable, because even if he did walk through the door right now, what was really going to happen?

In all reality, nothing.

But, whether it makes logical sense or not, I still feel it.

As we walk out the door, disappointment washes over me.

CHAPTER 15

"What a dump," Graham says as he guides me over to my car, his hand pressed possessively against the small of my back.

I roll my shoulders and arch forward, pushing away from him.

An appreciative whistle echoes from my right, causing both Graham and me to turn that way. He goes rigid at the sight of three guys circling his car, running their hands along its body.

Graham steps away from me and lets out an exaggerated sigh, like they're a bunch of schoolkids he has to go reprimand. He swaggers over to them and asks, "Can I help you with something?"

The guy crouching in front of one of the tires slowly turns to Graham, a smirk spreading across his face. He stands to his full height and somehow seems to look down at Graham, even being a few inches shorter than him. "Just admiring her," he says, matching Graham's defensive stance.

"Why don't you do that from a distance?"

The guy raises an eyebrow, throwing an amused look over his shoulder at his two friends. "We're fine right here, pretty boy." He pulls at the door, finding it unlocked, a laugh pouring out of him. "You rich kids just ask for it."

The guy drops into the seat, sliding his palms over the wheel, purposely pushing Graham, who takes the bait and closes the distance between them. "Get out of the car."

The guy only leans back further in the seat, getting comfortable.

"Fine," Graham seethes, pulling his phone out. "I'm calling the cops."

His friends circle the car, each taking one side and closing in on Graham.

"No, you aren't," the guy says from inside the car.

I can see the fear on Graham's face, and I know the men see it, too, but he only puffs out his chest further, trying to play someone he's not.

"Give me your phone," the guy on Graham's left says, holding out his hand.

Graham scoffs. "I'm not giving you my phone."

Stupid. He's being so stupid.

I guess that's what happens when you get everything handed to you—you always think things will work out in your favor. But there are some situations even money can't get you out of, and this is one of them.

Hands clamp down on each of his arms, and then he's dragged back away from the driver's seat, allowing enough space for the guy to climb out. Graham's eyes widen as if he's just now realized he's been playing with fire.

"We asked so nicely," the guy tsks as his friends' eyes light up with anticipation.

I take a step forward, knowing what's coming next, but before I can say anything, I hear a sharp demand.

"Back off, Wyatt."

Wait, I know that voice.

Wyatt shifts, pulling away from Graham and turning toward the approaching footsteps. I watch as Jameson stops in front of them, looking over Graham like he's nothing more than an inconvenience.

"What's going on here?" he asks.

This time, Graham keeps his mouth shut.

Jameson juts his head forward impatiently before Wyatt straightens.

"We were just checking out his ride. Shouldn't have been a problem."

"Uh-huh," Jameson grits out, clearly growing more irritated.

"The asshole threatened to call the cops," Wyatt explains.

Jameson moves toward Graham, and I swear he shrinks under Jameson's stare. "That really necessary?"

"They wouldn't get away from my car," Graham says. "I'm just trying to get home."

Jameson drops his eyes down to Graham's arms still being gripped by the two guys. He waves a hand. "Come on; ease up."

They drop their hold but don't move to step away.

Graham's shoulders lower as he rubs his hands against the spots they'd just been holding.

Jameson tips his chin toward Wyatt, who moves out of the path leading to the driver's seat. He opens the door, holding it for Graham, a clear signal that the interaction is over.

Cautiously, Graham steps forward into the waiting car, but before he can slide into his seat, Jameson stops him, gently placing his hand on Graham's chest. The move is somehow even more intimidating than the death grip the two guys just had him in. Graham stills as Jameson leans into his space.

"No need to make this an issue, right?"

Graham shakes his head, failing to meet Jameson's eyes.

"Good," Jameson answers with a patronizing pat against Graham's chest. "I'd hate for something to happen to such a pretty car."

"There's no issue," Graham chokes out.

Jameson nods and motions for him to get into the car. Once he's inside, Jameson closes the door and looks over at me, his eyes locking with mine. There isn't a hint of surprise on his face when he sees me, like he knew I was here the whole time.

The Porsche roars to life, and Graham wastes no time speeding away.

Jameson continues to watch me until I finally turn and walk the rest of the way to my waiting car.

Once inside, I watch Jameson head into the shop, the three others following behind him. Glancing around the empty lot, I give up any hope of seeing Billy and start to key my house into Google Maps. I'm picking a playlist for the drive when a tap against the window makes me jump.

I jerk my head up in surprise and am met with the smile that's been stuck in my head.

It's him.

I stare back at Billy until he motions for me to roll down the window.

"Hi," I breathe.

"Hi," he answers as he rests his arm on the roof of my car, leaning in closer. "I thought I was gonna miss you." When I don't say anything, he continues, "I had to run out to pick up a part, but when I heard you were here, I raced back."

"You did?" I ask shyly. "Why?"

"I wanted to see you."

"Really?"

He lets out a short laugh. "Yeah, Richie, really."

Did Jameson tell him I was here?

"You've got somewhere you gotta be?"

I nod. "A party." His smile falters, so I add, "But it's not until later."

He tips his head toward the passenger seat. "Can I sit?"

"Oh, yeah, sure," I sputter.

His smile comes back as he opens the door and drops down beside me.

I'm quiet as the space fills with his presence, feeling overwhelmed that he's really here. That it's just the two of us.

"I've gotta go back in soon, but I just—" He runs a hand through his hair. "I haven't been able to stop thinking about you since the other night."

My heart begins to race, never having expected to hear him say those words. I want to tell him that I haven't been able to stop thinking about him either, but I'm afraid to admit it. Afraid to make it real.

I search for something to give him, but before I get the chance, he continues, "I know I'm not *your type*." He says it like he still doesn't believe it's true. "But if that ever changes ..." He pulls a sharpie from his back pocket and finds a receipt in my center console. "Can I write on this?"

I nod, not trusting myself to speak right now, too worried it will betray my actual feelings.

He leans forward and scribbles his number on the receipt then turns to me. Grabbing my hand, he slides his thumb across my wrist then places the piece of paper in my palm and closes my fingers over it. "If that ever changes, call me."

"I ..." I flick my eyes up to meet his and clear my throat before trying again. "I will."

His gaze lowers to my lips, and it slows there for a moment before it drifts to his hand still circling my wrist. He pulls his hand away then turns to open the door.

I watch him as he steps out, closes the door, and leans into the open window.

"Richie?" he says, his voice low.

"Yes?" I manage to get out.

His eyes lock with mine. "I really hope you call."

Chapter 16

WHEN I GET HOME, I tuck the receipt with Billy's number on it under my bed, next to my acceptance letter to art school.

The whole drive home, I thought about whether I'd call and what it would mean if I did. I've imagined what it would look like, being with Billy, but it felt like a far-off fantasy, one that has no chance of happening. I didn't even know if he really liked me or if he was just that flirty with all girls.

But after what he just told me ...

After he gave me his number ...

The logical side of my brain crushes the thought.

So what if he did? What am I really going to do?

I can't picture any reality where Billy could actually become part of my life. For starters, my parents would never approve. My mother already warned me off *people like him* when Billy and Jameson dropped me off at home. Beyond that, I'm leaving for school in a few months.

He doesn't fit the plan.

He doesn't fit my life.

But sometimes, I really think about just abandoning it all. Going to art school instead of Brown. Not letting my parents decide everything I do. Finding friends who see me for who I really am.

But I'm too scared. Scared that it won't work, that I'll regret it, that I'm not capable of standing on my own.

So, instead of calling, I leave Billy's number under the mattress, along with my dreams for what could be, and get ready for Graham's party.

It doesn't take me long to find my friends. Graham's voice carries through the living room, competing with the steady thump of bass. There's a small circle around him, full of people with wide eyes.

"And I told them to back the fuck up," he tells his audience. "I would've let them look, but I wasn't about to let them scratch the paint."

His eyes flick up and land on me, everyone turning to follow his gaze. He reaches out his hand to pull me beside him, protectively tucking me under his arm. "I told Susan to stay where she was. I didn't want her anywhere near them."

I shrug out from under him while everyone practically ohs and aahs like he's some sort of hero.

"I can't even imagine what they'd do to a girl like you," he continues.

I take a step away from him, our blurred lines becoming too much.

One of the girls twirls her hair around a finger. "That's so scary."

"You've got to be careful around guys like that," he tells her, but it feels like his words are aimed at me. Scolding me for getting him into that situation.

"I'm gonna go get a drink," I mumble before slipping through the crowd.

I only get a few steps before I feel him at my back. He follows me into the kitchen, watching as I rummage through the fridge.

"What's your problem?"

I'm really not in the mood for this right now.

Turning, I crack open a seltzer. "I don't have a problem."

He scoffs. "Yeah, okay. 'Cause things between us are so great."

What does he expect?

I roll my eyes. "There is no *us* anymore, Graham.

"Come on. It was one time," he says, exasperated. "How many times are you going to make me say I'm sorry before we can just move on?"

"You can't just say sorry. That doesn't take it back."

He throws up his hands. "Well, it happened already. I messed up. I can't take it back now, so what do you want me to do?"

"Nothing."

"*Nothing*?" He takes a step toward me, his hand coming down on my arm. "We could be good together. We *were* good together."

"Then why'd you do it?"

His hand falls from my arm.

"You know what? Never mind. I don't want to hear your excuse."

He sighs. "I'm—"

"I'm gonna go," I cut him off.

"But you just got here."

I set down my drink. "I'm not up for it tonight."

I take a step back, but he catches my wrist. "Susan—"

"Stop touching me!" I snap. "I'm not yours anymore."

He shakes his head. "You'll change your mind. I'll prove to you that I can be better."

"Please," I whisper, "just let me go."

He pulls his hand back. "I'll text you tomorrow. See how you're feeling."

I shake my head but don't say anything. Stepping away, I shuffle through the crowd and back to my car. Closing the door, I let the silence wrap around me, take in a steadying breath, and turn up the radio until I can't hear my thoughts anymore.

The light in the front room of the house is on when I pull into the driveway. I slip inside and close the front door softly, hoping to escape up to my room unnoticed.

After sliding my shoes off, I only make it a couple steps before I hear my mother call out to me, "You're home early."

Pasting on a casual smile, I round the corner into the sitting room. "I just got tired," I respond. "I didn't sleep well last night."

She looks over the top of her laptop, assessing me as if she can sense the lie. "Is everything okay with you and Graham?"

My father glances up at the mention of Graham, his interest suddenly piqued.

I hesitate for a moment too long, and my mother's eyes narrow.

"Everything with Graham is fine," I lie.

I still haven't told them that we broke up.

"Good," she answers, leaning back in her chair. "You two make a great pair."

My father grunts in agreement.

"He'll be at the graduation party, yes?" she asks.

I nod.

Her lips twist in distaste as she fixates on my fidgeting hands. I immediately release them, dropping them down by my sides.

"Did you decide on a dress yet?"

"I think I'm going to go with the off-the-shoulder one."

"Are you sure?" she asks, picking up her glass of wine. "I thought the other one suited you much better."

Why does she even ask? Just for the illusion that I have a choice?

She watches me until I give her the response she wants. "I wasn't set on that one. I think you're right. The other one fits me better."

"Don't forget about your hair appointment, and I scheduled you with Danielle for makeup. Can you handle making your own nail appointment?"

"Yes."

"Okay, good. French tips would look best with the dress."

"That's what I was thinking," I answer, even though the thought never crossed my mind. Unlike my mother, I don't spend my time thinking about the future color of my nails.

"And remember what I told you," she says. "No painting the day before. I don't want your hands stained."

"I won't," I respond, not liking how weak my voice sounds.

"Well, I think that's everything," she says, more to herself. "Why don't you go get some sleep? You need to be well rested for your interview tomorrow."

"Do you feel prepared?" my father questions.

No.

"Yes," I answer.

He nods, turning the page of the newspaper he's reading, satisfied with my response.

I glance back at my mother and find her locked in on her laptop.

Taking it as my cue to go, I leave the room with the weight of their expectations sitting heavily on my shoulders.

CHAPTER 17

THE FINAL WEEKS OF school dragged on, each day seeming even longer than the last.

My interview for the internship went well. Based on what I told my father, he said I should definitely get it. Pride had shown on his face, and I hate that I let it get to me. That I allowed it to mean something.

All week, my mother has been nagging me. Just when I think she can't pick at anything else, she invariably finds something. I've been avoiding her, keeping to my room as much as possible when she's been home. But today, there's been no escaping it, not with my graduation this afternoon.

It all feels like too much, and it's only getting worse as the day gets later. My mind keeps drifting to the future, the plans I've made and the ones I've let go.

I've been sitting in my room for what feels like hours, my acceptance letter to art school and Billy's number mocking me from their place under my mattress. More than once I've thought about calling Billy. I even did call one time, but when he answered, I hung up before saying anything. I just didn't—

My door is pushed open, pulling me from my thoughts, and I turn to find my mother standing there with her arms crossed.

"What are you doing just sitting in the middle of the floor?"

I push myself up and mumble, "Nothing."

She eyes the dress that's still draped across my bed. "We need to leave in twenty minutes."

I begin to tell her that I'll be ready when her phone rings.

"It's the caterer," she says before taking a step into the hall. She grabs the door to pull it closed and warns, "Twenty minutes, Susan."

I hurry to get ready, slipping on my dress and running clear lip gloss over my lips. I stare at myself in the mirror, placing the cap on my head. I then slide the gown over my shoulders and finally place the various cords I've earned around my neck to finish it off.

"Susan!" my mother yells from downstairs. "I want pictures before we go."

I grab my phone and bag before heading downstairs where my mother impatiently waits.

Graduations are so boring. I'm the one graduating, and I can barely make it through without wanting to fall asleep. I mean, really, do they have to read out every single name? It takes forever before I'm finally called.

I walk across the stage, trying not to fall in the ridiculous shoes my mother bought me. Luckily, I get my diploma and make it back to my seat without tripping.

Finally, they finish calling all the names and tell us we're official. Everyone moves their tassels and throws their caps. I go through the motions, but it feels like I'm in a fog, like none of this matters.

I meet up with my friends and find my parents, Graham beside me through it all. When I confessed that I haven't told my parents we broke up yet, he was more than happy to play along.

We take rounds of pictures before breaking off to go to our various cars, all of us heading to my house for the party. My mother has been planning it for months. Luckily, she hasn't bothered to involve me in any of it. My job is to just show up and smile.

The house has been transformed in the few hours we've been at the graduation. Black and gold balloons line the front walkway, displaying our school colors and opening into the foyer with a blown-up photo of my senior picture. Waiters greet us with glasses of champagne and hors d'oeuvres—button mushrooms stuffed with something I'd rather not eat.

It's just as stuffy as I thought it would be. There isn't a detail out of place or expense that has been spared to put on a worthy display for my parents' friends.

My parents parade me around, and after one too many of the same conversations, I'm already ready for the night to be over. Finally, they seem to be satisfied that I've spoken with all the guests and go their own way.

I meander around until I find Graham sitting with Logan and Avery.

Avery turns to me and lets out a laugh. "I thought you'd never get away."

"This might be the lamest party I've ever been to," Logan says.

Graham swirls his drink. "No, nothing will ever top when Chip graduated from Yale. I literally fell asleep at that one."

I snort. "Oh, yeah, who could ever forget those speeches?"

"Hours," Avery groans. "They literally went on for hours."

"Well, your brother is very special," I tease.

She rolls her eyes. "He's only gotten worse since getting into med school."

Logan leans back into the couch, throwing his arm casually behind Avery. "I'm so not coming to that one, and I'm never calling him Doctor."

"How much longer do you think we have to give it before bailing?" Graham asks.

I look around for my mother, finding her talking with a group of her friends. "I think I've put in my time. We're probably good."

"Kennedy is having a party," Logan chimes in.

"So is Sebastian," Avery adds.

Graham glances up from his phone. "Lights Out, that local band my dad's working with, is playing at Red's. We should go."

Wait, Lights Out is the band Dylan is in, the guy who connected Graham with Jameson.

"Isn't Red's totally shady?" Avery asks.

Logan pulls her in closer. "Don't worry; I'll protect you."

"I'm serious," she groans.

"It's fine," Graham tells her. "My dad knows the guys who own it."

Of course he does.

He looks at me. "You in?"

I smile back. "Anything to get me out of this party."

It doesn't take much convincing for our parents to let us leave.

Avery and I ditch our heels and dresses, changing into something more casual. Logan and Graham lose their suit jackets, undoing a few buttons on their shirts and rolling up their sleeves. Within twenty minutes, we're on the road.

After circling a few times, we finally find a parking spot. Music and chatter filter out into the street as we make our way to the venue.

Graham slows in front of a packed building with a neon sign above the door. It shines against the black backdrop of night, showcasing a pinup girl with firetruck-red hair next to the glowing word *Red's*.

Instead of going to the end of the line that's snaking around the front of the building, Graham leads us all to another door, and after flashing something on his phone, we're let in.

We push through the crowd to find a spot, the space already full.

"How long until they go on?" I yell over the noise.

"They're on at nine," Graham answers.

I pull my phone out of my pocket to check the time, seeing that it's already ten past nine. Sure enough, just as we find a pocket in the crowd, the lights dim and the band comes out.

It's a group of four guys who all have a really grungy look. They immediately go into the first song, which is amazing. It has this sort of indie rock feel, with lyrics that completely draw me in.

It ends to a wave of applause, and then the lead singer says, "Thank you. We're Lights Out, from right over on Fairfax Ave."

The crowd erupts, and my stomach flutters, remembering their connection to Jameson.

To Billy.

I look around for either of them, knowing how unlikely it would be for me to see them. First of all, they might not even be here tonight, and I would also have to pick them out in a dark crowd of a couple hundred people.

I don't recognize any of the illuminated faces, which isn't much of a surprise, so I turn my attention back to the stage. Still, I'm distracted throughout the whole set.

After the show ends, Graham says we can go backstage to hang out with the band. He makes sure to remind us that he's already hung out with them and that, "They're really cool guys." He always makes it a point to talk about all the people he knows and the things he's done. Other people seem to eat it up, but it just gets on my nerves. Because what they don't seem to know is that name-dropping these people is his entire personality, and when your biggest accomplishment is that you've stood next to other accomplished people, it makes you pretty boring.

We have to wait for the crowd to clear out a bit, and then he brings us down a narrow hallway that ends in a big room.

The first thing I notice when we walk in is how smoky the space is and that it smells like weed and incense. The wall you see right as you step in is painted black and covered in signatures of varying colors. There's music playing, but a laugh pierces through it. I trace the sound, and my heart drops when I see who it came from.

Like he can sense my eyes on him, Billy turns his head, and a slow smile spreads across his face. He's leaning back lazily on a light blue velvet couch, the neck of a beer bottle dangling between two fingers. The lead singer is sitting to his right, clearly talking to him, but Billy isn't listening anymore.

Instead, he's watching me.

CHAPTER 18

THE ROOM IS EVEN bigger than I initially thought, and there's a good number of people scattered around, but Graham heads right toward where Billy is sitting.

I follow behind him while Avery and Logan go to the table with all the alcohol.

I have to remember to breathe as we walk over, each step feeling longer than the last.

Seeing us approach, the singer stands and grabs Graham's hand, pulling him into one of those bro hugs. "Thanks for coming, man."

"It was a killer show," Graham responds. "This is Susan," he adds, pushing me forward.

I concentrate on keeping my eyes off Billy as the singer asks, "How'd you like the show, Susan?" His voice comes out just as sultry when he talks as it did when he sang, walking a tightrope between gravelly and smooth, somehow settling on a mix of the two.

"I loved it, especially that one chorus about the match." I look up, trying to get it right. "'*You lit the match that set us on fire. Burn for me, baby, and bring me up higher.*'"

His eyes dance with amusement as he tells Graham, "Get this girl a job with the old man. She's got an ear."

"Oh, Susan's not into music like that," he answers dismissively.

The singer, whose name I still don't know, turns back to me with a questioning look. "I find that hard to believe."

That's because you're right, I want to say.

I love music, especially lyrics. My friends just don't know it because they've never asked. Graham doesn't care about the music when we go to things like this. For him, it's all about getting to meet people, and the more famous, the better.

"You sticking around?" the singer asks, his question directed at Graham this time.

"Yeah, we'll hang for a bit."

Since when does he talk like that?

The more I'm around Graham, the more I realize that he completely changes depending on who he's talking to.

I wonder how he changes around me.

"Derek's got the weed, so I'm about to go over there. You want in?"

Graham doesn't even spare me a glance before he accepts.

The singer looks over at Billy, but he waves him off, saying, "I'm good."

"I'll be back," Graham tells me as he takes off toward a group settled against the far wall.

Finally, I let my eyes drift back to Billy, and my skin heats when I realize he's still watching me.

He breaks contact for just long enough to drop his eyes to the seat next to him before bringing them back up to me. My body accepts his invitation before my mind can think about it, moving to sit down beside him.

I wait for him to ask me why I haven't called; instead, he says, "Didn't expect to see you here, Richie."

"Guess it's wrong to make assumptions about people," I answer.

He lets out a low laugh. "So, that's the ex?"

"Yeah," I mutter.

"Hmm."

"What?"

"You know what." He takes a pull from his beer. "He just left without even asking you."

"I'm not his mother. He doesn't need my permission." I shake my head. "And we're not together."

"But he wants to be, right? He must be trying to win you back."

I tuck a strand of hair behind my ear. "Why would you think that?"

"Well, he showed up here with you, didn't he?"

I nod.

He tips his beer bottle toward me. "And I mean, look at you. He'd be stupid not to try to get you back."

I look down, blushing.

"So, is he then?"

I slide my eyes back up to meet his. "Yeah."

"Then he made a big mistake."

I wait for him to explain, and when he doesn't, I inch my head forward. "What do you mean?"

"He just left you here alone"—he lowers his gaze to the floor before dragging it over me, not even bothering to hide his slow perusal of my body—"with me."

I let out a breath, feeling the space around us grow smaller.

He leans in closer. "If you were mine, I wouldn't let you out of my sight."

I shift in my seat, and he watches every movement, like the littlest thing I do is fascinating.

"Do you want a drink?" he asks, draining the last of his own.

I bite my lip. "Sure."

He stands and motions for me to follow.

I peek over my shoulder and find Graham leaning against the back wall, completely disinterested in what I'm doing and who I'm with.

So much for proving to me that he'd be better.

Looking back at Billy, it occurs to me that he was never actually introduced. Graham has no idea that it's him I'm with. What would he say if he knew Billy was the one I was with that night? Based on how easily he just left me, I'm not sure I care.

Billy leads us to a table that's lined with bottles. He grabs two Solo cups and fills them with Coke and then rum, one with about twice as much as the other.

He hands me the one with the lighter pour and says, "You'll like this."

I take a sip, and he's right, something I'm noticing he often is about me.

My lips tip up, and he mirrors my expression. He likes that he knew what I wanted.

I like it, too.

"Did Sam and Jameson come?" I ask.

"Yeah, they're somewhere around here. They tend to sneak off during things like this."

I want to ask about Sam but don't want to overstep.

He straightens like he can sense it. "What?"

I hesitate for a moment, taking another small sip of my drink. "Did everything end up being okay with her that night?"

He looks at me for a minute before nodding slowly, his expression turning distant. Finally, he says, "It was really cool of you to help out like that."

I shrug. "It was nothing."

"Don't downplay it. Not everyone would have done that. You barely even know her."

"I like her," I explain simply.

He snorts, and I roll my lips to hide a smile.

"What?"

"Come on; you know what. She's not exactly the warmest person when you first meet her."

"Well, at least she's genuine. It just makes me want to win her over. For her to accept me, I guess."

"If it makes you feel any better, I know she likes you, too."

"Really? How do you know?"

"She doesn't open up easily, which you probably guessed, so the fact that she let you go into her house means something. The fact that Jameson suggested it, even more. He's good at picking up vibes. He really trusts his gut, and she really trusts him."

"And I have a good vibe?"

He smiles. "Yeah, Richie, you have a good vibe."

I look up at him, matching his smile. "You do, too." Clearing my throat, I ask, "So, how do you know the band?"

Billy goes into a story about how they all grew up together. Of course, I knew that already, but what I didn't know was that Billy used to play with them. He was the drummer until he quit to work at his dad's garage. He glosses over those details, so I don't ask, but it seems like there's more to the story.

As he tells me about the things they got into as kids, I realize I could listen to him talk about it all night.

"What about you?" he asks. "How'd you end up here tonight?"

"I was at my graduation party—"

"Wait," he cuts in. "You graduated today?"

I nod.

"And you ditched your own party?"

"It wasn't—"

"Susan," a familiar voice calls, and I turn, finding Graham walking toward us, with Avery and Logan following behind him. "We're heading over to Sebastian's party. Come on."

Before I can respond, Billy says, "I can take her home."

Graham turns toward him. "Who are you?" he asks dismissively.

"I'm the guy who's been keeping her company all night."

Graham folds his arms over his chest. "Well, she's not going home with you."

Billy shifts forward. "Why not?"

"Because she's not. She came here with me, and she's leaving with me."

"*She's* right here," Billy grits out.

Graham glances at me briefly.

"Why don't you ask her?" Billy says, waving a hand in my direction.

Graham scoffs. "Don't be ridiculous. I'm not asking her if she wants to come with me. Of course she does."

"I really think you should," Billy pushes.

"I don't know what you think you're implying. Come on, Susan; let's go."

His words grate on me, making me feel like a child who's being dragged home.

Billy leans into me, his voice softening. "If you want to stay, I'll drive you home."

"Don't talk to her," Graham mutters.

Billy turns back to him. "I've been talking to her all night, remember? You've just been too busy to notice."

Graham steps forward and grabs my hand, pulling me to his side like I'm a toy he doesn't want to share.

Billy zeros in on the movement and snaps, "Don't touch her."

"She's my girlfriend," Graham says as if that's an excuse.

I tug my hand away. "No, I'm not."

Graham sighs. "You know what I mean."

I take a step away from him. "I want to stay."

He pulls his head back. "What?"

"I want to stay. Billy can drive me home."

Graham raises an eyebrow. "Do you know how that looks?"

A hollow laugh falls from my lips. "*That's* your response? Really?"

He takes a step back. "You know what? I'm over this. Do whatever you want. It's not like I haven't been."

My body tightens. "What does that mean?"

"Did you really think I would wait around forever?" He leans forward. "Do you know how many girls wish they were you? How many girls were practically begging   "

"That's enough," Billy cuts in.

"You told me it was a one-time thing? A mistake? How many times ...?" I look at Avery, waiting for her to stand up for me, to come to my side. But she says nothing, her eyes trained on the floor. "Why are you telling me this now?"

"I wanted you back," Graham says simply. Then he looks over at Billy and shrugs. "I don't anymore."

I open my mouth to respond, but nothing comes out.

"Have fun with the trash," Graham says over his shoulder as he strides away, Avery and Logan following behind him.

I watch them walk out the back door before turning to Billy. "I'm sorry," I whisper.

He shakes his head. "What are you sorry for?"

"That he talked to you like that. Like you were beneath him. He's such a—"

"Don't," Billy says, pulling me into his chest. "If anyone needs an apology, it's you. He shouldn't have said those things."

"Thank you," I mumble into his chest. "And thanks for standing up for me like you did."

He pulls away from me. "Anytime, Richie."

Without warning, an arm comes around Billy's neck, and he's pulled into a headlock. I jump back instinctively before realizing it's only Jameson.

Billy swings around and pushes him off, laughing the whole time, like this is a normal way to be greeted. Once free, he points at Jameson and says, "Back the fuck up." Then he looks between him and Sam, who's now pressed against Jameson's side. "Where've you two been hiding?"

She slides her hand into Jameson's back pocket, a dazed look on her face. Jameson gazes down at her then back to Billy.

"Oh, come on," Billy groans, rolling his eyes. "Can't you two ever use a bed like normal people?"

"We do that, too," Jameson says in a tone so dry that only the slight pull of his lips gives away the humor.

Sam slaps him teasingly on the chest. "Behave," she warns before turning her attention to Billy. "And it's not like you're one to judge. How many times have we caught you—"

She stops mid-sentence when Billy flicks his eyes to me, and it's just then she notices I'm here.

"Oh, hey," she says, glancing between Billy and me, as if wondering what we're doing here together. "Did you come alone?"

I hesitate before shaking my head.

"Then who'd you come with?" she asks.

"My friends," I answer. "But they, um, they left."

"*They left*?" She looks from me to Billy, her brow raising. "Without you?"

Billy wraps an arm around me, and I find myself leaning into him rather than pulling away. "I'm gonna take her home," he says.

Sam tracks the movement and nods. "All right, cool."

"Have you seen—"

There's suddenly a noise so loud that I can't even tell if it's my ears hearing it. It buzzes through my body before it fades out around me.

There are other noises, too. I think people are yelling, but it all sounds funny, like everyone is underwater.

I can see people moving, but my body remains still. I try to move my legs, but it feels like they're stuck to the ground.

I dart my eyes around frantically, but I can't figure out how everyone else can move. Is the air around them not as thick as the air around me?

The minutes feel like days, or maybe they're just seconds. Falling.

Why am I falling?

The air is knocked from my lungs as a hard and heavy body forces mine to drop to the ground.

I open my eyes, not even realizing they'd been closed. Then blink.

One time.

Two times.

Three.

Until the room comes back into focus.

Sam is crouched down behind Jameson, and a shudder runs through me when I see the look on her face.

If fear could be a person, it would be her.

Jameson has one hand snaked behind him, holding her by the waist, giving her some of his strength. In his other hand is a gun. It looks like an extension of him as he grips it with a knowing ease. There isn't the slightest tremble as he holds it up in front of him, his jaw set and eyes focused.

I barely see it coming—the slight movement of his finger.

Hands come down harshly over my ears, and I feel more pressure come on top of me. My whole body is now shielded by another, as if anticipating what's coming.

I hear that horrible sound again. Except, this time, it's somehow even louder than it was before.

I hold my body as still as I can for someone who's violently shaking.

Then I hear something fall.

No, *someone* fall.

It's heavy and happens all at once.

The weight moves off me and picks me up. The body starts running, holding me firmly against its chest. We're moving faster than seems normal. But then again, what even is normal?

I feel a cool breeze run over my skin. We must be outside. I'm put into the back of a car, one that smells like smoke and leather.

Above the ringing, I hear a voice ask, "What do we do?"

"I don't know," another says. "We just need to get the fuck out of here."

I try to make out what's happening. Who's talking.

Shock.

I must be in shock.

The car begins to move as an arm pulls me against a familiar body, the one that had just been on top of me, shielding me from that noise.

I adjust myself so my legs can come up onto the seat. My head lowers, and a hand begins to gently stroke my hair.

Slowly, I stop shaking and begin to return to my body. To my mind.

The repetitive movement of the hand against my hair calms me. A reassurance that I'm safe.

I don't know how long we sit like that before I finally tilt my head up and see Billy staring down at me.

Just one look at the expression on his face, and I somehow know that nothing will ever be the same again.

CHAPTER 19

WE PULL UP IN front of a small house, and Jameson leaves the car running while he goes inside. He returns a couple of minutes later with a duffle bag and a blanket. He places the blanket over Sam, who's staring straight ahead, eyes fixed on something that isn't there, and tucks it around her as if that will somehow make things better. His hand lingers on her like he's waiting for her to respond to his touch, for the gesture to work its magic. But her body remains rigid, her expression holding nothing but emptiness. Finally, he turns and hands the duffle bag to Billy, who sets it down on the floor, seeming to already know what's inside.

I watch them move around me, but nothing feels real. It's like I'm stuck in the same world Sam is in. A world where we don't have to process what we've just gone through. A world where we don't have to hear the thoughts screaming at us to listen. A world where we can just turn it all off.

I don't understand how Billy and Jameson aren't trapped in this world, too, but maybe they're just as lost as Sam and I are and are only better at hiding it.

Or maybe they just haven't let themselves lose it yet.

The car starts moving again, and I focus on the hum of the road and the lights that pass outside the window. I try to right myself, find something to hold onto, but my mind isn't working right. Everything is coming to me in little fragments. There are parts that are missing, that my mind won't let me see.

Nobody says a word as we drive, and the lights I was watching out the window eventually fade into empty back roads that leave me with nothing but darkness. It feels like we've been on the road forever.

I wonder how far away we are from home now. If I should tell them to stop and let me out. Or, if they even would.

The thoughts skate down my spine, prickling my skin. My hands curl in on themselves, and I breathe out as my nails dig into my palms.

Billy's hand comes down over mine, and I unfurl my fingers.

"You're safe," he tells me, the words no more than a whisper.

I feel his warmth as he pulls me in closer. My eyes close, and my racing heart begins to slow as I focus on the rough finger that's gliding back and forth over my hand.

I begin to slip into the moment, to let Billy's comfort wrap around me. The adrenaline is wearing off, and I feel myself start to succumb to the exhaustion. My body grows heavy as my mind starts to slow, but it's all ripped away by the sound of loud ringing.

I flinch at the noise, and my brain immediately returns to that sound, the one I never want to hear again.

Billy shifts under me as he tries to find his phone, and after looking at who's calling, he flicks his eyes up to meet Jameson's. He brings the phone to his ear but doesn't say anything, just sits there and listens, nothing but the slight bob of his throat giving away what's being said on the other side. Then he hangs up, not even saying goodbye, and nods his head stiffly once to Jameson.

"Fuck," Jameson mutters, running his hand through his hair, pulling manically, like he wants to feel the pain that comes with it. When that doesn't work, he starts hitting the steering wheel with the palm of his hand. Over and over and over again.

What's going on?

Sam sits next to him, completely still, eyes forward, as if she doesn't even notice him.

He pulls off onto the side of the road, and we sit there as he closes his eyes and takes long, steadying breaths. I count to forty-eight before he opens them again, no longer looking out of control.

He gave himself that one little outburst, and that's it. Now, the control he wears like an armor is firmly back in place.

Billy has become unnervingly still beneath me. I tip my head to look at him, but his full attention is on Jameson.

Waiting.

I understand why when Jameson starts rattling off instructions. "We need to ditch the phones. Especially hers," I hear him say.

Billy nods, handing his to Jameson. Then he taps my thigh. "I need your phone, babe." His voice sounds so soft, his tone so careful, like he's afraid that speaking any louder might break me open. "Do you know where it is? Can you find it for me?" he coaxes when I stay frozen in place.

Sitting up, I pull my knees to my chest and struggle to remember where my phone might be. I begin to speak, but it feels like I swallowed sand, my voice coming out low and strained.

Was I screaming before?

I clear my throat and try again. "I don't know where it is," I finally get out. "I just ... I don't remember. My purse. I think I left my purse."

"What about your pockets?" he asks. "It's important that we make sure it's not with us in the car."

I move my hands over my pockets and shake my head, telling Billy that they're empty.

Jameson turns around and uses the flashlight on his phone to check the floor.

What they're asking becomes clearer, and confusion sets in.

"Why do we need to get rid of our phones?"

"So we're not tracked," Jameson answers matter-of-factly.

I don't understand. Are there pieces in front of me that I'm not putting together? Is this the thing my mind won't let me see?

"The police are looking for us," Billy says.

I repeat the words in my head three times before they register.

The police are looking for us.

The police are looking for us.

The police are looking for us.

I flick my eyes between them.

"They know it was Jameson," Billy clarifies.

"What do they know was Jameson?" I ask, hoping the answer will be different than the image that's now playing in my head.

The image that my mind is finally showing me.

Different from what I saw right before I was picked up and carried away.

"They know it was Jameson who killed Carson."

Chapter 20

I'm trying to breathe, but it suddenly feels like I can't get enough air in.

Billy turns my head gently until his eyes meet mine.

I stare back at him.

"Breathe in," he tells me, his voice calming my racing heart.

This time, it works, and I inhale a deep breath.

"Good," he says, dropping one of his hands and grasping mine. "Now breathe back out," he utters as he brings our hands up to my chest and covers mine with his.

I let out a long breath and feel the panic start to slip away.

"Again," he whispers, and with each breath, the tightness in my chest begins to loosen. I begin to feel safe.

"You're all right," he states once my breathing comes back to normal.

I blink up at him, wondering how he did that. How he knew just what I needed. I've never been able to stop the panic that quickly, and I've never let anyone see me this way. But I let Billy.

Because I trust him.

Because I trust all of them.

"Thank you," I tell him hesitantly. I'm not used to being vulnerable with people or someone helping me like this.

He lowers my hand, still holding it firmly. "You don't have to thank me," he responds, shaking his head. "You shouldn't have to deal with this."

"Neither should you," I whisper.

I lean into him as Jameson says, "We need to figure out our next move." His words pull me out of the moment and right back into reality. "If Carson is dead, then this is worse than I thought it was."

"Wait, you didn't mean to kill him?" I blurt out, not thinking before I let the words slip.

"No, I did," he clarifies.

The blood drains from my face. It's one thing for me to assume it, but another for him to actually confirm it.

Billy winces, while Jameson's face is void of any expression.

It seems like after his outburst, he made the conscious decision to fully dissociate, to solve the problem in front of him and leave his emotions out of it.

"He didn't mean to miss the first time he shot at us," Jameson says. "He was just too fucked up to aim right. I wasn't about to wait around for his second try."

All my questions come out at once. "You really think he would have killed you? I mean, why would he just come and shoot at you? Why was he even there?"

"Yes, I think he would have killed me," he answers, his tone hard. "He's violent and unpredictable when he's high. Something happened a few weeks ago ..."

My eyes widen, and seeing it click, he nods, confirming, "It's why I couldn't go into her house that night. Why I thought Carson might be more on edge."

"What happened? What could make him that upset with you?"

"It doesn't take much with him," Billy mutters from beside me.

When I bring my attention back to Jameson, his is on Sam.

She looks like a shell of herself, and I can't imagine what it's doing to him to see her this way.

"This isn't the time to talk about it," Jameson snaps. "We need to get at least a few more hours out of town tonight, then we can stop and figure out what we're gonna do next."

I want to say something—anything—to make this better. I could tell them that we should go back, that what Jameson did was self-defense. But I'm way out of my depth, and with how on edge everyone is right now, I'm not sure that any of us are thinking clearly.

I look on as Sam continues to stare forward, and I watch as Jameson watches her before ripping his gaze away and turning the wheel left so we're back on the road.

Billy's hand grips mine tighter as if he needs something to hold onto.

I can feel their pain.

I can feel their fear.

But above all, I can feel their love for one another. The fact that they would do anything to keep each other safe. I can feel how they take on each other's emotions as if they were their own, how it's killing Jameson to see Sam like this, and killing Billy to watch the two of them. And in this moment, I share their same fears.

The fear of the unknown.

Fear of what the future might bring.

But what I'm not afraid of is the three of them.

If it weren't for Billy, I could be dead right now.

I just froze when Carson fired that first shot. I didn't drop down like the people around me.

If Billy hadn't pushed me down …

Covered me with his body …

He didn't have to do any of those things. He didn't have to protect me.

And Jameson …

If Jameson hadn't pulled that trigger …

If he hadn't killed Carson ...

How many more times would Carson have shot at us? Would one of those bullets have hit me?

Yes, those few minutes were the scariest moments of my life. But, being in this car, I feel safer than I ever have because, for once in my life, I'm sitting next to someone who risked everything for me.

He protected me, knowing what Carson was capable of.

He shielded me, knowing that Carson might shoot again.

And Billy never left my side, never let go of me, until he knew I was safe.

Chapter 21

I have no sense of time or where we are when we finally pull into a motel.

Jameson throws the car into park in front of the office. Billy opens the duffle bag and takes out a wad of cash held in a neat stack by a rubber band. He hands several bills to Jameson, who palms them then jumps out of the car and strides toward the front door.

I crane my neck to look into the bag, but Billy already has it zipped back up and is shoving it down by his feet.

How much money is in there? And why did Jameson have a bag full of cash just sitting in his house?

"You doing okay?" Billy asks, his voice low.

I shift so I can look at him. "I'm fine."

"That's good. Yeah, we're good. We'll just stop here and figure everything out. It'll all be good," he rambles, his words bleeding together.

Carefully, I ask, "Are *you* doing okay?"

Jameson slides back in his seat and closes the door quietly, his eyes immediately landing on Sam. The hope in them dies when he sees her looking the same as she did when he left.

Billy ignores my question altogether and instead says to Jameson, "They have a room?"

He cranks the key. "Yeah, we're all set."

We weave through the parking lot, turning around the back of a building before we pull into a spot. There's nobody else outside, making the sketchy exterior feel even more eerie.

Jameson gets out and rounds the car. He opens Sam's door, but she doesn't move to get out of her seat.

A panicked look runs across his face, but it falls away before he leans down and carefully unbuckles her seat belt. He moves it away from her body then kneels so he's eye level with her. Each movement he makes is so slow, so calculated.

"I'm going to get you out of the car now, okay?" he tells her, his voice as tender as I've ever heard it.

Still nothing.

He turns her, pulling her legs out the door, then cradles her in his arms and lifts her out of the car, careful to avoid hitting her head.

Billy looks away from them, as if he can't watch.

Instead of setting Sam down, Jameson continues to hold her as Billy lowers the seat in front of him. He grabs the duffle bag with one hand and drops mine for just long enough to climb out. I slide toward the open door and take his hand again as I get out behind him.

Jameson motions his head toward the floor of the front seat. "Grab her purse."

Billy snatches Sam's bag from the car and drapes it over his shoulder that's already holding the duffle bag.

Those two bags contain everything we have. I didn't think about it until now. How I literally don't have anything with me except the clothes I'm wearing.

Jameson leads the way to our room and mutters, "Back pocket."

We all stand and wait as Billy removes the room key and opens the door. Then he hits a switch, and the overhead light flickers a few times before finally filling the room with a harsh white glow. I squint my eyes, trying to acclimate.

Walking in, there's a strong smell of smoke mixed with stale air. The room is humid and stuffy, like a window has never been opened. There are two small beds, each covered by a thin bedspread with a dusty floral pattern.

Billy sets Sam's purse and the duffle bag down on the bed closest to the door then looks at Jameson expectantly.

As if feeling the weight of his stare, Jameson turns from Sam. "We're gonna go get some supplies." Something unspoken is exchanged between the two of them before Billy nods in understanding.

Jameson guides Sam through the front door and says over his shoulder, "Be back soon."

Right after I hear it shut, I ask, "Is she going to be okay?"

"She just needs some time alone with him," Billy answers.

"Have you ever seen her like this before?"

He runs a hand through his hair. "Once."

What happened that was as bad as this?

"Did Jameson make her better that time?"

"Yeah," he says, giving nothing else away.

I take a step forward. "I need answers, Billy. I know it's been a lot, and I understand why Jameson didn't want to talk about it in front of Sam, but I need to know why this is all happening."

"I know you do," he tells me.

"What happened a few weeks ago?"

He sighs, moving to sit down on the bed.

I follow, sitting down beside him. The bed is so small that my thigh grazes his as he turns toward me, and I realize that, other than the few minutes in my car, this is the first time we've ever been alone together.

It doesn't seem like we've known each other for such a short amount of time, but I guess when you go through a situation like this, time moves faster.

Even though he's facing me, his eyes won't meet mine. He stares at the wall behind me, his hand coming up to run through his hair again.

As I reach out and place my hand on his leg, I can sense his unease, the pain that's burning just below the surface.

All at once, his eyes become focused again, as if my touch brought him back from wherever he'd gone. And then, he starts talking.

He tells me everything that happened a few weeks ago, and once he's done, there's a part of me that wishes I never asked.

CHAPTER 22

"JAMESON GOT A CALL from Sam on a Tuesday, late in the afternoon," Billy starts. "Just that had me paying attention because she always works Tuesday nights, and by that time, she should have already been there. He only listened to her talk for maybe a few seconds before I knew something was off. He got this look on his face that I'd only seen a few other times, and when he gets that look ... Jameson didn't even have to say anything before I was following him out to the car.

"I still didn't know what was happening. I kept asking, but he wouldn't answer me. When he gets like that ... when it's about her ... he just loses it."

I think back to the diner. I've already seen firsthand how Jameson reacts when it comes to Sam.

"When we pulled up in front of her house, I knew it wasn't gonna be good. There'd been issues before, but nothing like what we walked into." His hand comes up to the back of his neck. "The whole front room was destroyed—furniture was flipped, and there was stuff everywhere. It looked like someone had torn through there completely out of their mind, like they'd really been looking for something. We both stopped for a minute, trying to figure out what we were dealing with when we heard him."

"Carson?" I ask, my voice quiet.

Billy dips his head. "Yeah. He was banging on a door and yelling something we couldn't really hear. Jameson went right for the stairs, but I grabbed his arm to stop him. I looked down to where I knew he had his gun tucked where he always keeps it and told him to give it to me. He hesitated for a second but handed it over. I put it in the back of my jeans and pulled my shirt down to cover it, and then followed him up the stairs."

"Why'd you make him give you the gun?" I interrupt.

He gives me a look like I should know better, and given what we're running from, I guess I should.

"Never mind," I mutter.

"When we got closer, we could hear Carson yelling, 'I know you fucking took 'em.' He just kept repeating it over and over again as he slammed his fist against the door. Once we made it to the top of the stairs, it wasn't just the pounding we heard, but crying, too. Jace was doing that wailing type of cry that babies do, you know, when it's so loud you can't even hear yourself think?"

I nod, even though I can only imagine what that's like.

"When we rounded the corner, Carson had his back to the stairs, and that fucker was right in front of Sam's room, losing his shit. It was like he didn't even hear the baby, like all he could think about was getting into her room. He started to get more and more impatient, and I was trying to figure out what he was going crazy about." He sighs. "I should have known when he started going on and on about how she took what was his."

Should have known what?

"He started messing with the door handle, pulling it in and out, using his body weight to try to break it down. I was waiting for Jameson to give me the go-ahead, and when Carson yelled through the door, 'Just give me my fucking pills, you junkie whore,' I knew that was it.

"I followed him over to where Carson was standing, and I didn't even hear Jameson flick open his knife because the crying and banging were so loud. You should've seen how fast he moved. How smooth he was as he pressed it against the front of Carson's neck. He never even saw it coming.

"Jameson leaned in close and told him to back away from the door. Carson's eyes got all big, and I thought he was gonna piss his pants. He was so shocked to see us. I stood next to Jameson, ready to jump in, but I knew he needed that first hit to be his.

"The second Carson turned and Jameson had a good shot, he punched him in the stomach, pulling the blade away. Carson fell to the ground, but got right back up, trying to look like he wasn't hurt. He started talking shit, asking who we thought we were coming into his house like that, telling us it wasn't our business." He shakes his head. "The guy was just asking for it.

"Jameson had the height, but Carson had probably fifty pounds on him. You've seen him—the guy's jacked. But it didn't matter because Carson didn't see Jameson coming and got cracked right across the jaw. He stumbled back and had to lean against the wall so he didn't fall on his ass.

"Since Carson was distracted, Jameson turned to me and told me to watch him. I stepped into the space where Jameson had just been, but Carson got back into it faster than I thought he would, and I had to dodge a punch he tried to land on me."

My hand tightens on Billy's leg.

"That's when it became obvious just how hopped-up he was and that he wasn't going to back down without a fight.

"I threw a punch back, and it landed, making him drop to his knees. He was breathing all heavy and tried to pull himself up, but the fight started to leave him. He just stayed down on the floor, saying a bunch of shit like, 'They always take everything,' and 'I just want what's mine.' He sounded out of his mind."

No wonder Jameson was so quick to fire back after Carson's first shot.

"I didn't know how long it was gonna be before he got up again. He looked like he was finally calming down, but that asshole is unpredictable, so I took whatever time I had to figure out the situation around me.

"Jameson had disappeared into Sam's room, so we were the only ones left in the hall. I tried to find out where Jace's crying was coming from and realized it was the bathroom across the hall. I yelled out to Cathleen, asking if she was in there with him. She opened the door and stuck her head out, but when she saw me standing in front of Carson, she came all the way out into the hall.

"She stood there with Jace in her arms, wrapped in a towel, and just stared at Carson. Finally, she asked him if he could see what he was doing to Jace. When Carson didn't answer, she told him that he was pathetic. She talked to him like she was his mother, which I guess she kinda was. Sam's mom split when they were pretty young, so Cathleen has always been like that, talking to Sam and Carson like they had to listen. Carson actually looked kinda sorry, like she was making him see how much of a fuckup he was being. But that went away real quick when Sam and Jameson walked out of her room.

"Carson looked over at Sam, and his eyes got that same crazy look again. He jumped up fast—well, as fast as he could after the hits we'd already landed on him, and Cathleen slowly moved back into the bathroom with her arms tight around Jace. Carson pointed at Sam and started saying that she had his pills. He was so mad that he was literally shaking as he yelled that it was her fault Jace was crying. He brought his hand up to his face, which was already starting to bruise, and screamed that was her fault, too."

How did Sam make it through living in that house?

"Jameson sounded like he was about to lose it when he tried to tell Carson that she didn't take his pills, that she isn't like him. Sam was standing right behind him, looking down at the floor, but Carson just laughed." Billy exhales. "I knew it was over for Carson before he even opened his mouth, but after what he said ... he had to have known what he was doing."

"What did he say?" I whisper.

Billy doesn't even have to think about it, like the words have been burned into his mind. "He stared right at Jameson and said, 'Bet you'll be right at home with her, won't you? All you have to do to see her future is look at your mess of a mother.'"

Yeah, he was definitely asking for it.

"Carson barely even got out the last word before Jameson went after him. He shoved him into the wall and pressed his blade against Carson's throat again. Jameson told him he knew nothing about Sam and nothing about his mother. He forced the blade against Carson's neck until he drew blood, but Carson jerked up his knee and got Jameson right in the balls, which is such a pussy move, but it made Jameson fall back a step and lower the blade from Carson's throat.

"I jumped in just before Carson's fist hit Jameson's face, pulling him out of the way and standing in his place. The swing meant for Jameson missed me, but I wasn't fast enough to dodge the next time he swung at me. He got a good hit in, but it wasn't bad enough that I couldn't keep going. It only made me want to knock that fucker out even more.

"By then, Jameson had gotten back into it, and between the two of us, we had Carson on the ground pretty fast. We were both unloading on him, but I could see that Carson was fading, so I pulled away. He clearly wasn't gonna get back up, but Jameson just kept going. He couldn't make himself stop.

"Sam was yelling his name, but even that didn't do it. She was getting desperate and started begging him to stop, screaming that he was gonna kill Carson."

Billy's expression becomes distant. "I've seen Jameson fight people a ton of times. I've even seen him lose control. But it was never like this. I really didn't think he was gonna stop, so I went back in and dragged him away. He was fighting me at first, but he eventually came back to himself.

"We both looked down, watching as Carson held his body in a fetal position, moaning in pain. Jameson pulled away from me then kneeled down next to him." Billy pauses. "He told him that if he ever pulled something like that again, he'd kill him."

I suck in a breath.

"Carson didn't respond—he just kept looking up at the ceiling—so Jameson leaned in real close and asked him if he understood. Carson was still for a minute before he nodded." Billy clears his throat before adding, "But it wasn't enough."

"What wasn't enough?" I ask.

He rolls his shoulders. "It's not that easy to explain."

"That's okay," I say, giving him an out.

Instead of taking it, he sighs. "Everything Jameson has, he had to take, and he learned young how to do it. Deep down, he really is a good guy." He looks at me, willing me to understand, so I nod.

"But he knows how to become what he has to be," Billy continues.

"I don't know what that means." Is he purposefully being cryptic?

"The reason Jameson is so intimidating isn't just because of the violence; it's because he knows how to take control of a situation, how to fully break someone. And for someone like Carson, being the one without the power is way worse than any hit we gave him. So, it wasn't enough for Jameson because Carson hadn't broken yet, and after what he did, Jameson wasn't letting him walk away whole."

"What did he do?"

Billy straightens. "He humiliated Carson. Made him feel small. Jameson told him to use his words, to tell him that he understood. Carson was still staring up at the ceiling, so Jameson grabbed his face so hard that he winced and told him to look at him when he was speaking, making sure to dig his fingers in where we'd already left a bruise on his cheek. I could see Carson's throat moving as he swallowed before he choked out that he understood. Jameson finally loosened his grip and warned Carson not to make him regret walking away with him still breathing."

It's so weird to be talking about this, knowing how everything eventually ended.

"Jameson stood and grabbed Sam's hand then turned over his shoulder to find Cathleen and told her to get the baby dressed and meet us downstairs. When we got down to the living room, Sam's dad was still passed out. Luckily, he'd been blacked out through the whole thing."

"It's a good thing he was passed out?" I ask. "He wouldn't have stopped Carson if he'd been awake?"

Billy fails to hide his disdain. "Her dad's always been obsessed with Carson. Sees him as some golden boy who can do no wrong."

I scrunch my eyebrows, confused.

"Sam's dad was a big football star in high school, but he was never good enough to get recruited. So, he pushed all that shit onto his sons; thought he could turn them into what he wasn't. Carson was the one who really had the skills. He was getting scouted by colleges since he was like sixteen. He was supposed to be their way out until an injury fucked up his knee and he lost it all."

"Wait," I interrupt. "You said 'sons.' Does Sam have another brother?"

Billy's expression is heavy when he answers, "That's a story for another time, babe. I can't deal with anything more than this tonight."

I nod, not wanting to push it, before asking, "So, just because Carson was some football star, her dad let him get away with whatever he wanted? That doesn't make sense."

"Her dad's not much better. The way he thinks isn't any different from how Carson does—or did ..."

"What do you mean?"

He lets out a breath. "Sam ended up staying over at Jameson's that night, but when she got home the next morning, her dad flipped out at her and blamed her for what we did to Carson."

My eyes go wide.

"Carson had convinced him that Sam took his Oxys, and her dad was pissed, saying that Carson needed them for the pain. That's what the whole thing had been about, why Carson had lost his shit." He scoffs. "Like he needed to be on that shit for an injury that happened over a year ago."

Hesitantly, I ask, "Did she take them?"

He looks at me like that question holds more weight than a simple answer. "She told us she didn't."

And you believe her? I want to ask but stop myself.

"Anyway, her dad laid down a bunch of threats, saying we couldn't step foot in their house again and that it was a family issue. I guess he even told her that he didn't want her seeing Jameson again." He rolls his eyes. "Like that would ever happen.

"Jameson wasn't having it. He tried to talk Sam into coming to stay with him, but she wouldn't do it. She was too scared her brother or dad would just come and get her."

"Wouldn't Jameson have protected her? Like he did that night?"

"That's what he kept telling her, but she still wouldn't do it. After seeing Jameson lose it on Carson, I think she was afraid of what he would do to them or what her dad and brother would do to him. She told Jameson that Carson wouldn't do anything to her after Jameson's warning, and it seemed like she was right. She promised us that things at home were fine, that Carson had left her alone."

I stare at him, and he looks back at me like he already knows my question.

"Then, why did he do it? Why did Carson come looking for Jameson?"

He holds my gaze for a moment before asking, "You didn't hear him?"

"Hear him when?"

"Right after he fired the first shot."

"No ..." I try to think back, but it's all a blur. "I just remember Sam's face, how afraid she looked."

"Carson kept yelling about how he didn't make promises to anyone. He was rambling, slurring his words. I'm sure Jameson could tell the second he saw him that he was out of it."

Billy's eyes darken. "I knew what was coming when Carson zeroed in on Sam and told her he was gonna make her pay before he leveled the gun in front of him."

Oh my God.

"Jameson didn't even take a breath before he fired."

A shiver rakes through my body as something occurs to me. "Do you think he came for Sam and not Jameson?"

"I don't know, but the second Carson looked at Sam that way, I knew it was over." He shakes his head. "Jameson doesn't make empty threats."

Chapter 23

"Thank you for telling me all that. I know it's probably the last thing you want to talk about after tonight."

"You deserved to know. I would've told you in the car when you asked, but with Sam like that …"

"It's fine. I completely understand."

He's running his hand through his hair again, a nervous tick that I'm quickly realizing both he and Jameson share.

The more I take him in, the more I notice just how much stress he's holding. His jaw is locked, shoulders hunched, and his other hand is gripping the comforter we're sitting on.

He clears his throat and shifts uncomfortably. "Well, this is fucking depressing," he tries to say with a laugh, but it falls flat. "Probably not the night you were expecting, huh?" He's trying to make a joke out of all of this, which seems to be his default. His coping mechanism.

Sam escapes through substances.

Jameson through aggression.

And Billy through pretending nothing is wrong.

He probably expects me to go along with it, just like I'm sure everyone else does, but I can tell how much he's hurting.

"You don't have to do that," I say, my voice gentle.

"Do what?" he answers, tilting his head to the side.

"You don't have to hide how you're feeling. I can handle it."

He continues to stare at me like he doesn't understand.

"You're trying to make light of all this so I won't have to take on how heavy it is for you. But you don't have to do that. You helped me. I want to help you."

"I didn't do anything special."

"Are you kidding me?"

He drops his eyes.

"I froze after that first shot, and you pushed me down."

He still isn't looking at me when he says, "Anyone would have done that."

"You covered my ears when you knew Jameson was going to shoot instead of covering your own. You carried me out of there. You stroked my hair when I was completely out of it and talked me down from a panic attack."

His eyes stay on the floor.

"Look at me, Billy."

Slowly, he moves his gaze up my body, stopping for a moment at my hand that's still on his thigh before landing on my face.

"Not everyone would have done that," I tell him.

He opens his mouth but then closes it again. "I just ..." he starts before stopping, never breaking our stare.

"You just what?" I whisper.

"I'm not used to talking about how I feel, okay?" He shakes his head. "People don't ask me about that."

"Well, I'm asking you."

"I don't have a good answer," he says defensively.

"That's okay. You can't say anything wrong. Just say the truth, and I'll listen."

"I'm pissed," he admits quickly, like he's afraid that if he doesn't just say it, he never will.

"Why are you pissed?"

He looks at me like I'm crazy and lets out a breathy laugh. "Why do you think, babe?" When I don't say anything, he sighs. "I'm pissed that all this bullshit keeps falling on us. It feels like it's one shitty thing after another. I see other people who get to be normal. Kids who didn't have to grow up so fast, like we all did. And now this. Now Jameson has to live with this. Sam's all fucked up. Like she hasn't dealt with enough. I don't want this for them."

"But what about you?"

"What?"

"You said you don't want this for *them*, but what about *you*?"

"What about me?"

"This happened to you, too."

"Not like it happened to them. I didn't pull the trigger. It wasn't my brother who died."

"Both of us were there, too, even if it didn't directly happen to us. You being upset about it doesn't mean that you can't still be there for them, too."

His eyes fall from mine, and again, they land on my hand that's resting on his leg. "You're nothing like I thought you'd be."

"Is that a good thing?"

He brings his attention back up to me. "Yeah, that's a good thing." He drops his eyes to my lips, and I grip the fabric of his jeans.

"Well, you're different than I thought you'd be, too," I answer, the words coming out breathless.

"Oh yeah?"

"Mmhmm" is all I can manage to get out as I fight against my body that's screaming at me to lean forward. "You're sweet," I tell him, my tongue coming out to wet my bottom lip.

I watch his throat bob, and my heart begins to pound.

The next thing I know, his hands are on my hips, and he's pulling me over to straddle his lap. My arms find their place behind his neck as he sweeps his lips over mine.

Chapter 24

I don't know how long we stay like that, our lips moving together as one.

Billy never pushes it too far, like he knows just how much to take. Just how much I need. The desperation in his kiss is greedy enough.

Of course, I've kissed other boys before—Graham and a couple of others—but it's never been like this. Not even close.

Those other times felt calculated, performative, like I was watching myself from the outside, thinking about what came next.

But with Billy, that all fades away.

It's the biggest rush I've ever felt.

My racing thoughts are replaced with only those of Billy, like in this moment, my mind has forgotten that anything else exists. All I can think about is how surprisingly soft his lips feel as they gently press against mine.

He moves slowly at first, but as I shift closer to him, his movements become more frantic. His tongue sweeps out and glides along the seam of my lips until they part to let him inside. We move in perfect rhythm, like we've been doing this together our whole lives.

He pulls my bottom lip lightly between his teeth, and I moan at the sensation, causing him to tighten his grip on my hips. I move my hands up without a second thought, sweeping through his hair and holding on as his lips continue to dance with mine.

I'm completely lost in the heat of his body and the way his fingers are pressed into my skin, like if he eased up just a little, I'd somehow float away.

I could stay like this forever, but the sound of a handle twisting and a door pushing open breaks the moment, making Billy and I lean back from each other.

Sam and Jameson walk into the room, and my face flushes at the idea that we've been caught, but Billy just continues to hold me against him like what we were doing is completely normal.

Something flutters inside me when I peer back at him and find that he's wearing a contented smile. He hasn't shifted me off his lap or dismissed me after they walked in. He's fine that they saw what we were doing.

I'm not naïve. I know that he's been with other girls, and after seeing him at that first party, I don't think he does anything more than casual. But that kiss didn't feel casual. None of this does.

"Well, that didn't take you long," Jameson calls out with a short laugh as he strides further into the room, carrying a brown paper bag.

Sam follows closely behind him, and I can immediately tell she's feeling better. She looks like herself again—her eyes are clear, and that unaffected expression she always wears is back on her face.

"I saw this shit coming from a mile away," she says.

I guess Billy wasn't kidding when he said Jameson could make her feel better.

I awkwardly slide off Billy's lap and stand next to him, unsure where to go or what to do.

Billy eyes the bag in Jameson's hand. "You get food?" he asks, unaffected.

Jameson nods, and Billy jumps up and makes his way over to where Jameson has just set the bag down.

Sam begins unloading all the items, the three of them now huddled around a small table in the corner. I suddenly feel out of place, my mind taking over again until Billy glances over his shoulder at me and tilts his head toward the table to come and join them.

Once I'm next to Billy, I look down and see a few bottles of water and two packs of cigarettes already laid out on the table.

Sam keeps pulling things out and adding them to the pile. Next is a Hershey's bar, which she sets down closest to herself. Then a loaf of bread, a jar of peanut butter, a jar of jelly, and finally, a flip phone.

Just when I think she's done, she begins rummaging through her purse, pulling out a bottle of vodka that's sticking out of the top, a set of utensils that's wrapped in plastic and, finally, a lighter.

"Everyone want one?" she asks, twisting open the jar of peanut butter.

I thought I wouldn't be hungry after everything that happened. Usually, when I'm anxious, the idea of eating makes my stomach knot up, but I'm unexpectedly hungry. And now that I think about it, I realize I don't actually feel all that anxious.

Sam opens the bottle of vodka, takes a long swig, and then starts making the sandwiches. Her hands are still shaking slightly as she spreads the peanut butter, but that's the only thing giving away what she's just been through. Well, that, and the few times she goes back for another drink.

She hands one to Jameson, then Billy, then me, and finally keeps one for herself. Once we all have our sandwiches, we sit around the room, eating them and passing around the bottle of vodka.

I wonder how they got liquor in the middle of the night until Billy takes a drink and winces. "Damn, that shit's nasty."

Jameson snatches the bottle from him. "Everything's closed. I had it in the trunk."

He passes the bottle my way, but Billy intercepts it. "No way you're gonna want that, babe."

"Why not?" I ask.

"'Cause straight vodka tastes like shit to start with, but warm vodka is even worse."

"How am I supposed to know if I never try it?"

"Wait, you've never had vodka?" Sam asks, her mouth full of peanut butter and jelly.

"I might have." I shrug. "At that party we all went to." I look at Billy. "Were the shots we did vodka?"

He keeps the bottle out of my reach. "Tequila."

"Oh," I mutter. "I don't think I've had vodka then." I shake my head. "I don't really drink."

Sam tilts her head. "But, I mean, what are you, like, seventeen? Eighteen?"

"Eighteen," I answer.

She stares at me in disbelief. "How do you get to eighteen without trying vodka?" Before I can respond, she says, "Well, you have to try it now."

"She's gonna hate it," Billy jumps in.

"Who cares? At least she can say she's tried it," Sam counters, grabbing the bottle from Billy and handing it to me.

I look around at the three of them as I tip the bottle to my lips. I take a small sip, but that's enough. I cough obnoxiously, wiping my mouth as the liquid dribbles from the corners of my lips.

"That's horrible! Why would anyone drink that on purpose?" I ask, taking a bite of my sandwich to try to chase away the taste.

Sam snorts, looking at me like I'm completely missing the point. "You don't drink it 'cause it tastes good."

I turn to Billy. "Well, you can rub it in my face now."

"I would never do that," he says, pretending to be offended, even holding his hand up to his chest to sell it. He passes me a bottle of water. "Here. I think this is more your speed."

"You said it was gross, too," I whine, throwing my hand in his direction.

"Sure, but I didn't drool all over myself."

I roll my eyes before grabbing the water from him. "Whatever."

I take a sip, and the room falls quiet. Sam grabs the bottle from where I've set it down and takes a quick drink. She hands it to Jameson, but he shakes his head.

His gaze shifts over each of us. "We've gotta figure some things out."

CHAPTER 25

"WHAT'S THE DEAL WITH your parents?" Jameson asks me. "Do we need to worry about them?"

My stomach clenches. "Worry about them what?"

"Coming after you."

"What do you mean, coming after me? Coming after me where?" My voice is edged with panic. "Aren't we going home?"

He stares back at me, his face void of all emotion.

I try to find some clue that will give away what he's thinking, but there's nothing. No tick in his jaw. No anxious movements. His lips are even set in a perfectly straight line.

I search for an answer from Sam or Billy, but it seems like they're both purposefully looking anywhere but at me.

"You didn't do anything wrong," I start. "Carson came after you first. It was self-defense. The police will understand if we just explain everything."

He scoffs. "You've clearly never spent any time with cops."

"My parents are lawyers," I quickly add. "I'm sure they'll help you."

That gets Sam's and Billy's attention, and their eyes snap to me.

I'm not sure if my parents will help, especially after how my mother reacted when Billy and Jameson dropped me off at home. But there's a chance they will. I have to believe that my parents wouldn't just turn their backs on us.

On me.

Jameson narrows his eyes. "I don't think you understand how this works. I don't have any money for fancy lawyers, and even if I did, it doesn't matter. The cops in town …" He drops his gaze to the floor. "Believe me; I'm not gonna get any favors from them."

Sam shifts, pulling her legs into her chest.

Billy catches the movement, his face falling, before he turns back to Jameson. "There were witnesses. People saw what happened."

"Carson never even got a hit on me, and I killed him," Jameson says. "*That's* what everyone saw. I'm supposed to argue self-defense for that?"

"You knew he was gonna shoot again."

"So what? I'm supposed to say I know the guy's a psychopath and 'cause I thought he was gonna shoot again, I killed him?"

"Yes," Sam answers quietly.

He turns to her. "You know that's not gonna work."

"It could if I testified. If I told them what he's like."

Jameson shakes his head. "I don't want you to have to go through that. And even if you did, we've been together forever. What if they think you're covering for me?"

"What about her sister?" I ask. "What if Cathleen said the same thing? She doesn't have any reason to protect you."

All eyes turn to me.

"If we had my parents, witnesses from the party, all of us, and Cathleen saying the same thing, it could work."

"And if it doesn't?" Jameson asks. "What then?" He starts to tap his fingers against the table lightly, the only thing giving away that he's beginning to lose control.

He shifts to look at Sam. "I'm not going inside. I can't do that to you."

She grabs the lighter from the table and begins fidgeting with it. Her hand is shaking so badly now that she keeps trying to strike the lighter over and over again, failing to produce a flame. "We don't have much of a choice," she says, her words muffled by the unlit cigarette dangling between her lips.

Jameson takes it from her hand and quickly lights the cigarette before tossing the lighter back onto the table. "We can just run. We don't have to go back."

"And do what? How are we gonna live?" Sam asks, throwing up her hand.

"We'll figure it out like we always do. I'm not gonna be another person who leaves you."

"No," she tells him, her voice firm. "This isn't like that."

"I can't risk it," he says roughly, bringing his hand down hard on the table. "I can't."

Sam jumps at the noise, and Jameson pulls his hand back, placing it on his lap. "Fuck, baby, I'm sorry," he tells her, trying to keep his voice calm. He rubs at his temples then runs his hands down his face, finally letting one rest gently on Sam's leg. "What if they don't believe us? Then I'm charged with murder. This isn't some petty shit. It's real time."

"We're not gonna let that happen," Billy cuts in. "But we need more information. Sam should call Cathleen to figure out what's happening there and if she'll talk. Then Susan will call her parents and see if they can help."

"I don't know," Jameson says.

"We can decide what to do after we have all the info. You don't feel okay with what's said during those calls, we'll leave," Billy tells him. "You know we'd never go along with anything that we think would land you inside."

Jameson looks to Sam for confirmation, which he gets when she gives him a quick nod.

Surprisingly, he moves to me next, gauging my reaction.

It's all too much to take in. There are so many different things running through my head. Up could be down for all I know.

I don't know how to help, but I meant what I said to Billy. *I want to help.*

I keep playing out all the scenarios, and proving that Jameson is innocent seems like the best option we have. My parents could be a big part of that. I could be a big part of that.

So, I nod, too.

Then I sit back anxiously as Sam dials her sister's number.

CHAPTER 26

THE PHONE IS RINGING in Sam's hand as we all wait to see if her sister will pick up.

Jameson already added the prepaid minutes. Apparently, we have sixty. He moved through the process easily, like he was used to setting up phones like this.

It's been ringing for a while now, and just when I'm afraid Cathleen won't answer, the call goes through.

"Sam?" she says, like she already knew who would be on the other line.

"Yeah," is all Sam seems to be able to get out, the word sounding broken.

"He's in a coma," Cathleen chokes.

Wait, what?

I'm still reeling when Sam asks, in a tone equally disbelieving, "What'd you say?"

"Carson. He's in a coma," she answers, her voice laced with confusion.

Sam turns, gaping at Jameson as she whispers, "We heard he was dead."

"The doctors got him stabilized, but they don't know if he'll ever wake up."

Sam just sits there, stunned.

After a long pause, her sister asks, "What happened? The cops said Jameson did it. Are you with him? Did you leave?" Her questions come one after another.

"Carson came after us. He shot at us and was making a bunch of insane threats. Jameson had to."

There's another drawn-out pause before Cathleen says, "Where are you now?"

Sam glances at Jameson, and he shakes his head. "I don't know. We just kept driving. We stopped at some motel."

"Good. You can't come back. You know that, right?"

"It was self-defense. There were witnesses. If we just explain what Carson is like, if we tell them what happened the other night—"

"I can't do that," Cathleen interrupts her.

Sam closes her eyes at her sister's response.

Cathleen continues, "I have to live here, Sam. I have Jace. I can't give this up when I have no other options. Dad knows Jameson did it, and he knows that you were there. Cops showed up at the hospital. They were asking a lot of questions. He was already spiraling when we got the call about Carson, but when they told him that you were there, too, he lost it. You don't want me to tell you the things he's saying about you. How you betrayed us by leaving with Jameson." She takes a breath. "I have to stay on this side of it. I'm sorry."

It sounds like she's forcing out the words when Sam answers, "It's okay. I understand."

Cathleen clears her throat. "You'll be okay. You've always been tough, especially when you have the two of them by your side."

I look between Jameson and Billy, who are both watching Sam.

"Yeah, I know," she says, her eyes fixed on the floor.

"I love you," Cathleen tells her. "I'm sorry I couldn't protect you from him."

Sam twists the ring on her finger, shaking her head. "You always gave everything you could." She pulls her bottom lip between her teeth, holding back the emotion that still creeps into her voice. "I love you, too."

Jameson is on the bed next to her the second she closes the phone. His hand is on her back, rubbing slow circles as she grips the phone tightly. "She'll be okay," he soothes.

"How's she supposed to handle all of this by herself? She doesn't have anyone there for her."

"She's dealt with plenty and is still standing. She'll get through this, too," Jameson assures her.

"I wish I could be there," Sam says, her hands fidgeting in her lap.

She goes to stand, but Jameson lightly pushes her back onto the bed. "I'll get it," he insists.

"And my—"

"I know," he cuts in.

A second later, he returns with the bottle of vodka, a pack of cigarettes, and her lighter.

He drops down next to her then turns to face me and Billy, the scowl on his face seeming to say, *"See? I told you this wouldn't work."*

"I can still ask my parents to help," I offer.

Sam peers over at Jameson, her eyes glassy.

"Yeah, all right," he says.

She hands me the phone, and I dial my mother's number, glad that she's had the same one since I was a kid. It's one of the only phone numbers I know by heart.

She answers on the second ring. "Cecilia Parker."

"Mom."

"Susan? Why are you calling me in the middle of the night?"

"I ..." I start to answer before she cuts me off.

"Are you not home? And whose number is this?"

Where do I even start?

"Something happened tonight. It's kind of a long story, but I need your help."

I hear blankets rustling as she tells me, "Hold on." Another minute goes by before she says, "I'm listening."

I quickly explain what happened, how Carson came to the party, shot at Jameson and Sam, that he was threatening them. Then how Jameson fired back and that Carson was in a coma. I explain how Carson had been violent toward them before and that he'd been using drugs. How I was right there when it all happened and how Billy protected me. Then, finally, how we ran, not knowing what else to do.

"That's clearly self-defense, right? You could prove it, couldn't you?" I ask.

Slowly, she says, "Are you with these people right now?"

I don't miss the way she refers to them as "these people."

I look up, and Jameson shakes his head.

"No, I'm alone."

"And where are you?

Again, Jameson shakes his head. "I'm not sure."

"What do you mean, you're not sure? How can you not know where you are?"

"I'm at a motel. I just don't know where it is. We drove for a while."

"Figure out where you are, and we'll come get you."

A wave of relief washes over me. "So, you'll help them? You think it'll be seen as self-defense?"

She laughs, and it instantly turns my stomach sour. "You were stupid enough to get yourself mixed up with these kids, even after I told you what would happen if you associated with people like them, but I know you're smarter than this. Don't insult me by asking questions that you already know the answer to."

When I don't respond, she says, "Why did this boy even take you with him? Why didn't he leave you at the party?"

"He ..." I begin to answer, but I don't know what to say.

Why didn't he just leave me there?

"I was in shock, and I already told you he covered me when Carson shot at us."

"Are you two in some sort of relationship?" she sneers.

How am I supposed to answer that? I don't even know what me and Billy are.

"And what about Graham?" she asks. "Where was he when all of this happened?"

Now doesn't seem like time to tell her that Graham and I broke up.

What's he going to think when he finds out about this? What's Avery going to think? Does it even matter anymore?

I'm trying to find the right words, when she cuts in, "You know what? It's irrelevant. Here's what's going to happen. You're going to tell me the name of this motel where they've taken you, and I will inform both your father and the police.

When we get there, you'll say that you were without your faculties and didn't know what was happening when you got into the car. You will explain to them that once you came to your senses, you called us and asked to be taken home."

I refuse to look at anyone in the room when I ask, "But what about Jameson?"

"Who?"

"Jameson, the one who shot Sam's brother," I reply, irritated.

"It really doesn't matter to me what happens to Jameson. I care about what happens to you. I will not let you ruin your life because you were in the wrong place at the wrong time."

We were all in the wrong place at the wrong time.

Jameson stands and says, "That's enough."

But I need to finish this conversation, so I shake my head.

"Give me a minute," I tell him quietly.

He peers down at me, locking his arms across his chest, but he doesn't say anything else.

"Susan!" my mother yells.

"I'm here," I clip back at her.

"Was that him? I thought you said you were alone," she accuses.

I don't answer her question. "I'm asking you, Mom, to please help them. It's important to me. Think about if it was me who fired that shot. Would you help then? What if it was me who was facing jail time?"

"Oh, don't be absurd," she says. "You would never do something like that."

"Only because I've never had to. Some people don't get that luxury. He's the same age as me, Mom. Think about that. He has his whole life ahead of him."

She lets out a bitter laugh. "I doubt he's on his way to becoming an upstanding citizen. He might have killed someone, Susan, or are you forgetting that part?"

"Of course I'm not forgetting that part!" I shout. "I was there, and it was traumatizing, which you wouldn't know since you never even asked me if I'm okay, because that's not what concerns you, is it? You don't actually care how I'm feeling, or how this affects me, or that these people matter to me. You're just worried about how this is going to look when everyone finds out that I'm involved."

"What has gotten into you? Why are you acting like this? I'm just trying to protect you. You know that telling the police is the right thing to do."

"Is it?"

"Of course it is," she says, exasperated. "You're letting the things that you think you feel about these people, or for this boy, cloud your judgment. I thought I raised you better than that."

I scoff. "Are you kidding? You would have actually had to be around to raise me. And if this is how you react when people need help, thank God you weren't. You're the most selfish person I've ever met."

"Sometimes life isn't fair, Susan," she hisses. "I'm not going to ruin my name by representing someone like that, and I'm not about to ruin yours by letting people know that you're in any way willingly associated with them."

I'm so embarrassed that they're all hearing her speak about them like this.

"I care about them," I tell her.

"That's enough. You need to get it together. You have a life that you've built. You *actually* have a future, unlike this boy. The honest truth is that it doesn't matter what happens to him because *he* doesn't matter. I've seen plenty of kids like him go through the system, and most of them deserve to be there. Don't delude yourself into thinking that these people are something they're not."

I wince, meeting Jameson's stare. He doesn't look surprised at all by what she's saying, like he expected it.

Like he's heard it all before.

"Now," she says, "tell me where you are."

Her words hit me as my life flashes in front of me. How unhappy I always am. How pointless it all feels. The pressure my parents put on me. The words my mother uses like swords.

How I never do anything to stop it. I just take it. Day. After day. After day. And it suffocates me.

I think about the future that's been forced on me, regardless of if I want it or not. How nothing feels like it will ever change. How nobody has ever asked me what I want, how I feel. How it's made me into a shell of myself. And how incredibly, painfully lonely I've been.

I didn't realize how empty I've felt until something started to bloom in that space. I never knew what true friendship, sacrifice, and connection looked like. Felt like. Until now.

"No," I say, the word leaving me with a breath.

"Excuse me?"

"I said *no*." Each word comes out firm, intentional, strong.

"Yes, I heard you, but what exactly does that mean?"

"It means I'm not telling you where I am, and I'm not coming home."

"You either tell me where you are now or you are completely cut off. Do you hear me?"

"I don't want your money."

"This is not a joke."

"I didn't think it was."

"You can't give up your entire life. Your family, your friends, your future."

"I never had any of that, not really. I've seen how a family treats each other, and it's not how you treat me."

"Oh, come on; don't be so dramatic. You have a family. Of course you have a family."

"I only have a family when it's convenient for you. When it benefits you. You don't actually care about me."

"Don't be ridiculous."

"Tell me you'll help him, and I'll come home."

She remains quiet.

"You can't, can you? Because right and wrong don't matter to you. It's always been about your reputation, your job. That's always come before me, and it always will."

She huffs. "I don't need to prove anything to you."

"Then don't," I snap.

And for the first time in my life, I hang up on my mother.

CHAPTER 27

WE EACH SIT WITH our thoughts, absorbing what was said and what it means.

That we're all out of options.

"Well ..." Billy says, drawing out the word, "she's a sweetheart, isn't she?"

I hear a quick burst of laughter before I realize it's coming from me. The room feels so heavy that it's a wonder the sound doesn't just get swallowed up in it.

Glancing to my left, I'm met again with Jameson's stare, but this time, his stern face has slipped into a look of amusement.

Still, seeing him brings me back to our situation and what my mother said about him.

"I'm sorry she talked about you like that. You know I don't believe any of the stuff she said."

His expression shifts as his eyes bore into me. His energy is so intense that I have to force myself not to look away. Finally, he speaks. "I know. How you handled that call says a lot." His attention drifts from me to Billy. "We made the calls. You with me now?"

"Yeah, I'm with you," Billy answers before glancing at the phone in my hand. "I need to call my dad. Let him know what's going on."

Jameson nods as he moves to sit back down next to Sam, and I pass the phone to Billy.

It only rings once before it picks up, but he doesn't say anything. There's a stretch of silence before a gruff voice says, "That you, kid?"

Billy sighs. "Yeah, Dad, it's me."

"You okay? Are all of you together?" I can hear him trying to hold back his panic.

"We're okay, and yeah, we're all here." He runs a hand through his hair. "How do you know what happened? Have the cops already been there?"

"They just left. Came here after your aunt Aubrey's."

Jameson goes rigid.

"What happened, Billy?"

He explains it all in far more detail than Sam and I had. It's clear that he trusts his dad and thinks he needs the full story. Like maybe he can help us.

When he's finished, his dad says, "I would have done the same thing."

Jameson exhales an audible breath as Sam places her hand over his.

"I agree, though. You can't come back. There's too much risk." He pauses. "You have any cash with you?"

I remember the duffle bag.

Billy looks to Jameson, and he holds up two fingers.

"Yeah, 2K."

His dad doesn't ask how they have that kind of money. Instead, all he says is, "Good. That'll get you to where you need to go. A buddy of mine from the Army opened up a shop down in Florida. He's good people. I trust him with my life, and 'cause of that, I trust him with yours. I'll call him in the morning and explain the situation. He can set you and Jameson up with jobs at the garage."

"Thank you."

"I'll call this number tomorrow morning with an address."

"I'm sorry this happened," Billy mutters.

"Don't be. You were protecting each other, just like I raised you to do." His dad clears his throat. "Can you give the phone to him?"

"Yeah, hold on," Billy answers before passing the phone.

"Hey," Jameson says.

"You holdin' up okay?"

"I'm fine."

A gravelly laugh comes down the line. "I don't know what I expected asking you a question like that." His voice sobers. "I just want you to know that I'm here for you, like always. No matter what, you hear me?"

"I hear you," Jameson responds. He straightens before he mumbles, "Can you … uh … can you check in on her for me? I left her some money, and I'll send more when I can, but I just need to know that someone's making sure she's good."

"I promised your dad that I'd look after you both. Nothing's changed. Don't worry about anything back here. I've got it."

"Thank you," Jameson forces out.

The words come out slow, tentative, as Billy's dad asks, "Have you called her?"

"No."

The line is quiet, but the silence holds a whole conversation.

Finally, Jameson relents. "I will."

"Good. Now put Sam on, will ya?"

"She's here," Jameson says.

"Hi, Luke," Sam greets him.

"Hey, honey," he replies, his voice lighter, gentler. "I'm so sorry."

It's easy to forget that the person who's in a coma is her brother, or how it must feel that her boyfriend was the one who put him there. I mean, how do you even begin to wrap your head around that?

She seems to be trying to work through it all as she searches for a way to respond. "It just doesn't seem real," is what she settles on.

"Nobody should have to go through something like this, but you're getting away from all of it. Maybe this was the only way that would have happened."

"Yeah, maybe," she says, her voice far away.

"You're going to get through this. All of you, all right?" I can feel the emotion in each word, the pain, and the love when he adds, "You're all good kids."

Jameson flinches like the words struck him, while Sam's eyes remain glassy.

"Thank you," she pushes out. "For everything."

"Of course," he answers. "You all stay safe. I'll call with the address as soon as I have it."

Sam closes the phone as Billy says, "Guess we're going to Florida."

CHAPTER 28

Sam turns to Jameson. "Are you going to call her?"

He runs a hand through his hair.

Once.

Twice.

Three times.

Blowing out a breath, he nods. Then he hovers his thumb over the phone, but it never comes down on a key.

"I'm right here," Sam reassures him.

"She's gonna blame me," he says, his voice heavy.

"You had no other choice."

He clicks his tongue. "She won't care. That's not how she'll see it."

Sam leans forward. "Look at me, Jamie."

His eyes remain glued to the phone. "She's never gonna forgive me for leaving."

Sam places her hand on his cheek, tilting his face so he's looking at her. "You can't take care of her from inside a prison. What you're doing isn't selfish."

"That's not what I—"

"Yes, it was," she interrupts. "For years, you've been trapped. You can't make her better, but you can't let go either."

"She needs me."

"She's your mother, Jamie. She was supposed to take care of you. *You* needed *her*."

He brings his elbows to his knees and drops his head, the heels of his hands sliding up and down his forehead.

Sam gives him space, like she knows he needs it, not even touching him anymore, until finally, he says, "I'm never gonna get that from her. I don't even know why I'm bothering to call."

"Then don't," Sam answers, her tone devoid of all judgment. "Whatever you wanna do is okay."

"Fuck," he breathes, shutting his eyes, just like he did in the car. Once they open again, his face is set, his expression empty. "No. I've gotta call. I have to be the one to tell her I'm leaving." He dials the number, and I'm surprised when I can clearly hear it ringing.

We decided to put the other calls on speaker because we were looking for information that we all needed to know, but this call seems far more personal, like it's just for him. I should have known that he'd want Sam and Billy to be with him through it, but it doesn't escape me that he trusts me enough to hear it all, too.

I'm realizing just how much support they get from each other. It's almost like they're pieces of the same person, feeding off one another and filling in the missing spaces. It feels like maybe I'm starting to fit in as one of those pieces, too.

The phone continues to ring until it goes to voicemail. He looks at Sam, and she squeezes his thigh before he dials again.

It rings a few more times before a voice filters through. "Yeah."

With that one word, she somehow manages to sound both desperate and disinterested all at the same time.

When Jameson doesn't answer right away, she says, "Who is this?"

"It's me, Ma," he says, blowing out a breath.

"Jameson?" she asks, and his jaw ticks at the question.

"Who else would it be?" he mutters.

"The cops were here. They're looking for you."

"I know."

"They said you shot Carson, that you put him in a coma."

Jameson stays quiet.

"Well, did you shoot him?" she bites out.

"It was either me or him. I had to."

His mother exhales. "This is real bad. Really fucking bad, Jameson."

"You think I don't already know that?" he snaps back at her.

"Well, what are you gonna do?" she asks him in a tone that implies he better figure it out.

"I need to get out of town for a bit," he tells her, squaring his shoulders like he's waiting to be hit.

He was right. That's not the answer she wanted to hear.

"No, no, no," she pleads. "You can't do that. I need you to come home. Just come home, and we'll figure this out."

"There's nothing to figure out. People saw me shoot him."

"You can't just leave! Where are you gonna go?"

"If I come home, I'll probably go away. You want me to risk that?"

"Not again, not again," she begins to rant hysterically. "Everybody leaves. They all leave. You said you wouldn't do this to me. You said you wouldn't leave me like him."

I jump when something shatters on her end of the line.

"What are you doing? Calm down," Jameson tells her, bringing his thumb and index finger up to pinch the bridge of his nose.

"What am I supposed to do now, hmm? Tell me, Jameson. What am I supposed to do?" Something else shatters as she says, "God, you're just like him. I should've seen this coming."

He closes his eyes as he sighs. "Don't say that."

"Why not? You don't like hearing the truth, do you? You never have. Well, go ahead, just keep lying to yourself."

"Please, just calm down."

"Don't you tell me to fucking calm down! How am I gonna get by? You left me with nothing. I have nothing now. How could you do this to me?"

"I didn't leave you with nothing," he grits out. "There's still money in the safe."

The line goes silent before she says, "Well, then give me the code."

"That money has to last a bit. I won't be able to send any more for a while, and I'm not gonna let you spend it all at once."

"I'm not gonna spend it all at once," she says like the accusation is ridiculous.

"The last time you had access to that safe, I came home to it empty. You remember that?"

"Oh, come on; that was one time. One mistake, and you never let me forget it," she scoffs. "Like you're some sort of saint. You want me to start talking about where that money comes from, huh?"

"I don't hear any complaints while you're spending it."

"Just give me the code, Jameson."

"No. I'll give it to Luke, and he can manage it."

"That's just fucking great. Another man I get to beg for money from. You love to keep me weak, just like your father did, don't you? I know what you're doing."

"What are you talking about? I'm trying to take care of you," he tells her, his patience running thin.

"No, you're not. If that's what you were trying to do, you wouldn't have been stupid enough to shoot someone in front of a room full of people."

"I had no other choice."

"Sure, keep telling yourself that. I know how smart you are. You could've found another way." She's quiet for a beat. "You've been waiting for an excuse to leave. Well, now you've got one. I bet you're happy to be rid of me."

Jameson shakes his head, his grip on the phone so tight that his knuckles are turning white.

"I know you think I'm a burden," she adds, her rage turning to tears.

She's completely losing it.

He tilts his head up toward the ceiling as he draws in a steadying breath, seemingly trying to prepare himself to say what he knows she needs to hear. "I'm not choosing to leave. I have to. And I don't think you're a burden. You know I don't think that."

She's fully crying now, like something inside her broke open.

"I'm not leaving you. I just have to go away for a bit, okay?" he says, attempting to calm her.

She doesn't respond. The only thing she gives him is tears.

"I'll always make sure you're taken care of. Luke is gonna come by and check in on you. He'll make sure you have everything you need."

Her words are muffled by tears when she says, "You're never gonna come back."

He doesn't answer.

"Jameson ..." she pleads.

"What?" he answers, his voice strained.

"Tell me that you'll come back."

He shuts his eyes. "I'll come back."

"Tell me you love me."

His shoulders slump forward as his chin comes to his chest. "I love you, Ma." Before she can answer, he says, "Look, I'm gonna run out of minutes." He swallows. "I'll check in when I can."

"Don't disappear on me."

"I won't," he says then hangs up.

Reaching over Sam, he grabs the bottle of vodka from the nightstand and drops the phone down in its place. He takes a long drink, and just after he pulls it away from his lips, he launches the bottle across the room.

I watch as it hits the wall, the sound of it smashing into pieces echoing around us.

Just like that, the reality of the situation comes crashing down on me.

There's nothing to hide behind now.

We've all made our calls.

Said our goodbyes.

Now all that's left is the road ahead.

CHAPTER 29

"WHAT TIME IS IT?" Billy wonders aloud.

I follow his gaze as it lands on an alarm clock sitting atop the nightstand. Somehow, it's already past four in the morning.

Seeing the time, Jameson says, "We should try to get a few hours of sleep before getting on the road." His voice is taut, controlled, like he's keeping all that rage just below it.

He stands stiffly, rolling his neck, before muttering, "Be back in a minute."

Without a word, Sam follows behind him, and they slip out the front door.

I turn to Billy and find his attention on me.

"Do you, um, want to shower or anything before going to sleep?" He sounds uncharacteristically nervous, like he's afraid at any minute I'm going to realize the situation we're in and want to get out of it. It's like now that things have settled down, they're getting more real. But as real as it's becoming,

I still don't want to go back. And I can't decide if that makes me crazy or not.

"Susan?" Billy prompts. "You okay?"

I blink up at him, realizing I never answered his question. "I'm fine. A shower sounds nice, but I can wait if someone else wants to go first."

He shakes his head. "Nah, it's all yours, babe."

I move to get up from the bed, but he grabs my wrist, keeping me in place.

"Really, are you good? 'Cause we can—"

"I'm good," I cut him off. "I promise."

He watches me for a drawn-out moment before finally nodding and releasing his hold on me. "Just checking," he says, attempting to sound casual.

I linger, wondering if I should say something else. How do you even navigate a situation like this?

"Go ahead," he tells me, patting my leg, seeming to be able to read what's running through my head.

I smile shyly at him before making my way to the bathroom, careful to avoid the broken glass on the floor.

Once I'm alone in the small room, I let out a long breath and pull off my clothes, carefully hanging them over the towel rack.

It's weird to have nothing with me, no change of clothes or toiletries.

Waiting for the water to heat up, I bounce from foot to foot on the cold tile until it eventually warms enough to step in.

The hot water beating down on me relaxes my muscles as the hum of the bathroom fan lulls me into a sense of calm. My mind starts to slow as exhaustion finally begins to wash over me.

I quickly move through the motions, suddenly eager to get into bed.

After stepping out, I begin to dry off, not looking forward to putting back on the tight jeans and halter top that I wore to the concert, but I don't have any other option.

As I grab for my jeans, there's a knock at the door.

"Yeah?" I yell over the noise of the fan.

"Can I come in?" Billy asks.

I set my jeans back on the rack, wrap the towel tightly around myself, then open the door and peek my head out. Immediately, I'm met with Billy's bare chest. I try to look up at him, but I can't stop staring. My eyes dance over his tan skin, landing on a tattoo over his heart. The word "*Loyalty*" written above angel wings. I have to keep myself from reaching out and running my fingers over it. I want to see if his skin is as smooth as it looks.

He clears his throat, and my eyes snap to his.

He's smirking as he holds out the T-shirt he was wearing. "Thought you might wanna sleep in this."

"Oh, um ..." I stutter. "That's okay. I don't want to take your shirt."

"You'd be more comfortable sleeping in this than you would in jeans and that little shirt you had on, wouldn't you?"

"I mean ..."

"Yes or no, babe."

I bite my lip and nod. "Yes."

"Good, then take it," he says, handing it to me.

"Thank you," I respond, my words coming out breathless. "I'm gonna ..." I tip my head back toward the bathroom, and he steps away, allowing me to close the door.

Pulling the shirt over my head is like wrapping myself in Billy. He must have just taken it off because it's still warm from his body heat. I fold my arms around myself, inhaling the scent of him, then neatly stack my clothes before stepping into the main room.

Because of Billy's height, the shirt falls just above my knees, so I don't feel uncomfortable walking out in it. But with the way his eyes slide up my body when he sees me, I might as well be naked.

He's lying in bed with the covers pulled up to his waist. His hands are behind his head, and the position shows off a body that I can only imagine he got from working on cars all day.

I look over and see that Sam and Jameson are already in the other bed, his body curled around hers, with his back to us.

The blinds are closed, and all the lights are off except for the lamp between the two beds.

I bring my focus back to Billy, feeling a little awkward. I linger in the space between the bathroom and bedroom, playing with the hem of his shirt.

"Come to bed," he says softly.

He watches me as I walk over, pulling the blankets up for me to climb in. Once I'm lying at his side, he switches off the light and shifts his body next to mine.

The bed is small, so there's no getting around being pressed together. I realize he's stripped down to just his boxers when his bare leg brushes against mine. It all feels incredibly intimate, even though we're not doing anything more than just lying next to each other. Maybe it's the way he drapes his arm around my waist, pulling me against his hard chest. How his thumb draws lazy circles against my skin. Or how I can feel his hot breath on my neck, the sound of him breathing against my ear.

But more than anything, it's how, instead of feeling nervous or wanting to pull away, I only want more. To be even closer. I've never experienced anything like this. I didn't know that feelings for someone could hit you so fast or so hard. That you could trust someone you just met as much as I trust him.

Wrapped up in his arms, my body becomes heavy as I let go. Sleep begins to take me as he murmurs, lips pressed against my ear, "I'm really glad you're here with me."

I wake up to the sound of hushed voices. The fog of deep sleep still weighs down my mind, keeping me from making out the words.

It takes me a minute to remember where I am.

Why I'm here.

I blink my eyes open and drag a hand down my face. Turning my gaze to the left, the motel room comes into focus. Billy and Jameson are hunched over the small table, talking quietly, as Sam remains curled up in bed.

I let my eyes close again as memories from the day before dance around in my head. I try to grab a hold of them, but they're all moving so quickly that I can't get any thought to still for long enough to make sense of it. I'm left with only fractions of moments passing by.

Things said.

Promises made.

Billy's body crashing over mine as that horrible sound rang out.

The look on Sam's face right before Jameson fired back.

Being in a car without knowing where we were going.

The fear in Jameson's eyes when he realized what he'd done.

How scared Billy was for his friends. The way it felt to see him that way. To feel his vulnerability, his pain.

The moment he pressed his lips against mine.

The calls we all made, but especially the conversation I had with my mother.

That's the thought I grab onto the tightest. The one I make myself fully see.

I run through everything she said, how I physically felt the weight of her words. And what I'd said in response.

"I'm not coming back."

But, did I really mean it? Am I really not going back?

Maybe she was right. Maybe I am being ridiculous, unreasonable.

Am I actually going to run away with them? Leave my entire life behind?

I had a whole future laid out in front of me, but the idea of living that life made me feel like I was suffocating. I've always felt it but pushed those feelings down, thinking I was wrong for not wanting something other people would be lucky to have.

My parents always told me that I should be grateful for the lifestyle they provided, and I was. I know how privileged I was to grow up with the money and opportunities I've been given. I just wasn't happy, and I could never figure out why.

My entire existence has been based on the idea that happiness comes from building a life like my parents have. That if I do what I'm told, go to the right school, get the right job, and marry the right guy, I'll be set. I'll be living the dream. It's what everything has been based on. What every choice I've made has been rooted in.

But those "right" things never felt like they were the right thing for me. That life didn't feel like my dream.

I've always assumed that I was the problem. That I would learn to want those things. But last night, when I dropped to the ground with Billy's body over mine ...

When I realized the sound I heard was a gunshot ...

That more could be coming, and I might never leave that room ...

I was hit with a horrible sensation. An overwhelming feeling of regret.

Regret that I'd never lived the life I wanted.

I realized that if it all ended in that moment, I only ever lived my life for other people. Done what they wanted. Became the version of myself they wanted me to be.

I don't want to do that anymore. I want to learn who I am. What I want. What I'm capable of. Who I can be.

The open road ahead is scary. Not knowing what comes next is scary. But it's not as scary as going back to a life that isn't mine. A life I know I don't want.

Who knows if I'm making the right choice by leaving, but at least the choice is finally mine to make.

Chapter 30

Billy turns to look at me, hearing the sound of sheets rustling against the bed as I move to sit up. He smiles, causing my lips to pull up in response.

I step out of bed, tugging his shirt down to make it cover as much of my legs as it can, and walk over to him.

The small table he and Jameson are sitting at can only fit two chairs, so I stand between them, wondering if I'm interrupting. They were clearly in the middle of a conversation that stopped when I came over.

My uncertainty disappears when Billy gazes up at me, eyes gentle, and says, "We're just figuring some things out." Then he pushes his chair back and tells me to sit, his eyes dropping to his lap.

I hesitate and glance at Jameson to see if he'll object, but the hard look on his face softens, and he lowers his chin in a slight nod.

His show of acceptance eases a fear I didn't know I was holding onto—that even after last night, Jameson still doesn't trust me.

I remember what Billy told me about how hard it is for Jameson to let people in, yet when they continue talking like it's no big deal I'm here, I realize I might fall into that small group.

Grinning to myself, I sit down and lean back against Billy's chest, his arm coming around my waist, anchoring me to him.

I tune into their conversation, hearing Jameson mid-sentence. "... been playing through all the scenarios, and none of them are good. The best I've come up with is to get to Florida as fast as we can without getting pulled over and ditch it as soon as possible."

"Ditch what?" I ask.

"My car."

"Why don't you just trade it in for another one?"

"Don't have the title. Plus, I don't want any paper trails right now," he says, flicking the lighter in his hand open and closed.

Billy gives him a look that must hold a question because Jameson adds, "If we stole a car, we'd be in the same spot, driving around with plates that we don't want cops running." He pauses. "We're fucked no matter what way we do it."

"So, what? We just hope we make it to Florida without getting stopped?" Billy asks.

Jameson pushes his chair back. "No, we *make sure* we make it to Florida without getting stopped, and the sooner we get there, the better."

Billy rubs the back of his neck, his body shifting against mine before he nods.

Jameson strides over to where Sam is still sleeping, throwing over his shoulder, "Let's leave in ten, yeah?"

"Yeah," Billy replies.

I turn in his lap so we're face-to-face. He assesses my expression like he's searching for something. I'm not sure what, but the tightness in his body relaxes when he doesn't seem to find it.

He calls to Jameson, "We'll be outside."

Billy's leaning against the wall next to me, bringing his face eye level to mine. "How'd you sleep?"

The question seems so normal after everything.

"Better than I thought I would," I answer honestly. I hadn't expected to be able to sleep at all.

"Good," he responds, like what he really wants to say is buried beneath the word.

I place my hand over his, silently inviting him to share what he's holding back.

He follows the movement, letting his attention linger for just a moment before meeting my stare. "You can still go home."

I tense, and I know he notices it because he clarifies, "I mean, only if you want to. I just don't want you to feel like that's not an option anymore."

My body stills. I don't know if he realizes how much those words mean to me. That he's making sure I know the decision is mine. That he's giving me a choice. Like maybe he knows how few I've been given. How many have been made for me.

His eyes are clouded with worry when I don't respond. "I'm not asking because I want you to go home. You know that, right? I just need you to—"

I don't quite know why I do it. Maybe it's because I want to take that worry away from him. Or because nobody has ever cared enough about what I wanted to ask me what I wanted. Or because even though I know he would rather I stay, he asked if I wanted to leave, anyway. Whatever the reason, I lean up and press my lips against his, cutting him off mid-sentence.

For just a moment, I doubt myself. I've never been this bold before. I've never made the first move like this. What if the kiss last night was just a one-time thing? A reaction to all the emotions swirling around us? What if he—

My thoughts shut off as his lips begin to move over mine. He shifts so he's in front of me, my back now to the wall, as he presses his body into mine.

The way he's kissing me leaves no room for doubt. No room for thought. No room for anything but this moment. No room for anything but him.

Chapter 31

We all load into the car, taking the spots that practically seem assigned at this point—Jameson driving, Sam in the passenger seat, Billy and me in the back.

We haven't heard from Billy's dad yet, so I'm not sure how Jameson knows where he's going. We have no GPS or map to go off, but within a few minutes, we're on a highway that I can only assume leads to Florida.

A couple quiet hours pass, all of us keeping to ourselves, when Jameson exits the highway and slows onto an access road.

"Where are we going?" I ask.

"There's a toll coming up," Jameson mutters.

My brows pinch.

"Tolls have cameras," he clarifies.

Oh, right.

We're just pulling back onto the highway when the burner phone finally rings.

Jameson pulls it from his pocket and hands it back to Billy, who listens for a minute before saying, "Okay, thanks." Another pause, and then, "Yeah, we're on the highway. We slept some at the motel and left maybe two hours ago." He nods at whatever his dad is saying on the other line before telling him, "We will."

Billy closes the phone, tucking it into his pocket. "It's a straight shot until we cross over into Florida. He said to call again when we get to the state line, and he'll give us directions. He talked to his friend who has the shop, so the guy knows we're coming."

"All right, good," Jameson answers, mindlessly drifting his hand to rest on Sam's leg.

She looks up from the book she's been reading for just a moment, letting their eyes catch. He pulls his hand away to switch on the radio before placing it back on her thigh. Music begins to fill the car as a warm breeze drifts in through the open windows. I watch as cars move past us, letting my mind still.

Billy starts drumming his fingers against the back of Sam's seat to the beat of the song, just like he did the first time we rode in the car together.

I look at each of them and am hit with a feeling of déjà vu. It's almost identical to the first time I was in the car with them—Jameson's hand on Sam, Billy drumming to the music, and Sam oblivious to it all, like they've lived this same moment countless times before. I guess they probably have.

"How long have you all been like this?" I ask Billy.

"Been like what?" he answers, dropping his hands from the back of her seat.

"Together."

He smiles and looks between the two of them. "Well, Jameson and I grew up like brothers. He's only two months older than me."

I try to picture them as kids. It's not hard to see Billy as a little boy, with his puppy dog eyes and easy humor. But Jameson's more difficult to picture, like maybe he skipped childhood altogether.

"How old are you?" I ask, realizing I don't know.

"Nineteen. And you're eighteen, right?"

I nod.

"When's your birthday?"

"March nineteenth," I mumble. I've never liked my birthday.

Wanting to shift the conversation away from it, I ask, "What about Sam?"

The highway noise and music seem to cover our voices because neither Sam nor Jameson have turned around at the sounds of their names.

Billy looks up, as if trying to recall a memory. "It feels like she's always been around, but I guess it was only a few years ago that we all started hanging out.

"How'd you guys meet?"

"We went to school together, but she was a year below me and Jameson, so we didn't really know her." He looks unsure before adding, "Her brother started working for Jameson's dad, and not long after, Sam got a job at the garage, too. She worked the front desk. After that, the three of us were always together."

"Carson worked for Jameson's dad?"

Billy clears his throat. "No, her other brother, Johnny."

I remember our conversation from last night. How Billy said Sam's "brothers." He didn't want to talk about it then, so I decide not to press him about it now.

He sees the expression on my face and says, "It's not that I don't want to tell you about it. It's just not my story to share."

"No, I know," I tell him. "I understand."

"What about you? Do you have any siblings?"

"Nope, no siblings. One kid was more than enough for my parents." I mean it as a joke, but it doesn't come out sounding that way. A pained look passes over his face, and I start to ramble, attempting to bury the truth I let slip. "I do have a best friend, though." I wring my hands, "Or, I did. Remember Avery? She was with Graham at the party. The blonde girl."

He nods.

"We've been best friends since we were little. She's just kind of always been there, you know?"

Billy nods again, watching me carefully.

"Although, I guess I'm starting to realize that maybe we weren't actually friends at all."

He lowers his eyes to my fidgeting hands, and I drop them out of habit.

"She was never really there for me, especially after things with Graham ended. She kept trying to convince me to give him another chance. I think she just wanted things to go back to how they were." My shoulders sag forward. "I guess I can understand that, but she just made me feel ..."

"Made you feel what?"

"I don't know ..." I shake my head. "I just never felt like I fit. It's like I was always pretending." I look over at him. "That probably sounds stupid."

"No, it doesn't," he says. "I know exactly what you mean."

"You do?" I ask. "You don't seem like someone who pretends."

"That's because I don't when I'm with you."

Before I can respond, he claps his hands together. "Okay, next question."

"Next question?"

"Yeah, babe, haven't you ever played the question game?"

"Um, I don't think so."

"Well, it's real easy. I ask a question, and you answer. Then you ask a question, and I answer."

"Isn't that just a conversation?"

He snorts. "No, it's the question game."

I smile back at him. "All right, what's your question?"

He thinks for a minute before asking, "If you could only eat one food for the rest of your life, what would it be?"

The question seems silly after what we've just been talking about, but I answer right away. "That's easy. Chocolate cake."

"Of course you love sweets."

Immediately, my mind goes to all the times my mother has pointed out what I was eating, told me a portion was too big, or asked me if I was *sure* I wanted dessert.

My body folds in on itself, worried that's what Billy means. But then he says, "You are what you eat, right? And I've never met anyone as sweet as you."

I can't help the laugh that falls from my lips, my worry instantly gone. "I think that's the cheesiest thing I've ever heard."

"Got you to laugh, though," he says, looking triumphant.

I blush. "You're ridiculous."

"I know," he answers, an energy radiating off him that you can't help but get sucked in by. "All right, next question."

"How many questions are there?" I ask.

"As many as it takes.

"Takes for what?"

"Until I know everything there is to know about you."

242

CHAPTER 32

WE STOP A FEW times to get food or go to the bathroom, but the rest of the day is spent driving. Billy and I never stop talking. His questions for me are endless. Some of them are easy, like my favorite color, book, or movie, but he doesn't just stay on the surface. He asks about my parents, my friends, the relationships I've had, what I want in the future, and what I don't.

I tell him about my art, even revealing that I got into my dream school. He's the only person I've told, but he just makes me want to keep talking. He listens to my answers like he's hanging on to each and every word. Like he can't wait to hear what I'll say next.

For every question he asks, he answers one, too, and I end up learning just as much about him as he does about me.

The questions start off simple, like his favorite color. It's red.

When I ask him why, he says, "It's the color of my bike."

Then I learn that he fixed up an old Harley a few years ago, and it's what he's driven ever since. I can tell how much he loves the thing by how his face lights up when he talks about it. He goes on and on, explaining all the changes he made. I have no idea what any of it means, but I nod, anyway, encouraging him to continue, just so I can keep watching the look on his face.

When I ask about his family's garage, he tells me how his dad inherited it when Billy was a kid, after his grandpa died. And that when his dad took over, it was so in the hole that they almost lost it. He starts to close up after that, so I don't push for more.

He tells me about how his mom left, but he doesn't go into any detail. When I ask him if he knows where she went, all he says is, "No."

I can see the pain he's trying to mask, so I quickly ask him something lighter, thinking that he can tell me more about it another time, if he wants to.

"If you could only listen to one band for the rest of your life, who would it be?"

"That's easy. Led Zeppelin," he answers without a second thought.

"You're kidding."

"What—you like their stuff?"

Unable to hold back a smile, I say, "Yeah, they're my favorite band."

"Nuh-uh."

I nod enthusiastically.

"*Your* favorite band is Led Zeppelin?"

"Is that so hard to believe?" I ask, feigning offense. I know exactly why he would never assume that's my favorite band.

Finally, I've got him. An assumption he guessed wrong.

"Just wasn't expecting that."

"And what were you expecting—Taylor Swift?"

He fights a smile, motioning in my direction. "I mean ..."

I can't help but sound smug. "What did I say about making assumptions about me?"

"That I'm always right?" he replies, his voice cocky.

I bite my lower lip to keep from laughing. "No. Try again."

"Hmm," he says, pretending to really think it over.

I slap him playfully. "Not to make them."

"Oh yeah. Now I remember," he answers, grabbing the hand I just hit him with and pulling me in closer. "I just can't help myself." Our bodies are suddenly pressed against each other's, and he looks down at me with heated eyes. "Like right now," he says against my ear. "I'd bet anything I know what you're thinking about."

"What am I thinking?" I ask, my heart starting to race.

His voice is low when he says, "All the things I'd do to you if we were alone in this car." He moves in even closer before asking, "Am I right?"

I feel my cheeks heat, too embarrassed to respond.

He leans back, gazing down at me. "You don't have to say anything. I know I'm right just by that look on your face, babe."

He releases me, and the only thought I'm left with is: *What exactly would he do to me if we were alone in this car?*

Chapter 33

THE SUN IS FINALLY starting to set on the day.

Ever since Billy and I ended our game of questions, we've all drifted between a comfortable silence and easy conversation. But my mind keeps wandering back to those last words he said to me. How they made me feel things I didn't know only words could make you feel. I try not to show how much he affected me, but each time I catch him looking my way, I wonder if he can see the thoughts written all over my face.

"I know I'm right just by that look on your face, babe."

I'm pulled from my thoughts when Sam squeals.

Billy looks just as surprised as I am to hear a sound like that coming from her until he sees what she's pointing at and laughs.

It's a big sign advertising a Cracker Barrel in two miles.

"Can we stop?" she pleads to Jameson, who looks wary. "Oh, come on, we have to eat." He still doesn't look sold, so she adds with a bit of a pout, "It's been a shit few days. This'll make me happy."

He glances over at her and sighs. "Yeah, all right."

Confused, I look to Billy.

His face is still amused as he explains, "She loves Cracker Barrel. Anytime there's a reason to go out to eat, that's what she picks. We go every year for her birthday."

The image of them all sitting around a table together each year warms something inside me. That sounds like the perfect way to spend a birthday.

Jealousy creeps in, and that hollow feeling I'm so familiar with replaces the warmth in my chest. I try to shake free of its hold, but I can't stop myself from wishing that I had what they all built together growing up. That I had people who knew me well enough to make my birthday feel special. Instead, it's always been a time that highlighted how alone I was.

My parents would get me an expensive gift that showed just how much they didn't know me when all I really wanted was their attention. Each year, I always thought that would be the one that was different. That they'd plan something for us to do together, or I'd open a gift that proved they listened to the things I talked about. That they knew what I liked.

I finally gave up hoping when I turned fifteen. That year, I got home from school and found a pair of diamond earrings on the dining room table with a note that read, "*Happy Birthday*," written in my mother's perfect handwriting.

That was all it said.

I looked around the house for them before realizing they weren't home. They had already left for work by the time I'd come downstairs that morning, so I hadn't seen them yet.

I had just settled in with a book when I got a text from my mother saying a last-minute work dinner came up and it couldn't be canceled. That was the only thing she said to me all day. I never heard from my father, and I never saw either of them.

I know it sounds dramatic, and it probably is, but I couldn't bring myself to wear those earrings. Every time I looked at them, I thought about how it felt when I realized they were choosing work over me, that they didn't care enough about me to even see me on my birthday.

My friends weren't much better. Every year, they'd throw me a big party, which I know sounds nice. It's just that if they knew anything about me, they'd know I hate big parties. Or maybe they did know and just didn't care. It was clear that nobody was actually there for me. It being my birthday was just another excuse for them to have a good time. And Avery was usually chasing after a guy, leaving me to spend the night with people I barely knew and wishing I could just go home.

Each year, I was surrounded by gifts and people, but all I ever wanted was for someone to see me. To actually understand me enough to realize that was the last way I wanted to spend my birthday.

"Babe. *Babe.*"

"Huh?" I reply, turning my attention to the voice at my side.

"Where'd you go in there?" Billy asks, brushing a loose strand of hair behind my ear.

I blink, willing myself back to reality.

"We're here," he tells me.

I look out the window and see we're in the Cracker Barrel parking lot.

Billy slides out of the seat and extends his hand to me. Once I'm standing at his side, he lowers it to the small of my back and leans into me. "You okay?" he questions, low enough that only I can hear him.

"Yup," I say, but my response comes out a bit too fast and high-pitched for it to be believable.

He narrows his eyes slightly, but he lets it go, leaving his hand firmly planted on my back as we walk inside.

I look around, not understanding as we step into what I thought was going to be a restaurant and instead is a big country store. But I can smell something sweet and buttery, so maybe the restaurant is in the back?

Billy smiles so wide that I swear it takes up his whole face, and his eyes are teasing as he says, "Of course you've never been to a Cracker Barrel."

"Who says I've never been here?"

He laughs. "You couldn't look more out of place if you tried."

"Okay, fine. I've never been here," I relent.

"That's just sad."

"What's sad?" Sam asks.

Billy tips his chin in my direction. "She's never been to Cracker Barrel before."

Sam cocks her head to the side in disbelief. "How is that even possible? Everyone's been here."

I look between the two of them and shrug. "My parents are huge snobs."

Billy snorts.

"This explains so much," Sam says. "What other normal things have you never done?"

"It explains so much that I've never been to Cracker Barrel?"

"Uh, yeah," she says, dead serious. "Have you ever been to a Walmart?"

I don't respond.

"Taken the city bus?"

I shake my head.

"Had a Big Mac?"

When I only stare back at her, she says, "That's just insane."

Billy laughs. "This is gonna be fun."

"What is?"

"Getting to show you all the things you've been missing out on."

I understand now why Sam loves this place. I eat so much that it feels like I'll never be hungry again.

Once we've all cleared our plates, Billy and Jameson go up front to pay the bill while Sam and I use the bathroom before getting back on the road.

We come out to find them waiting for us by the front door, Jameson holding a brown paper bag and Billy with one hand behind his back.

Sam lights up when Jameson hands it to her, finding the bag filled with old-fashioned candy and seeming particularly excited about one that's wrapped in yellow and red. The tension his face usually holds fades as he watches her pop the caramel in her mouth and moan in satisfaction. Then she leans up on her tiptoes and lightly brushes her lips against his.

I begin to follow them out the door when Billy grabs my arm. "I got you something."

I beam up at him. "You did?"

He pulls out the hand he was hiding behind his back, and my heart flips when I see he's holding a candy necklace. He takes it out of its packaging and places it over my head, careful to pull my hair out of the way so it doesn't get caught.

I run my fingers over the little colored candies. "I love it," I tell him, and I really mean it. The fact that he was thinking of me, that he wanted to give me something he knew would make me smile, makes my stomach flutter.

He runs a hand through his hair and rocks back on his heels. "I know it's not much, but—"

I grab his hand, cutting him off. "It's perfect, Billy, really."

"Yeah?" he asks.

"Yeah," I whisper as he pulls me into him and throws his arm over my shoulders.

"I'm glad you like it," he says, leading me out to the car.

Sam turns around as we pull into a Walmart parking lot. "We're already checking another one off the list."

Jameson raises an eyebrow.

"She's never been to Walmart," Sam explains then adds, "Or anywhere, really."

"I've been to lots of places," I huff.

"I bet you have," she teases. "Just nowhere normal." Then swings her door open and steps out of the car.

Once inside, Jameson grabs a cart and says, "Just the basics."

We follow him around the store, grabbing things like toothbrushes, toothpaste, and some clothes. It's still so surreal that none of us have any of our stuff, that we left with nothing but Sam's purse and the cash Jameson somehow had stashed away.

Once we have what we'll need for the next couple of days, we pay and head back to the car.

We drive for a few more hours then pull into another motel. After spending the night, we get back on the road and repeat the process once more before finally, we see the sign that reads, "*Welcome to Florida.*"

CHAPTER 34

BILLY CALLS HIS DAD and gets directions to his friend Lou's garage. We find out we only have a few hours left until we reach the place that will be our new home. I try not to think about how crazy this all is as I watch the busy roads fade into ones less traveled.

After days of driving on the highway, it's nice to be surrounded by open space. I focus on the little details we pass, letting them center my racing mind. There are too many questions I don't know the answers to and too many things about the future that are unknown.

Seeing that "*Welcome to Florida*" sign stirred up so many conflicting emotions that I don't even know how to start untangling them. So, rather than letting myself get lost in my thoughts, I watch the things that pass by.

Eventually, the sky starts to turn a bright pink and orange, and the air that drifts through the open windows begins to chill.

I've only seen a few cars drive past the whole time I've been looking out the window, so when I notice a car pulled off on the side of the road, it catches my eye. There's just enough light still in the sky to make out an old-looking Buick. The front door is open, but I can't see if anyone is inside.

I tap Billy's arm and point to the car. "I think someone's in there."

"Jameson," he says.

"Yeah, I see it."

They must have heard us approaching because an older woman steps out of the car and begins waving her hands, signaling that she needs help.

Instead of slowing or pulling onto the side of the road, Jameson keeps driving.

"You're not gonna stop?" I ask.

Jameson's grip tightens on the steering wheel. "We can't risk any attention."

"But there haven't been any cars for a long time," I push.

"And it's gonna be completely dark soon," Billy adds.

"Someone else will help," Jameson answers, seeming to try to reassure himself more than any of us.

"Jamie," Sam urges.

He turns to her, and she only has to give him a look before we're turning around.

We all get out of the car and are greeted by a woman who introduces herself as Eileen.

Her eyes stay on Billy as she explains that her tire blew out, and she couldn't put the spare on by herself. When she tried to call for help, she realized there wasn't any service. "I thought I was going to be stranded out here," she says, her voice shaky.

Billy politely introduces himself and explains that he's a mechanic, assuring her that he can get the tire on in no time. His warm tone seems to put her at ease, but I don't miss the few times her gaze quickly slides to Jameson, warily eyeing his tattoos.

She glances at each of us. "Thank you for stopping. You're the fifth car to drive by and the only one to stop."

"It's no problem," Jameson surprises me by responding. I can tell he's trying to sound gentler, like he knows he intimidates her.

I wonder what it must be like to always get that response from people? I've seen him use it to his advantage, but I wonder if it ever bothers him.

Eileen smiles back at him before he heads over to help Billy grab the spare out of the trunk.

Sam and I introduce ourselves and chat with her while they change the tire. We make small talk, but I keep getting distracted, stealing glances at Billy. His brows are furrowed in concentration as he works to get the tire off like he's done it a thousand times before.

I turn back when Eileen asks if we're in school. Sam explains that we just graduated and are here on vacation to celebrate. I've never met anyone who can lie as easily as she does.

The humid air sticks to my skin as I swat the mosquitoes swarming around us away. I look back over at Billy and find him stripping his Henley off, so he's left wearing only a thin white tank that clings to his sweaty chest. I quickly bring my attention back to the conversation, seeing Sam smirk at me out of the corner of my eye.

"Almost done," Billy yells out.

I turn as I hear someone coming down the road, and my body tenses when I see it's a police car. I know Sam sees it, too, but she doesn't let any panic show on her face.

I try to focus on Eileen's words as I wait for the car to pass, but instead of continuing down the road, the lights turn on, and it pulls in behind us.

Blue and red flashes against the night sky, and my stomach sinks.

CHAPTER 35

Gravel crunches as tires slow behind us, and then I hear a car door slam shut.

Oh God, this is it.

I glance over at Sam, but she gives nothing away, appearing completely unaffected. Jameson straightens as Billy stands, and his eyes catch mine. He tips his chin, trying to reassure me that it's all right.

The officer walks toward us and, with each step closer, my anxiety gets worse. We should've listened to Jameson.

He slows, taking in the scene. "What's going on here?"

"I got a flat tire, and these nice kids stopped to help me," Eileen tells him. "If it weren't for them, I could have been stuck out here all night."

He looks between Sam and me before focusing on Jameson and Billy. They're both still standing on the other side of her car with the tire between them.

I try to keep myself calm as he stalks over to them, waiting for the questions to start, but all he says is, "Need a hand?"

If Jameson is surprised, he doesn't show it. Instead, his voice is steady. "We just finished getting it changed out. She should be all good to go now. We were just about to get this in the trunk."

"Good deal," the officer replies as he clasps him on the shoulder. He looks between the two of them and says, "The world needs more upstanding young people like you. Thanks for helping out."

Something flashes across Jameson's face for just a second, and then it's gone.

"We're happy to help," Billy says, carrying the tire to the trunk of Eileen's car.

The officer distractedly tells us to have a good night as he gets another call, quickly making his way back to his car.

I finally let myself relax as his taillights fade into the distance.

Billy tells Eileen she needs to get to a mechanic as soon as she can to get off the spare. She assures him that she'll go in the morning and thanks us again before heading to her car.

"He was nice," Billy says once we're on the road again.

Jameson scoffs. "That back there is exactly why we don't take stupid risks."

"Nothing happened."

"We were lucky this time, that's it. It could have gone the other way back there, and you know it," Jameson snaps.

"Not everyone and everything is out to get you."

Jameson pins Billy with a deadly glare. "Don't start with me."

Billy shakes his head. "Whatever."

"We're so close, and we're not gonna fuck it up by being reckless."

"So what? You would have rather just left an old lady stranded?"

"Yes," Jameson answers.

Billy pulls his head back. "Fuck that."

"Someone else would've stopped to play the hero, like that cop you think is so nice."

"It was the right thing to do."

"No, the right thing to do would've been to keep driving. The people I need to take care of are in this car. That's my number one priority." He pauses. "My only priority." The car is quiet until Jameson says, "We've gotta look out for ourselves 'cause nobody else is gonna do it. We can't go trying to save the world when we can barely save ourselves."

CHAPTER 36

JAMESON'S WORDS LINGER AS we drive, adding to the tension that's building as we get closer to our destination. The only times the car isn't silent are the few calls Billy makes to his dad to ask for directions. It all seems to be catching up to us.

The exhaustion.

The fear.

The anticipation.

Not knowing what's coming next.

But we keep driving, and I keep hoping that this all wasn't one horrible mistake.

It's close to nine when we finally pull into the empty lot of a mechanic shop. It looks similar to the one Billy's dad owns, except a little bigger and a little better taken care of. We were told that Lou would be waiting for us, so we all head inside.

We're almost to the front door when it swings open and a man walks out. He's around the same height as me and has a beer belly that his tucked-in shirt can barely contain. His skin is leathered, like he's spent far too much time in the sun, and his face is made up of hard lines that seem permanently etched into place.

He points at Billy and says, "You must be Luke's boy."

Billy nods. "Thanks for helping us out."

Lou stares at him for a moment, as if lost in a memory. "You look just like him when he was your age." Then he sweeps his gaze over each of us and says, "All right, come on in."

He moves slowly as he leads us into a small break room, dragging his left leg with effort. There's a woman sitting at the table, and her head jerks up when she hears us approach. The dingy room lights up with her smile, and her energy fills the space as she stands.

Lou sweeps his hand in her direction. "This is my girl, Candi."

She walks over to us, her wedges clicking against the tile. Her hair is blonde and teased, and her makeup is caked on heavily, as if it'll conceal her age. She's wearing bootcut jeans and a little pink cardigan with the top buttons left undone, causing her huge fake boobs to spill out of the top.

"It's so nice to meet y'all," she says with a sweet southern drawl. She looks funny standing next to Lou, his complete opposite. "Come sit," Candi tells us. "I'll make some coffee. Are you hungry? You must be hungry after all that driving." Her words come out a mile a minute.

We all take a seat around the table, Billy sliding his chair close to mine. "Coffee's good, thank you," he tells her.

She rummages around in the cabinets before dropping a tin of cookies and a bag of chips on the table. "Just in case," she says with a wink then goes back to the coffee.

Lou clears his throat and looks between us before landing on Billy. "Your pop told me about the trouble you're in."

Jameson is sitting completely still, like he's bracing himself for the words that are coming next.

Lou shifts his attention to him, but the wariness that so many people greet Jameson with is missing from his face. "Sometimes life puts us in shitty situations. Forces us to make choices we don't wanna make. You got dealt one of those choices, but don't you regret for one minute doing what you had to do to protect the people you love. You hear me?"

Jameson nods stiffly.

"You ain't gotta worry about any judgment from me," Lou tacks on.

Jameson nods again, the movement seeming to release some of the apprehension he's been holding since we walked in here.

"All right, now let's talk about what comes next." He keeps his attention on Billy and Jameson as Candi sets down the pot of coffee. "I can get both of you set up with jobs at the shop." He tips his head toward Billy. "I know you know your way around a car." Then turns to Jameson. "What about you?"

"Not as much as him, but more than the basics, and I learn fast."

That seems to be enough for him because Lou says, "Good. You both start tomorrow. Be here at nine."

Candi sets down six mugs, sugar, and cream, and then she drops into the chair next to Lou.

Billy pours me a cup before filling his own. The exhaustion of the last few days is starting to wear on me, so I forgo my no-caffeine-after-two rule and mix in some cream.

"I got you an apartment," Lou starts, and all of our heads whip in his direction. "It's a one-bedroom, but it comes furnished, and it's only a few blocks from here. I'll take the money I paid for the deposit out of your paychecks, and then you'll pay me the rent each month. This way, nothing is in your names, and you don't have to worry about getting approved."

"Thank you," Billy says. "That's really generous of you."

"Don't mention it."

"How much a month?" Jameson asks.

"Rent's nine hundred."

Sam leans forward. "Do you know any restaurants hiring?"

Candi thinks for a moment before answering, "Yeah, there's a little place called Eloise's Café. I saw a help wanted sign last time we were there."

"Okay, thanks," Sam says as she dunks a cookie into her coffee.

"It's on the main street in town. You can't miss it."

Lou sets down his mug. "That's all I have. Any of you got anything else?"

"Yeah," Jameson says. "We need to get rid of our car. You know anyone who'll buy it without asking questions or a place I can just sell it for parts?"

Jameson holds his stare, and they seem to be having a silent conversation until Lou says, "I've got someone. You can have my truck until you get it sorted."

"You don't have to—" Billy starts to say, but the look on Jameson's face cuts him off.

Lou jumps in. "It's fine, really. I've got my Harley, or I can catch rides with Candi."

Billy glances at Candi, and she nods reassuringly.

"That should have you all covered. We can talk more tomorrow and get all the details figured out," Lou says.

"Y'all must be tired and want to get settled," Candi adds as we stand to leave.

As if on cue, I yawn.

Billy looks down at me and says, "Come on; let's get you home."

As he leads me out toward Lou's truck, that word tumbles around in my head.

Home.

CHAPTER 37

WE WALK THROUGH THE front door of the apartment, and all just stand there, staring. It's small and a bit run-down, but it's ours.

It looks like freedom.

Billy and I begin to explore, but I stop when I see that Sam is still standing by the door, Jameson leaning against the wall beside her.

Her eyes are wide as she glances around, moving through each space in the room and then back over them again. It's like she's committing everything to memory in case it all disappears. Like she can't believe it's real.

I try to busy myself by opening cabinets in the kitchen, but I turn when I hear a muffled cry.

Sam's pressed against Jameson's chest, shaking, and he's holding her so tightly I wonder if she would sag to the ground if he let go.

I'm not sure what to do, so I turn to Billy and find him watching them, mirroring my uncertainty.

He starts to take a step toward them but stops himself. Instead, he shifts his attention to me and tips his head toward the bedroom, so I follow him in.

Closing the door, he lets out a long breath.

"Is she okay?" I ask. "Do you know why she's crying?"

He runs a hand through his hair. "I think it's all hitting her. She holds a lot in. I've ..." He sits down on the bed. "I've only ever seen her cry once before."

I think back to the motel when Billy told me that he'd only seen Sam that upset one other time. Was that the one time he saw her cry?

Billy looks at the door. "I don't think she ever thought this would actually happen."

I sit down beside him. "That what would happen?"

"That we'd get out of there." His eyes find mine. "I don't think she even let herself imagine leaving."

"And you?" I ask. "Did you ever think about leaving?"

"I never let myself imagine leaving, either. It just always seemed like that was going to be it for us. I accepted it and told myself it was fine, that we'd all stay in Crestview forever, but now that we're here ..."

I take his hand, shifting closer.

"Now that things are different, it's a lot to take in"—he hesitates—"and I just feel so guilty."

"Why do you feel guilty? You didn't do anything."

"I know we left for all the wrong reasons, but I just feel so relieved, like I can finally breathe. I didn't realize how trapped I felt. How suffocated."

Without thinking, I squeeze his hand. "I know exactly what you mean."

"You do?"

I nod slowly. "I keep thinking that I should feel more scared or more nervous, but I don't. I've never felt so ..."

"Free," Billy says for me.

I pull my bottom lip between my teeth and nod again. "I always knew what was coming next, and I thought I found comfort in it, needed it even. But now that I don't have that, I've realized that wasn't true at all. I could never understand why I was so unhappy, why I had that same suffocating feeling. But I get it now. After everything that's happened ..."

It's Billy who squeezes my hand this time.

"After everything that happened ... I realized that it was because I was living my life for other people. And that, after so many years of living like that, I became the person they made me rather than who I really am." I feel like I sound crazy, but I peer up and find Billy watching me with a look like he completely understands. It's that look that makes me say, "And

I think you see me for the person I really am." I pause before adding, "You make me want to be that person. You make me want to be me."

CHAPTER 38

WE GO BACK OUT into the living room once we hear Sam and Jameson moving around the space. Billy opens the door, and Sam's laughter fills the room.

"What's so funny?" he asks, sounding grateful that the mood has lightened.

"Don't say it," Sam says, pointing a finger at Jameson.

Billy looks between them, Jameson putting up his hands in mock defeat, while Sam stares him down, trying to look serious.

They watch each other silently, waiting to see who will crack first. Surprisingly, it's Jameson. A laugh slips from his lips so fast that if I wasn't paying attention, I would have missed it. Sam is quick to follow, her lips tipping up as she affectionately says, "You're an idiot."

Jameson slings his arm over her shoulders, pulling her into his side and using his other hand to ruffle her hair.

I glance over at Billy, and his eyes are bright as he takes the two of them in.

Jameson releases his hold on Sam and focuses on all the details of the room. It's like he didn't really see it until now, until he knew she was okay.

He nods to himself as he mutters, "This'll work." Then he walks over to the couch, removing the cushions and pulling it out into a bed.

"You guys can take the bedroom," I say, motioning to Billy. "We can take the couch."

Jameson's hands still, and his head snaps up, his eyes finding mine. His face is tight, brows drawn together, like he's waiting for the catch.

A part of me breaks for him, for the life he must have lived to make him this way.

Billy jumps in, "Really, take it. It's no big deal."

Jameson still doesn't seem convinced, so Billy adds with a grin, "I'm more than happy to have to snuggle up close to Susan."

"Thanks," Sam says, cutting in.

The sound of her voice has Jameson turning toward her, and just then, it seems to occur to him that the bedroom would be for her, too. That must be all the convincing he needs because his shoulders drop as he mumbles, "Yeah, thanks."

"You should go crash. You look wiped," Billy says.

He really does look tired. He drove the entire way here. I don't know if it's because we were in his car or if he just needed to feel like he was in control of something.

Jameson dodges the suggestion entirely. "We should figure out the plan for tomorrow."

Sam leans casually against the side of the couch. "I want to apply for that waitressing job, so maybe you can drive me during your lunch break?"

"I'll ask Lou. Shouldn't be a problem, though."

I shift on my feet. "I'll go, too."

I expect some snide remark or assumption that I've never had a job, but I get neither. Instead, Sam asks, "What about money until our first paychecks?" She glances toward the kitchen. "We'll need groceries and stuff."

"We still have some cash left. It should be enough to get us started," Jameson answers. "We can go after Billy and I get off tomorrow night. Anything else?" he asks, looking at each of us. When we all shake our heads, he says, "Good, 'cause I really am fucking exhausted."

I make up the pull-out sofa while Billy showers, and I've just settled under the covers when I hear the bathroom door close.

He saunters into the room, a towel wrapped around his waist, stopping at the Walmart bag to pull out a pair of boxers. I'm glad his back is to me so he can't see the blush that's surely coloring my face.

He drops the towel, and it takes all I have to hold back a gasp. After quickly stepping into them, he turns to face me, his lips pulling up into a knowing smirk.

He heads to the kitchen, and I watch him the whole way there, unable to look away. He stops at a cabinet and pulls out two glasses, his arm muscles flexing in the process. He then walks to the sink and fills them both with water, his eyes flicking up to meet mine. I immediately drop his gaze and look down at my hands, wishing I had my phone or a book that I could pretend to focus on.

I hear his footsteps approaching, and my body tingles with anticipation, but he says nothing as he sets one of the cups down next to me then walks around to his side of the bed.

His warmth envelops the small space as his body slides up behind mine, and I feel his hot breath against my neck when he says, "I saw you watching me."

I try to respond, but the words disappear when he brings his hand up and grazes the side of my face. He slowly slides his thumb over my cheek, down to my bottom lip. With his other arm, he pulls me in closer as his mouth comes down on my neck, trailing kisses along my skin until he reaches my collarbone. "So sweet," he mutters softly.

A moan escapes my lips, and something snaps inside of him, his movements turning rushed. Suddenly, I'm on my back with Billy hovering over me. He finds the hem of his T-shirt that I'm wearing and slips his hand underneath, sliding up my body.

"This okay?" he breathes against my lips.

I wrap my legs around his back and pull him closer to me in response.

He grinds against me, and I push myself into him, desperate for more.

"You're killing me," he groans as he grips my hips, moving me to the pace he's created. Then he drifts his hands lower, and his eyes again meet mine, but this time, they're holding a question.

"Please," I answer.

That one word sets him into a frenzy, and I thread my fingers through his hair as he rakes his gaze down my body, stopping where his fingers have just gone. He watches me as I move under his touch until my eyes close and my body begins to shake.

I try to steady my breathing as I open them again and find Billy looking at me like he would devour me right now if I told him to.

I swallow hard, dropping my eyes lower then back up to his face. Reaching out, I run a hand up and down his chest, tracing the tattoo over his heart. He grabs my chin, pulling my mouth to his, before letting go and flipping our positions on the bed.

Now it's me who's hovering over him, and I let my hands trail lower until I hear him suck in a breath. I give him what he gave me and watch as his eyes close just as mine did. A few drawn-out seconds pass before he blinks them open, as if pulling himself out of a fog.

"Perfect," he whispers. "You're perfect."

CHAPTER 39

I FEEL A HAND lightly brush over my cheek, and someone quietly says my name. I turn over and find Billy standing over me.

"Jameson and I are heading out," he tells me.

I move to sit up, but he stops me. "Keep sleeping, baby. We should be back at lunch to drive you and Sam over to the diner."

The blanket that was draped over us has become a jumbled mess, so he takes it and spreads it back over me, tucking it around my sides. I feel his lips on my forehead. "I'll see you later."

Before I can respond, I'm already drifting back to sleep.

I wake up to bright morning light filtering through the curtains. Stretching my arms overhead, I can't remember the last time I slept this well.

Suddenly realizing how thirsty I am, I grab the glass of water that Billy left on the side table for me. Gulping it down, I glance around, finding the apartment empty. How long have I been asleep?

I reach for my phone to check the time before remembering I no longer have one. Instead, I stand, squinting to read the clock on the microwave, and my eyes widen when I see that it's ten forty-eight. I don't think I've ever woken up this late. I must have been really tired, or maybe I was just relaxed after spending a night wrapped up in Billy's arms.

Turning, I see that the bedroom door is cracked open. I knock twice before hearing "Yeah," from Sam and push inside.

She looks up from the book she's reading and says, "I thought you'd never wake up."

"I don't know what happened. I never sleep in this late."

She rolls her lips. "From the look on Billy's face this morning, I'm not surprised you needed the extra rest."

"We ... uh ... we didn't," I stammer, failing to find the words.

"Calm down." She laughs. "I'm not judging you. I think you're good for him."

"You do?"

Setting the book down on her lap, she tips her chin toward the end of the bed, and I walk over to sit across from her.

"Yes," she answers, the teasing tone gone from her voice. "He needs someone like you."

"Someone like me?"

"Yeah, someone like you. Someone loyal and kind. He needs someone consistent."

I smile at her words. She doesn't seem like someone who gives out compliments often.

"What do you mean *consistent*?" I ask.

"You've seen the type of girls he messes around with."

I remember back to the party we went to, and the girl who practically dry-humped him, trying to get his attention.

I nod.

"None of them are serious. None of them last."

"Why not? I mean, hasn't he ever had a girlfriend?"

She shakes her head. "There've been plenty of girls."

I flinch, thinking about how many girls he's done the things we did last night with.

"But he's never had a real girlfriend. He's never had something like me and Jameson have." She fidgets with her ring. "I've always wanted that for him."

"How come he's never ...?"

A sadness washes over her, and it's then that I understand. "Because of his mom?"

Her eyes snap up to meet mine. "He told you about her?"

"Not a lot, just that she left. He said he would tell me more about it later, and I didn't want to push him to share anything he wasn't ready to."

She stares at me in disbelief. "He doesn't ever talk about his mom."

My heart skips a beat, thinking about what it means that he shared that part of himself with me.

"But yeah"—she nods—"I think that has a lot to do with it. It can be hard for him to let people in."

"That's understandable."

"Once he lets you in, though, he'll hold onto you with all he has. If you guys are gonna move forward." She searches my face for confirmation. "Are you gonna move forward?"

"Um," I start. "I don't know. Do you think he wants that? I thought you said he doesn't do girlfriends."

"He doesn't." She pauses. "Or, he hasn't. He's different with you, though. I've never seen him this way before."

"Different how?"

"He's never tried before. It's always been"—she hesitates—"difficult to watch him move from one girl to the next. There's never any emotion. It's all about distraction with him. He likes the attention and the affection, but he's always left feeling empty. It's like he's been looking for something he couldn't find." Her eyes meet mine. "Until you."

My stomach flutters as her words sink in.

"Why me? I'm nothing special."

She shakes her head as if dismissing my response. "You see him for the person he really is, not the person he pretends to be."

What I said to Billy last night echoes in my mind. *I think you see me for the person I really am. You make me want to be that person. You make me want to be me.*

"He's more sensitive than people think he is. He plays it off with his jokes, but there's a lot more to him than people see," she says.

"I know."

"I know you know. That's why I think you're good for him. Anyway," she continues, "if you're gonna move forward together, make sure you're ready for what comes with it."

I look back at her, confused.

"Once Billy's in, he's all in. He'll give you everything he has, even if it leaves him with nothing." She pins me with a hard stare. "Don't leave him with nothing."

"Sam," a low voice calls from the front door.

Jameson stops in the doorway, looking between the two of us. He seems surprised to have found us sitting together, talking.

Before he says anything, he and Sam have one of their silent conversations. It's like they have their own language that they can use whenever they want to keep their thoughts private, which I'm finding out is most of the time.

I look behind Jameson, wondering if Billy will come in after him.

Tracking my gaze, he simply says, "He's at the shop."

My shoulders drop, disappointed that he didn't come, too.

Sam must give him some kind of look because he rolls his eyes and clarifies, "Lou had him buried in something that needed to be finished by tonight."

I nod, feeling better that he didn't have a choice in not coming.

Jameson motions toward the front door. "Let's go hit the diner. I told Lou I'd be fast."

I look down at myself. I'm still in Billy's T-shirt and haven't done anything with my hair or makeup. "I need five minutes."

"Go quick," he grunts.

I slip past him and into the living room then rummage through my plastic bag of clothes and pull out the nicest thing I have—a pair of jeans and a white T-shirt. It'll have to do, I guess.

Sam comes up behind me and hands me a brush, a tube of mascara, and lipstick that she must have found in the endless black hole that she calls her purse. As much as I want to make fun of her for all the stuff she carries, it really has come in handy.

I thank her and rush into the bathroom, trying to make myself presentable enough for an interview.

I think about the time I used to spend getting ready and the obsession my mother put on my appearance. I wonder what she would think if she saw me now.

Brushing the mascara over my lashes, I push the thoughts of her away.

"Time's up," Jameson yells out.

I walk out into the living room, still running the brush through my hair, and find him standing with the front door open.

I follow Sam out and wait for Jameson to lock up before trailing behind them to the truck.

I spend the whole drive to the café stuck in my head, running through all the questions I might be asked and how I should respond.

Is there even going to be an interview today? Do you have an interview right away, or do you have to apply first? Am I going to get laughed at when I say I have no work experience? Maybe I should talk about all of my volunteer experience. Does that count?

I think about asking Sam for advice, but I don't want to make it obvious that this will be my first job.

The engine cuts off, and I glance up to see a pastel sign that reads, "*Eloise's Café*." It's situated next to other small business-es that line what must be the main street in town. Each of them appears old but well taken care of. It's all really charming.

Maybe I have nothing to worry about.

"I'll wait here," Jameson says as Sam pushes open her door.

A bell chimes overhead when we walk into the café. The space is bright and teeming with energy, the sounds of silver-ware clanging against plates and lively conversation filling the space.

As I follow Sam up to the counter, I notice that most of the booths and tables are full. A woman is moving swiftly between customers, trying to keep up with the demand.

We wait until she rushes behind the counter and sets down a pitcher of water. "Can I help you?"

"We saw the help wanted sign," Sam says, angling her head toward the sign hanging on the front window. "Are you still hiring?"

"Oh, thank God." The woman sighs. "You girls have expe-rience waitressing?"

Sam takes a step closer. "I do."

The woman turns to me.

"I learn quickly. Or, I can wash dishes. Whatever you need."

"I'll take whatever I can get," she says. "One of my waitresses just had a baby, and she's not coming back to work. Another one left me high and dry. Just stopped showing up. I've been drowning here."

"That's so stressful. I'm sorry," I respond, genuinely feeling bad for her.

"Thank you," she answers, her voice warm with appreciation. "So, when can you two start?"

That's it? We're just hired? I guess she really is desperate.

"As soon as you need us," Sam tells her.

"What about now?"

"Yeah, we can start now."

"Great," she says, clearly relieved. "Give me a couple of minutes to check on everyone, and I'll be back to get you set up." She wipes her hand against the apron tied around her before sticking it out. "I'm Carol."

Sam and I both shake her hand and tell her our names.

"We're just gonna go tell our ride he can go," Sam says before Carol turns, rushing over to a couple trying to get her attention.

My stomach sinks as the nerves creep back in. I didn't prepare myself for this. I didn't think we'd start right away. What if I look like an idiot who has no idea what they're doing?

As if reading my mind, Sam says, "Calm down. I'll help you. She's not gonna just throw you right in without any training."

"Thanks," I mutter, but my anxious mind still isn't convinced.

Sam knocks on the driver's side window of the truck, and Jameson rolls it down. "We're starting now," she tells him.

Unfazed, he asks, "When're you done?"

"She didn't say. I guess just swing by when you guys are finished for the day."

"All right," he answers, but before rolling the window back up, he quietly adds, "Come here."

She steps up on her toes, leaning in closer, and he grabs her face, pulling her into a kiss.

I drop my eyes to give them some privacy until I hear him call out, "See ya," as he throws the truck into reverse.

Sam comes up next to me. "Come on."

I walk in behind her to start my first ever day of work.

CHAPTER 40

I'VE BEEN SHADOWING SAM at the café for a couple weeks now, and I'm finally starting to get the hang of things. The customers are all locals and have been patient with me. I've started to get to know some of them and look forward to when the regulars come in.

Carol has been so nice, answering any questions I have and telling me repeatedly that I'm doing a great job. Between her and Sam's encouragement, I feel a lot more confident than I did when I started.

The afternoon rush today went by quickly. Lunch was a madhouse, but Sam and I fell into a groove, moving from one table to the next.

It's just past five o'clock now, and Carol tells us that we can be finished for the day. Billy and Jameson still aren't here yet, so we offer to help out with whatever is needed until they get here.

Carol lights up at the suggestion, and we spend the next hour or so refilling sugar containers, condiment bottles, and restocking things behind the counter.

I'm clearing off a table when I feel arms wrap around my waist. My body goes rigid until a familiar voice says, "I missed you today."

My lips pull into a smile as I turn and see Billy staring down at me. "I missed you, too."

"You ready?" Jameson asks, coming up beside us with Sam right behind him.

"Let me just clear this table, and then we can go," I tell them.

"All right, we'll be in the truck," Jameson says, draping an arm over Sam's shoulder.

Billy stays back to help me finish up, and after saying good-bye to Carol, we head out.

"What do you want for dinner?" Sam asks.

We all think until Billy drums his hands on the back of her seat excitedly. "Pigs and potatoes!"

Pigs and potatoes?

"Oh ... fuck yes," Jameson agrees with as much enthusiasm as I think he's capable of.

Sam laughs. "Okay, sure. I can make that."

"What's pigs and potatoes?" Should I know what that is?

"One of the best things you'll ever eat! That's what," Billy answers. "It's one of her specialties."

"I came up with it one day when I was trying to pull dinner together," Sam says. "We didn't have a lot of groceries, so I just kinda made it up."

"One of her best inventions yet," Billy cuts in.

"Well, everything else you've made has been good," I tell her. She's been cooking dinner every night since we've gotten here. Nobody asked her to, but she just kind of assumed the role.

Jameson looks over at her with adoration. "She's the best."

"I'm not the best. I just throw stuff together. It's nothing fancy."

"Just 'cause it's not fancy doesn't mean it's not good," he responds. "I can't cook for shit."

Billy snorts, amused.

"You're not any better, asshole," Jameson spits back.

"Yeah, I am."

"Oh yeah? What can you cook?"

"Eggs. Pasta." He pauses. "Beans and franks."

"That's not cooking."

"It's better than what you can do."

"Will the two of you stop?" Sam teases. "I wouldn't eat anything either of you cooked."

Billy turns to me. "What about you?"

I shake my head. "I'm probably just as bad as you."

"Probably?" Sam asks.

I shrug. "I've never really tried before."

"Right, I forgot you have a mom," she says with a hint of bitterness.

"Oh no, my mom doesn't cook," I clarify.

"So, who does? Your dad?" she asks, like she can't picture a man in the kitchen.

"No, he doesn't either."

"What—do you rich people just not eat?"

"I get takeout a lot. Or, we go out."

"That must be nice," she says, the bitterness in her voice growing thicker.

"It sounds that way, but it gets old. I can't remember the last time we all ate together at home. We only go out to eat as a family if we're meeting people or are putting in an appearance somewhere." I clear my throat. "Most of the time, it's just me."

She's quiet after that.

"Well, not anymore," Billy says, squeezing my hand. "You've got us now."

We stop at the grocery store, and Sam grabs everything she needs to make dinners for the week. It's like she's made a whole meal plan in her head, navigating the store like she's been cooking for a family for years. I guess she probably has.

The rest of us stick to just throwing snacks into the cart, Jameson putting back half the stuff Billy adds, telling him we don't need it. I look at everything they pick up, almost all of them things my mother would never have allowed us to have in the house.

After Sam says that she's got everything, we go to check out. I help unload the cart, thinking about how ridiculous the Lucky Charms look next to the big case of beer, both added by Billy. Sam asks the cashier for a carton of cigarettes, and while waiting for him to return, she adds three bars of chocolate to our growing pile of food.

As the cashier walks back with the cigarettes, he sweeps his gaze over her appreciatively. Jameson steps in closer and possessively snakes his arm around her waist. The cashier zeros in on the movement and immediately drops his eyes.

Sam only smirks at the exchange.

The cashier is probably around twenty, small, and about the least intimidating person I've ever seen. I notice that he doesn't ask to see any I.D. when he scans the beer. If I were him, I would take one look at Jameson and "forget" to ask too.

He reads out the total, telling us it'll be one hundred twenty-seven dollars and eighty-two cents, and looks up in surprise when Jameson hands him cash, both of the bills hundreds.

Jameson arches a brow as he waits for him to take the money and that quickly gets the guy moving. He makes our change, counts it twice, and then hands it over, looking relieved when Jameson pockets it without complaint.

Walking out to the car, Billy says, "I'm surprised the kid didn't piss his pants after how you looked at him."

"I don't know what you're talking about," Jameson answers.

Billy bites back a grin. "Sure you don't."

Jameson stops in front of the car. "I didn't like how he was looking at her."

Sam rolls her eyes. "You're both being dramatic."

"I'm not being dramatic," Jameson huffs.

"*You* overreacting about Sam?" Billy says sarcastically. "Never."

Jameson tosses the bags into the trunk. "Shut up. He was practically eye-fucking her."

Billy laughs. "Dude, that's how everybody looks at Sam."

"They do not," Sam says at the same time Jameson snaps, "They better fucking not."

"People at home just hide it better 'cause they know you're with Jameson."

Sam turns toward the passenger seat, trying to hide her embarrassment. "Whatever. I'm hungry, and the casserole will take an hour."

I follow behind her, and as I'm sliding into the back seat, I hear Jameson ask Billy, "Who looked at her like that back home?"

Chapter 41

Pigs and potatoes ends up being a Spam and tater tot casserole. I was wary when I realized we'd be eating canned meat for dinner, but based on how good the apartment smells right now, I'm becoming a lot less skeptical.

Sam pulls it out of the oven and calls out, "Food!"

Billy shoots up from beside me on the couch the second the word leaves her mouth. He walks to the fridge, grabs three beers, then turns to me. "You want one?"

I shake my head. "I'll just have water."

He jerks his chin toward the kitchen table. "Sit. I'll get it for you."

I join Jameson at the table, and Sam follows behind me with the casserole. Billy hands out our drinks then returns again with plates and silverware.

I scoop some on my plate and feel them all watching me, waiting for my reaction. I take the first bite and don't even finish chewing before I moan out, "Mmmohmygod."

Billy laughs. "Told ya."

"You should make this every night," I tell Sam.

"I wouldn't complain," Billy chimes in.

"It really is so fucking good," Jameson follows.

Sam smiles. "I'm glad you guys like it."

"How was work today?" Jameson asks, turning to Sam. "Everything go good?"

I have to keep myself from correcting him as my mother's words enter my head. *It's well, Susan, not good. Say the sentence again, but correctly this time.*

"Yeah, lunch was crazy, but the rest of the day wasn't too bad," she answers.

"What about your day?" I ask, glancing between Billy and Jameson.

"It was awesome," Billy responds enthusiastically. "Lou really is such a nice guy." He takes another bite before adding, "Oh, I didn't even tell you both yet. He has an old bike that doesn't run anymore, and he said that if I can fix it up, I can have it!"

"He's just going to give it to you?" I question.

"Well, I'll have to buy whatever parts I need, but I checked it out, and it shouldn't be too much. I just have to do all the labor, but it's nothing I can't handle."

"Wow, that's amazing," I say.

"I know! After I get it running, I'll take you for your first ride."

I look back at him nervously. "I don't know if I'm a motorcycle kind of girl."

"There's nothing to be scared of, baby. I'll do all the work. You just have to hold on tight."

My face heats at the double meaning in his words.

Sam laughs. "Jesus, Billy, do you hear half the shit that comes out of your mouth? Do you even think before you talk, or do you just say everything that comes into your head?"

"Everything that comes into my head," he replies easily.

She shakes her head with a smile then turns her attention to me. "It looks scarier than it is. It's actually really fun."

"You ride motorcycles, too?"

"Only on the back," she clarifies. "I don't drive."

"At all?" Jameson always drives, so it's never crossed my mind that she doesn't.

She shakes her head.

"Do you have a license?"

"I have a fake," she answers.

"Why don't you drive?"

"It freaks me out." She waves her hand between Jameson and Billy. "And I've always had them to drive me around." She looks up defensively, even though I haven't said anything. "I'm gonna get it. I just haven't yet."

"I don't really like driving either," I say, hoping it will make her feel better.

Her face softens as she takes another bite of her food.

"Really, it's a good thing that you don't drive. Because if you did, I wouldn't have given you a ride home from the food bank. And if I didn't give you a ride home, we wouldn't have driven over that median." I look at Billy. "And then I never even would have met you guys."

Billy points at me. "Good fuckin' point, babe."

He turns to Sam. "Guess I owe you."

Jameson and Billy clean up from dinner while Sam and I take turns showering. I go last, and when I come out into the main room, I find them all sitting around the kitchen table again, with cards spread out in front of them. The window is open, letting in a warm breeze and the hum of cars passing by on the street below.

I sit down in the empty seat next to Billy, and he pulls my chair in closer to his then leans over and kisses me on top of my head.

"What was that for?" I ask, looking up at him with a smile.

"'Cause you're just so damn cute I can't help myself," he says then returns back to the game, grabbing a card from a pile in the middle of the table.

Every time I think he can't get any better, he does little things like this.

"What are you playing?"

"Gin. You ever played?"

I shake my head.

"It's easy. I'll teach you if you wanna join in."

"I don't want to slow you guys down. I can just watch."

"Just a yes or no question, babe. You don't have to over-think it," he tells me gently. He then picks up another card, rearranges the ones in his hand, and turns to me, waiting for my answer.

"Yes," I say simply.

He grins. "Good."

Shifting even closer to me so I can fully see his cards, he explains how the game works. "You can watch this round, and then we'll deal you in on the next one."

I watch them play and begin to get it, but they move so quickly I worry I won't be able to keep up.

"Do you guys play this a lot?"

"Yeah, we've been playing since we were kids. We haven't played in a while, though, but when I saw the cards at the grocery store tonight, I thought: why not?" He shrugs. "We usually play for cash," Then he nods toward Sam. "This one always walks away with all our money."

Sam bites back a grin.

"Who taught you how to play?"

She picks up a card. "My brother taught me, and I taught them."

"You didn't teach us," Billy scoffs, setting down his beer.

"Fine, you knew how to play, but you weren't any good."

"Whatever," Billy mumbles. "You just thought you were hot shit 'cause Johnny used to take you to his games."

"'Cause I *was* hot shit," she brags. "Like you just said, I always beat the two of you." She shuffles around the cards in her hand and says, "And I still do." Then she lays them down and calls out, "Gin."

Billy throws down his cards. "You little shit."

Jameson laughs at the two of them then gets up as Billy begins shuffling the cards and returns with three more beers.

Sam has just lit another cigarette when the phone rings.

I jump from the noise, not having expected to hear it, and we all look at each other with concern on our faces.

We purposefully haven't been talking about Carson and whether or not he'll come out of the coma, but we all seem to have the same feeling.

That the person on the other end of the line is about to tell us.

Jameson slowly rises from his seat, grabs the phone on the kitchen counter, and answers it. "Hey," he says, his voice hard. There's a pause before he asks, "What does that mean?"

Minutes go by that feel like hours as he waits for who I'm assuming is Billy's dad to explain. His back is to the table, the phone pressed against his ear rather than on speaker. His body is rigid, shoulders pulled up to his ears. He's completely isolated himself.

I can't imagine how much this has been weighing on him. What must it feel like to know that one phone call is all that stands between knowing if you've killed someone or not?

He's pacing back and forth but stills when he chokes out, "You sure?" Another beat passes before he mutters, "Yeah, you, too," and then hangs up the phone. He stands there for a moment, not moving.

I look between Sam and Billy. Their eyes are glued to his back, both just as still as him. It's like the world around me has frozen, time utterly suspended.

Jameson exhales audibly, a tremor running though his body. The room snaps back to life when he turns around and says, "He woke up."

CHAPTER 42

THE WORDS BEGIN TO sink in as I watch everything unfold around me.

He woke up.

He woke up.

He woke up.

That means Jameson didn't ...

He pulls out the chair next to Sam, the legs dragging against the floor. Dropping down with a *thud*, his elbows find the table, and his head falls into his hands. His breathing is quick and shallow as he repeatedly runs his fingers through his hair like the motion is his only tether to reality.

Nobody says anything as we all work through what those words mean.

Jameson closes his eyes as he leans back. I don't know where he goes inside himself, but it doesn't take long before he opens his eyes and is back in control.

He pulls out a cigarette and lights it, each motion quick and steady. Tossing the lighter back onto the table, he says, "He's supposed to make a full recovery. Something about where …" He glances at Sam then drops his eyes to his hands. "Something about where the bullet hit him. I didn't really understand what Luke was saying when he tried to explain it." He exhales a cloud of smoke. "Luke said that since he'll be okay, all the drugs they found in his system, and all the witnesses that said he fired first …" He pauses, clearing his throat. "Because of all of that, they don't have a case." He finally looks up, focusing on Sam. "Luke said they won't pursue charges."

Her body goes limp as she lets out a strangled gasp.

Billy finds my hand and squeezes it, the only movement he's made since the phone rang.

With his eyes locked on Sam's, Jameson holds out his hand for her to grab. She takes it and whispers, "They're not coming?"

He shakes his head.

"They're not coming," she repeats, like she's trying to get herself to believe it. "They're not gonna take you away from me." She tightens her grip on his hand. "Are you sure?"

"Yeah, I'm sure," he tells her.

He pushes back his chair, keeping her hand in his. She stands and closes the space between them, settling in his lap, her back against his chest. Jameson closes his arm around her waist, pulling her against him. Then his attention shifts to Billy, who's sitting completely still by my side. A look passes between them, and understanding flashes across Jameson's face.

"I'm not going anywhere."

"I know," Billy answers, but his voice sounds small, broken. Like a little boy who grew up to not believe those words.

I run my thumb back and forth along his hand.

It's quiet for a minute before Sam blurts out, "I don't want to go home."

We haven't talked about what we would do if this were the outcome. If we weren't on the run. If there was nothing keeping us here but our own decision.

"We don't have to go anywhere," Jameson says. He looks between me and Billy. "Right?"

Billy turns to me, the scared look he had earlier returning to his face.

"Right," I say, surprised at how easily the word slipped out. Billy nods.

"It's always gonna be the three of us," Jameson says, looking between Sam and Billy, but then his eyes land on me, on my thumb sliding back and forth over Billy's hand. His expression softens, and he dips his head slightly, as if thanking me. "The four of us," he corrects.

Chapter 43

SAM AND JAMESON HEAD off to bed, which leaves Billy and I alone at the table.

We sit together, our breathing the only sound in the room, as Billy keeps his attention fixed on his hand in mine. I know he needs time to process everything that's happened, to work through the fear he's been holding on to. So, I give it to him.

Finally, he shifts toward me, and his eyes begin to trail up my body. He moves so slowly, as if he's trying to memorize every inch of me until, finally, his gaze locks with mine. The vulnerability, the fear on his face nearly cleaves my heart in two.

"I'm here," I whisper, and I know he realizes I mean more than just that I'm here beside him.

He closes his eyes at my words, like they're too much for him. "You can't say things like that to me if you're not ..." He swallows, his eyes finding mine again. "I don't know what to do with this feeling. With what you're doing to me."

I'm quiet, waiting for him to continue.

"I've never felt … this." He shakes his head. "And I don't know if I want to."

"You don't know if you want to what?" I ask, my voice cracking.

He looks away from me as he says, "Love you. I don't know if I want to love you."

I blink back the tears that are welling up. "Why?" is all I can think to say.

He loves me. He just told me that he loves me.

He quickly glances at our hands again, waiting for me to pull away. When I only tighten my grip, he lifts his eyes. "Because I'm scared," he says softly. "I'm so fucking scared that you'll leave me, and I can't put that on you." He runs a hand through his hair. "I know I can't put all my baggage on you like that. It's not fair."

"I know who you are, Billy, and nothing about you makes me not want to love you."

"You …"

I nod. "I love you."

A single tear falls down his face, but he doesn't wipe it away, like those three words I just said are all he can think about.

"I don't know what's going to happen in the future, and I'm scared, too," I tell him. "I've never felt this way, either, and it all feels so fast, but I'd rather try than never know." I press my body closer to his. "I *want* to love you, even if it hurts in the end, because even then, it will have been worth it for what I feel right now."

"I want to love you, too," he answers, his voice strained. He pulls me into his lap and brings his lips to mine, saying the words again between kisses. "I want to love you, too."

I feel tears on my face, and I'm not sure if they're mine or his.

Our lips begin to move faster as he folds his arms around me.

"I need you," he moans into my mouth.

The breathy whimper I give in response has him standing with me in his arms, my legs wrapped around his waist. In a few quick steps, we're at the bed, and he lays me down gently, positioning his body over mine.

He begins to trail his lips down my body, stopping just above my jeans. He looks up at me in question, and I shift my hips up in response. He undoes the button and slowly slides them down my legs then traces the tips of his fingers back up my body until they slow at my waist. He hooks his thumbs under the band of my underwear and pulls them down, too.

I blush as he rakes his eyes over me, never having been this exposed before.

I feel his hands move under my shirt, and a strong arm comes around my back, pulling me up until I'm sitting. He drags my shirt over my head. Then, with a quick flick of his fingers, my bra is falling off me, too.

He releases his hold on me and leans back. I hear a sharp inhale of breath as he looks down at me.

"So beautiful."

Grabbing the back collar of his T-shirt, he pulls it over his head. Before I can reach for him, he's already pressed against me again, his skin flush with mine.

"I can't get close enough to you," he groans.

I wrap myself around him, feeling the same way. It's like my body is begging for more.

"I want all of you," I tell him, barely able to get the words out. "I *need* all of you."

He goes still. "Are you sure? We can wait."

"I'm sure," I answer without a second thought.

He gazes down at me like he can't believe I'm real, like he can't believe that any of this is real.

I reach out, lightly sweeping my hand from his cheek down to his chest. His throat bobs as he swallows, and I lean forward to press kisses up the length of it until I've reached his lips.

"I want you to love me," I breathe.

He sags against me before pulling back and searching my eyes once more, as if maybe I didn't really mean it, like the words might have all just been in his head. Whatever he sees in my face must be enough because, all at once, the apprehension is gone, and I'm being pushed back against the bed.

The next minute, he's gone, and I hear plastic bags being sorted through. He's back as quickly as he left, stepping out of his jeans.

I bite my lip as I take him in, standing in front of me without an ounce of shame.

The bed dips under the weight of his body, the old springs creaking as he moves over me.

"I've never ..." I start, barely hearing my words over the pounding of my heart.

Leaning in close, he traces the curve of my jaw with his tongue. "I'll go real slow," he says into my neck, and I moan as his mouth comes back down against my skin. He pulls away from me for just long enough to put on a condom, and then his mouth is back at my ear.

I feel him start to fill me, and my body tenses at the pressure. "You okay?" he asks.

I nod against his chest.

He pushes in further then stills, letting me adjust. Then, sucking in a breath, he begins to move.

I meet him in the rhythm he's created, dragging my nails down his back. His hands are moving over me like he wishes he could touch me everywhere all at once. I thread my fingers through his hair as I pull his face down to meet mine.

The sting has faded into a warm pulse, and I begin to roll my hips against him. "More," I plead.

With that one word, he lets go, and my eyes roll back as he unleashes himself. A heat starts to build within me, and I begin to shake just as he does, my name falling from his lips as he drops down against me.

"That was ..." He pauses, gently sweeping a strand of hair from my face. "I didn't know it could be like that."

I blink up at him, absorbing his words.

"Thank you," he says, lowering his forehead to mine.

"For what?" I whisper.

He presses his lips lightly to my neck. "For wanting me to love you."

Chapter 44

I wake up to the smell of bacon and a heavy arm draped over me. Turning to my left, I'm face-to-face with Billy.

He stirs, feeling me shift, and a slow smile spreads across his face. "Morning, gorgeous," he says, his voice raspy.

I start to tell him, "Good morning," but my words become muffled as his lips sweep over mine.

He pulls away, lifting his arms overhead in an exaggerated stretch. Then, leaning over me, he quickly kisses my forehead before slipping out of bed.

"Jesus, Billy, put some fucking clothes on," Sam groans from the kitchen.

Looking over, I realize he's still completely naked from last night.

He shrugs. "It's not my fault my bedroom is the living room."

Well, I guess there's no hiding what we did last night.

He pulls on a pair of jeans and leaves one of his T-shirts on the bed for me before striding into the kitchen.

I pull the covers up over my head, giving myself some sense of privacy, before wiggling into Billy's shirt. Then I reluctantly drag myself out of bed and pad into the kitchen, motivated by the smell of coffee brewing.

Right as I turn the corner, I have to step back as Billy dodges a spatula that Sam's swatting at him. He holds up his hands, a piece of bacon in one of them, and waits for her to turn back to the stove. Then he ducks around her and steals another piece.

"Get out!" she yells, pointing the spatula at him.

I hold back a laugh as he slinks away, joining Jameson at the table.

"What can I do to help?" I ask.

"I'm almost done," she says as she pulls a tray of biscuits out of the oven.

My eyebrows rise as I take in all the food she's made.

"I thought I'd do a big breakfast since it's the weekend," she explains.

I look over and find her eyes drifting around the apartment, settling on Jameson and Billy, sitting together at the table.

I remember her reaction when we first walked into the apartment, what Billy said about how much being here meant to her. How much it meant to her that we were all here together.

"We should try to do this every Saturday. Maybe you can teach me." Motioning to the stove, I say, "I can't even make eggs."

She snorts. "That's just embarrassing." Then she turns to open the fridge, pulling things out and handing them to me before she finally says with a hint of a smile, "I like that idea—the Saturday breakfasts."

Once again, all of us are sitting around the table, devouring Sam's delicious cooking. We're quiet as we eat, Sam seeming satisfied with the silence.

Eventually, Billy shoves back his empty plate and grabs the cup of coffee in front of him. "I want to go to the garage and start working on the bike today. You guys wanna come?" He looks at Jameson. "I could use a hand."

"Yeah, sure," he answers.

Billy looks between Sam and me.

"I'll hang out," she says. At the same time, I nod.

"Sweet!" he replies, reaching for the coffee pot and refilling his cup. "Lou gave me a key, so we can go whenever."

Sam pushes back her chair, beginning to clear the dishes, but Jameson stands, reaching out a hand to stop her. "Go get ready. I'll clean up."

She eyes the table filled with dirty dishes. "I can do it."

He shakes his head. "That's not how this is gonna be. You cooked, so you don't clean." He raises an eyebrow. "Yeah?"

Her face brightens as he holds out his hand for the plate she's carrying. "Yeah."

She heads for the bedroom, and I stand, grabbing my plate.

"Leave it," Billy says. "We've got it."

Jameson passes behind us, his hands full.

"Are you sure?" I ask. "I don't mind helping."

He smirks. "Yeah, I'm sure." Looking down at me, he adds, "You should go get dressed. If I have to keep watching you walk around in my shirt, we'll never leave." I melt against him as he leans in closer and says, "After last night, all I can think about is getting you underneath me again." He tilts my chin back so my gaze can meet his.

I sweep my tongue over my bottom lip, and his eyes follow the movement.

Jameson comes back in, and Billy releases his hold on me, turning toward the table and grabbing the empty tray of biscuits. I stay stuck in the spot he left me, any rational thought suddenly gone.

He looks over his shoulder at me, his face smug. "You okay?"

"Mmhmm," I answer, trying to shake myself out of the stupor he left me in.

"Well, get going then."

An hour later, we're walking into Lou's garage.

Billy unlocks the front door, flicks on the lights, and leads us all over to the back corner. He can barely contain his excitement as he gestures to a beat-up-looking motorcycle. "Here she is," he says, focusing most of his attention on me.

I don't know anything about motorcycles, but it looks like it will take a miracle to get this one running. I guess it's written all over my face because he adds, "Like I said, it needs a lot of work."

Sam snorts. "That's an understatement."

He glares at her. "It's not even gonna look like the same bike when I'm done with it."

I give him an encouraging smile as Sam tips over a milk crate and drops down to take a seat.

Billy begins walking around, collecting tools and turning on a couple of fans. Thank God for that, because I'm already sweating. I don't know if I'll ever get used to the Florida heat.

I'm looking around for another milk crate when he comes up behind me. "I got something for you."

I turn to face him. "Really?"

He runs his hands up my back. "Surprised you haven't spotted it yet."

I search the room until I see it, and my eyes go wide.

An easel set up with a canvas and a box filled with paints.

"Billy," I whisper.

"You told me how much you love to paint. How much it means to you."

"How? When did you get all of this?"

"I went on my lunch break yesterday."

"Thank you," I breathe. "This is the best surprise I've ever gotten."

He slows his hands as I look up at him, my eyes glassy.

"It's just paint," he says.

"It's not. You know it's not."

"I want you to be happy here," he says quietly. "And I really want to see your art."

"You do?" Nobody has ever cared about my paintings.

"Of course I do. I want to see everything you make."

"Me, too."

He smiles.

"I mean, with your bike and all that. It's really cool," I say, fumbling my words.

His smile grows. "I'll set you up by me." He leans in and presses his lips against my hair then helps me get settled right next to where he's working.

CHAPTER 45

M‌Y BRUSH HITS THE canvas, and my mind clears.

When I paint, the process takes over. I never know what I've made until I step away and look at it. I've always gravitated toward abstract art. Even when I'm painting portraits or landscapes, I tend to veer out of the lines. It's the one thing I have in life that allows me to let go, to just be, to create. I didn't realize how much I missed it until Billy gave it back to me.

I relax into the process, listening to the clank of tools and occasional curses that come from Billy and Jameson when something doesn't work.

Every so often, I feel Billy's eyes on me, looking over like he wants to remind himself that I'm still here. Each time our eyes meet, his face brightens. Sam has been reading since we got here, barely glancing up from her book. We're all just existing together. I don't know if I've ever felt this at peace.

Before long, sweat is dripping down my back and I'm in desperate need of a drink. I set my brush and palette down, asking Billy, "Are there waters inside?"

"Yeah, and some sodas, too."

"Can you get me a Coke?" Sam mutters.

"Sure," I answer, turning back to Billy and Jameson. "You guys want something?"

"Water," they say at the same time.

"Do you remember how to get to the break room?" Billy asks.

I nod, thinking back to the first night we came here. I can't believe it's only been a few weeks. It feels like a lifetime ago.

Billy calls out, "Want me to come help you carry every-thing?"

"I should be fine," I tell him, already starting toward the door. "Thank you, though."

He rolls his neck, stretching his arms overhead. "Just yell if you change your mind."

I find my way to the break room and grab the drinks, pressing the cool can of soda against my forehead. I tuck the waters under my arms, grab another can of Coke for Sam, then head back to the shop.

The door swings shut behind me, and my steps falter when I see Jameson and Billy both standing with their shirts off, using them to wipe the sweat off their bodies. I hand them the waters and try to keep myself from staring.

Normally, Billy would have all of my attention, but it's Jameson who I find it hard to look away from. I knew he had a lot of tattoos, having seen the ones on his arms and hands, but I didn't realize just how many he has. I take them all in, but it's the big tattoo that spans his chest that I can't stop looking at.

Angel wings wrapped around the word "*Loyalty*." The same one Billy has.

I look at the tattoo over Billy's heart, and tracking my gaze, he tells me, "We all have one." I turn from him to Sam, as he says, "Show her yours."

I've seen a couple tattoos on her but never this one.

She stands and lifts her shirt, angling her body so I can see the small tattoo on her ribcage.

"When did you get them?" I ask no one in particular.

It's Sam who answers. "A couple years ago ..." She pauses, glancing between Billy and Jameson. "A couple years ago, we all went through some stuff that left us in a hard place, and the only thing that got us through it was each other."

When she doesn't explain, I turn to Billy. His eyes are fixed on nothing, like he's caught up in a memory.

"What happened?" I ask.

Nobody responds right away, and I shift on my feet, anxious that I might have overstepped. I quickly backpedal.

"You don't have to tell me if you don't want to. Sorry, I shouldn't have asked. I know it must be personal." My words come out one after another, bleeding into a jumbled mess.

Billy leans closer to me. "You're allowed to ask questions. Sometimes they're just hard to answer."

Something passes between the three of them before Sam pushes out a breath. "My brother, Johnny, used to work for Jameson's dad. He was ..." She looks to Jameson, like she doesn't know how to explain it.

"My dad ran a crew of guys who did a lot of different things to make money. Officially, they were mechanics," Jameson finishes for her.

Billy tenses beside me.

"But, unofficially ... they stole cars, chopped them up, and sold the parts. He had us doing some other stuff, too, but most of the money was in the cars."

Us? Did Jameson work for his dad?

Did Billy?

"He used Baxston & Sons as a cover for everything."

Billy's dad's garage. But I guess since Jameson's and Billy's dads are brothers, that makes it Jameson's dad's garage, too.

I peer over at Billy and find his face clouded in anger.

"Luke didn't like it. He wanted the business to be legitimate."

"Then why did he let your dad use it like that?"

He laughs, but there's no humor in it. "Why else? Money." His shoulders fall back as he adds dryly, "And my old man could be very persuasive. He wasn't really someone you said no to."

He wraps his arm around himself, resting his hand on his left rib cage. Sam follows the movement before she drops her eyes to the ground.

"Johnny started working for him, and he was good, real good. I've never seen anyone who could boost a car as fast as he could."

The sound of a lighter sparking cuts through the room as Sam brings a cigarette to her lips.

Jameson gives her a look that seems to ask if she wants him to stop, but she jerks her chin up, prompting him to keep going.

"One night, they went out. It was just my old man and Johnny. That's how it would usually go. Like I said, Johnny was the best he had."

My stomach drops, anticipating what he's going to say next.

"That night, neither of them came back."

Chapter 46

Not wanting to see the pain that I know must be on Sam's face, I keep my focus on Jameson as he explains, "The cops chased them until they were surrounded." His voice is flat, the slight tick of his jaw the only sign of emotion. "There was no getting out of it, no way to run, but the old man tried, anyway. Pulled out his gun and shot at a cop." He runs his fingers through his hair. "They shot back."

I tense, waiting.

"They killed him."

I blink, absorbing his words before finally letting my eyes drift over to Sam. She's staring forward, her expression blank.

I turn back to Jameson, asking the question I'm scared I already know the answer to, "What about Johnny?"

"After my old man went down, Johnny tried to run. He managed to get back in the car. He even got a few blocks away, but he lost control of the car and hit a tree." Jameson's voice drops, quieting. "He died on impact."

I swallow hard, barely pushing the words out, "I'm so sorry." I look between the two of them. "For both of you."

Jameson dips his chin, but his attention is on Sam.

I turn to her. "Were you …?" I clear my throat. "Were you and your brother close?"

"Very," she says, exhaling a cloud of smoke. Her voice is even, too even. It's like she's completely locked this part of herself away.

"He was older than you?" I assume.

Sam nods. "By five years." She drops her cigarette, crushing it under her shoe. "Growing up, he was like a father to me. Always made sure I was looked after." She twists the ring on her finger, her eyes welling up. "He was the best there was."

I feel a tear fall down my cheek and quickly wipe it away. "I'm sorry I didn't get to meet him. I wish I had."

"You would have liked him," she says, her face softening. "He didn't always make the best choices, but he always had a good reason for making the bad ones." She smiles, and it's the saddest thing I've ever seen. "He gave up his life trying to give me a better one. I'll never forget it." She shakes her head. "And I'll never waste it."

She looks up, her eyes meeting Jameson's. History passes between them, and she repeats her words, this time a whispered promise, "I'll never waste it."

Jameson shifts closer to her.

"What about you?" I ask him. "Were you and your dad close?"

He pulls a pack of cigarettes from his back pocket and lights one. Each movement is slow and controlled, like he's giving himself time to come up with an answer. "We had a complicated relationship," he says on an exhale. "I was ..." He pauses, running a hand through his hair. "He saw me as what I could be, what he could make me into, instead of who I was." He hesitates. "I think, in his own way, he was trying to prepare me, but I didn't want all he was preparing me for. Then he left, and I had no other choice but to be ready."

"After ..." Billy starts, as if not wanting to say the words. "After what happened that night, everything went to shit."

"Like it wasn't already shitty enough," Jameson mutters.

"Without Jameson's dad, there wasn't any money coming in. It affected all of us. My dad was left with a shop that was in debt, and even though he always wanted the business to be legit, it was hard to make it without that money. It took a long time to turn it around. I started helping out even more after school, but even with that, money was still really tight." He looks over at Sam and Jameson. "For all of us."

A lighter sparks again, and I turn in the direction of the noise.

"Johnny brought in almost all of the money then," Sam starts. "My dad couldn't ever keep a job for long, so sometimes he'd have money, but a lot of times, he didn't. And even when he did, we usually didn't see most of it. Cathleen wasn't living at home then, so Johnny was the only consistent thing we had." She exhales. "He was all we had. So, after he ... after he was gone, the money was gone, too."

"What did you do?"

"My dad fell during a construction job a few weeks after everything with Johnny happened. He started getting disability, so that was a steady check. I got my job at the diner and started taking all the shifts I could. It wasn't much, and sometimes, it wasn't enough, but we made it through."

Wait.

"What about Carson?"

"Back then, he didn't work," she says. "Both him and my dad decided that he should put all of his focus on football. That was before he blew out his knee. They thought he'd get recruited, and that would be our ticket out."

"So, only you worked?"

She nods.

"How old were you when ...?"

"Sixteen," she answers. "At least I still had Cathleen." She slides her eyes toward Jameson. "She didn't move back home for another year, but she helped as much as she could."

I turn to Jameson. "Do you have any siblings?" It's so weird how much I still don't know about them.

He shakes his head.

"So, it was just you and your mom?"

"Yup," he says, and that one word somehow holds a lifetime of resentment.

"That must have been hard."

He scoffs. "You could say that. After my old man was killed, she lost it." He flicks the ash off his cigarette. "She wasn't much of a mother before that, but after, it was like she just gave up. It took a long time for her to come out of it. Even now, she's … well, you heard what she's like."

All I can think to do is nod.

"I tried to stay in school, but I realized pretty quick that wasn't gonna work. I made it a couple months before I dropped out. I couldn't even get my mother to leave her room, so her getting a job wasn't gonna happen. My old man had some cash stashed, so we had that for a bit, but it wasn't enough to last us. I tried to get a regular job, a legal one, and I ended up working on a construction crew, but they didn't always need me, and the money sucked. I thought about getting a second job once I quit school, but I was just so fucking tired. It was so easy to slip back into the things my dad taught me and the people I knew.

"After what happened, I didn't want to mess with cars, so I started dealing. I told myself that I would just do it for long enough to get us through, until I could find something better, until my mother got it together. But"—he straightens—"I should have known better."

"You did what you had to do," Sam cuts in. "Just like you always do."

I stare at the tattoo inked across his chest, now beginning to understand just how much the word means to them. Then I turn my gaze, settling it on Billy's tattoo, knowing there's more to his story. Knowing that losing the money wasn't what broke him.

The question is sitting there, waiting for me to ask it. I almost bury the words, but then I remember what he said earlier. *You're allowed to ask questions. Sometimes, they're just hard to answer.*

So, I ask it.

"Is that when your mom left?"

CHAPTER 47

A MINUTE PASSES BEFORE he says, "Yes," the word sounding
like it had been lodged in his throat.

I give him the space to answer, letting him decide how much
he wants to tell me.

He takes a breath and starts talking. "My parents started
dating in high school, and my mom got pregnant with me her
senior year. They got married, and she obviously had the baby,
but I know it wasn't what she wanted."

"How do you know?"

He doesn't look at me when he whispers, "Because she told
me."

My shoulders sag forward as I search for something to say,
some way to make it better, but he keeps going like he needs to
get it all out.

"It always felt like she had one foot out the door, but my dad
loved her. Honestly, I don't know why, but for some reason, he
really did. He tried to do whatever he could to make her happy,

to keep her from leaving." He runs his fingers through his hair, rolling his shoulders back, his movements mirroring the ones Jameson made earlier. "Even before everything happened, she was spending money we didn't have. But once everything shut down, we really didn't have anything extra to spend, so my dad had to cut her off. They started fighting all the time, and she started spending more time out of the house, giving excuses that were clearly lies."

"Did he confront her about it?"

Billy shakes his head. "I don't think so. He wasn't home much, either. He had to let two of the other mechanics go, so he used to work crazy hours back then. That's when I started helping out a lot after school, but he would never let me stay as late as him.

"It became pretty obvious what she was doing when she wasn't home. My dad never said anything, but I think he knew. Even before she left that note, I think he knew she was seeing someone else.

"One day, I came home after working at the garage," he starts, his voice hard. "She worked as a hairdresser, and the salon closed at five. It was just before eight when I pulled into the driveway, so she should have been home by then. I remember being annoyed. More than annoyed actually. I was pissed. I couldn't believe she was doing this to my dad after everything he'd done for her, and I was pissed at my dad for doing nothing about it, for burying his head in the sand and pretending it wasn't happening. At first, I didn't even realize she'd left." He tries to laugh, but it comes out as little more than a push of air. "I was in the house for hours before I figured it out. It got to be past ten, and she still wasn't home. I started to get worried that something happened to her, so I called her cell."

He looks at the ground like he's trying to keep down the emotions that are coming to the surface. Seconds pass before he looks up again, his gaze landing on Jameson. Billy tips up his chin, and Jameson answers by handing him his pack of cigarettes and the lighter.

It's still so strange to watch them do that—communicate without having to say anything.

It takes Billy a few tries to spark the lighter before he finally lights the cigarette. He inhales, closing his eyes before he speaks again. "When I called her, I got a message that the number was no longer in use. I didn't get it at first. I thought maybe we didn't pay the phone bill, and they shut off the line or something. But then I realized that we were all on the same plan, so if my phone was working, hers should be, too.

"I remember sitting on the couch, barely able to move when I realized she had changed her number." He grinds his teeth. "That she changed it without telling me, and that the only reason she would do something like that was if she didn't want to be found.

"I couldn't make myself get up. I just sat there until my dad got home. It only took one look at me, and he knew. He didn't even say anything before he was running to their room. I sat there as he yelled, hearing things being thrown, shit crashing into the wall." His hand shakes as he brings the cigarette back up to his lips. "I sat there as I heard him begin to sob. I'd never heard my dad cry before, but even if I had, I'm sure it wouldn't have sounded like that. It was …" He runs his fingers through his hair. Again. And again. And again. Pulling at the strands. "I just wanted it to stop. I just wanted all of it to stop."

He exhales. "Finally, I got up and went to their room. He was asleep on the floor, everything around him destroyed. His hand was at his side, clenched in a fist, holding a note she had written him. I cleared away the stuff around where he was lying, put a blanket over him, and went to my room. Right when I stepped in, I saw it. There was a note on my bed, waiting for me, too.

"I told myself I wouldn't read it, that it didn't matter what she said. I tried to go to sleep for the night, but all I could think about was what she might have written in that letter. I thought maybe …" His voice cracks. "I thought maybe it would say that she was coming back, or at least where she went."

"What did it say?"

"It was just a bunch of bullshit."

"Tell me," I press gently.

He sighs. "That she wasn't happy. That she hadn't been for a long time. She said she met someone, and she was going to live with him."

"She didn't say where?"

"No," he responds, his tone cold. "She didn't say a lot of things, which is fine. I didn't need to know where she was going or if she was coming back. I didn't need her to say goodbye or that she loved me." He stomps his cigarette out under his boot. "I didn't want her to love me, anyway."

With those words, my heart breaks for him.

CHAPTER 48

OUR CONVERSATION IN THE garage seemed to be the last piece that was missing to finally bring me into their group. I know I'll never have their history together, but I also know how important it is that they trusted me enough to share their stories with me. Ever since, there's been an openness like we didn't have before, and not just between me and Billy. It changed the dynamic between all of us.

Even though I didn't go through those things with them, the fact that I know about them now has made us all closer.

A little over a week has passed since that afternoon we spent in the garage, and things have been great. More than great, actually. We've spent our days working, which I really enjoy. Carol is amazing, and it's nice to get to work with Sam. Whenever we have breaks, we fill the time reading or talking about books.

Billy and Jameson pick us up after work every night, and then Sam cooks dinner, which I can tell is the highlight of her day. She tried to teach me, but after I nearly burned the apartment down searing chicken, we gave up on that.

We play gin and talk around the kitchen table most nights, which is my favorite part of the day, when we're all together, just hanging out and laughing. Well, either that or when Sam and Jameson go to sleep, and Billy carries me to bed. After that first time we slept together, we haven't been able to stop.

I've never been happier than I am right now. It scares me because I've never had anything or anyone I was this afraid to lose. It's all happened so quickly, so unexpectedly. It makes me worried it will all come crashing down just as fast.

That's where my thoughts have drifted off to as I'm lying in bed, unable to sleep.

I feel Billy's arms come around me, sliding along my bare skin. The sun is just rising as he says, "What's bothering you, baby?"

"Nothing."

He loosens his hold. "Look at me," he breathes.

I turn around so I'm facing his chest then tilt my head so I can meet his gaze.

He searches my eyes and asks, "What is it?"

"I just ..."

He gently cups my face before he begins to trace his thumb along my jaw. I close my eyes and lean into his touch, trying to find the words to explain how I'm feeling.

"I've never been this happy," I tell him, repeating my thoughts from before.

His thumb stills on my face. "Me, neither."

"I'm afraid that it won't last, that something will happen to make it all go away."

He nods. "I know. I feel the same way."

We're quiet for a long time before he says, "I think happiness is a choice." His eyes are full of promise as he looks down at me. "Whatever happens, whatever comes our way, I'll always choose you." He presses his lips lightly over mine. "Because you're my happiness." He kisses me again, his words playing in my head like the greatest love song.

Because you're my happiness.

Because you're my happiness.

Because you're my happiness.

He brings me back against his chest, curling his body around mine, then begins running his fingers lightly through my hair. My eyes grow heavy from the warmth of his skin, the soft sound of his breathing, and the caress of his fingers. I'm surrounded by him, and I've never felt more safe, more cared for, more loved.

The fear of the unknown and the what-ifs begin to slip away. A sense of calm washes over me as he whispers, "It's all going to be okay."

I smile and let the truth of his words sink in.

It's all going to be okay.

CHAPTER 49

BILLY IS IN THE bathroom, showering, when the phone rings. By the ringtone, I know it's not one of the two iPhones Jameson came home with one day, but the burner phone.

Billy gave his dad our new number, and Jameson also gave it to his mom, so that only leaves two options for who could be calling.

Sam hasn't heard from anyone in her family, including her sister. I know it bothers her that Cathleen hasn't called, even though she pretends it doesn't. But whenever the burner phone rings, it's always Sam who makes a point to see who it is.

Me, I never answer.

This time is no different. The phone rings, Sam picks it up, and then her eyes slide to meet mine.

I shake my head, just like I do every other time my parents have called.

She pulls it away from her, covering the phone with her hand. "You're gonna have to answer at some point."

I sigh. "No, I don't."

"Don't you want to know why they're calling? Why they won't stop?" she asks. "It's not like you can't just hang up on them again."

I stare at the phone in her outstretched hand, and my stomach tightens. My fingers curl into a fist, and I drag my nails over my palm, my mind racing. I've thought through every possible way this conversation could go. The hopeful part of me holds on to the idea that they might be calling to check in on me, to see how I'm doing. However, the logical side of me knows they're most likely calling to convince me to come back.

But I'm not the same girl I was before.

These last few weeks have given me a perspective I've never had. I'm finally doing what I want to do rather than being the girl they want me to be. It's given me a sense of power, and I don't want to give it back.

I glance at the phone that's still in Sam's outstretched hand and realize she's right—they're not going to stop calling. At some point, I have to tell them that I'm not coming back, even if speaking that truth scares me. It's my final step. The last piece holding me back from living a life that's finally on my terms.

So, I take the phone from her and hold it up to my ear. "Hello."

"Susan," my mother says, my name coming out like an accusation.

I already want to hang up. But I won't. I can't.

Sam looks at me and tilts up her chin, asking if I want her to stay with me.

I wave her off and mouth, "*I'm fine.*"

She goes back to doing dishes as my mother mutters, "Well, are you going to say anything?"

Realizing I haven't responded, I quickly answer, "Sorry, I'm here." I instantly regret starting the conversation by apologizing.

She puts on her concerned mother voice. "How could you just disappear and then never answer any of our calls?"

You mean, like you did to me my whole childhood? I want to say.

"I wasn't ready to have this conversation," I tell her instead.

"And what's that supposed to mean?"

I take a breath as that concerned tone she put on already begins to slip back into the harsh condescension I grew up with. "It means that I wasn't ready to have a repeat of the last time we talked."

"Oh, you mean the time you hung up on me?" she huffs. "Really, Susan, how childish can you be?"

"Why don't you just tell me why you keep calling?" I reply, my words sounding harsher than I expected.

She tsks. "How can you ask a question like that? Did you think we would just let you run away and leave behind everything we've worked so hard for?"

"No, that's why I didn't want to have this conversation. I knew you wouldn't listen to anything I have to say."

"I told your father we spoiled you. I should have known something like this would happen. You were always so ungrateful."

I brush off her words, refusing to let them have the impact she intended. If I'm going to get through this, I need to be strong. I can't let her get to me.

"I appreciate everything both of you have provided for me, but you never gave me a say in anything."

"You're a child. You don't know what's right for you or what you need." She lets out a patronizing laugh. "You more than proved that with this little detour."

I dig my nails into my palms so hard I wince. "It's my life," I tell her. "I should be able to decide how I live it."

"You can start to make your own choices when you can provide for yourself."

"I do provide for myself. I haven't used any of your money since leaving."

"Yes, well, I'm sure that won't last. I can't imagine you're enjoying living with nothing. Do I even want to know how you've been paying for things since you left?"

"I work as a waitress."

She's quiet for so long that I almost repeat myself.

"*A waitress*?" She says the word like it's dirty. "You're supposed to be going to Brown this fall, Susan. That is what you are giving up. You do realize that, don't you?"

"How could I forget when it's all you and Dad talk about?" Then I add sarcastically, "And it's what we've worked so hard for."

"Don't take that tone with me!" she snaps.

I know I need to tell her the truth, but it feels so foreign to stand up to her, like I'm hardwired to do the opposite. So, I push out the words before I can take them back.

"I'm not going to Brown."

"What do you mean?" she counters. "Yes, you are."

I hold firm. "No, I'm really not."

I can hear her begin to pace. "What's it going to take to get you to come back, huh?"

"I don't know how many different ways I can say it. I don't want to come back. I'm happy here, in case you're wondering." It hasn't slipped my attention that she never asked.

"Where is here? Where are you?"

"Florida," I answer.

"*Florida*!" she practically shrieks. "What in God's name are you doing all the way down in Florida?"

"Billy's dad has a friend who gave Billy and Jameson jobs here."

"The murderer?" she asks, disdain blanketing the question. "Or did you think I forgot that little detail?"

I try to keep my voice steady. "He's not a murderer. Cason, the guy he shot, is going to make a full recovery."

"Do you even hear yourself?" she asks. "This is the life you've chosen? One where you have to clarify that the person you're living with didn't kill someone they shot?"

"He was protecting himself. He was protecting all of us, actually, and he's been nothing but nice to me. All of them have. So—"

"None of these little details matter since you're coming home," she says, cutting me off. "Your father and I will forgive you. We'll forget all of this happened if you just come back and get your life on track."

"These *little details* are my life. I can't just forget they happened." I exhale. "I don't want to go back to how my life was before."

"Oh, because your life was so hard," she mocks me.

"The fact that you won't even ask me or talk to me about why I wasn't happy proves the point. You don't care how I feel. You never have, as long as I'm following the path you laid out for me."

"I didn't realize you were so unhappy here. You never told me."

"When would I have told you? You were never home."

"I won't apologize for working hard to provide—"

"I tried," I interrupt her.

"Excuse me?"

"I tried to tell you how unhappy I was, and even if I hadn't, all you had to do was look at me."

"What are you implying?"

"Just that ..." I let out a breath. "I'm telling you now. You can listen to me now." I hate how desperate I sound.

"I have listened to everything you've said," she replies. "And do you know what I hear?"

I keep quiet, knowing she's not really looking for an answer.

"I hear a naïve girl who has no idea what she's getting into or what she's giving up. It may seem all new and shiny now, but how are you going to feel in a few years when you're still working as some waitress? How are you going to feel when you have no education, no career, and nothing to fall back on?" I let her words sink in as she adds, "You know you're making a mistake, and frankly, I won't watch you do it."

My stomach sinks as she gives me the ultimatum I feared was coming.

"You either come home and get your life back on track, or I'm sorry, but we're done." Her voice is distant, completely unattached.

I swallow. "What do you mean *we're done?*"

"I mean you either come home, or you're no longer a part of our lives."

Is this actually happening?

"Well?" she prompts.

"I'm not saying I don't want you and Dad in my life. I'm saying I want my own life." I pause, willing the panic out of my voice. "You can still be a part of that life, Mom."

"I'm afraid that's not an option."

My words come out pleading. "Why not?"

"Because it's just not," she says. "Now, answer my question, Susan."

Suddenly, it becomes hard to breathe. That feeling I'm so familiar with comes crashing over me. I don't want to have to make this choice. It doesn't seem fair to have to choose.

My parents and I obviously don't have the best relationship, but they're still my parents. Am I really going to walk away from them?

"What about Dad?"

"What about him?"

"If I don't come home, is he going to stop talking to me, too?"

"Your father and I are in agreement about this."

"Where is he?"

"What?" she asks.

"Why isn't he with you right now? Why isn't he talking to me about this, too?"

"He's in his office, on a call. I don't want to interrupt him for a conversation that I'm sure he'd be disappointed to be a part of."

My disbelief morphs into anger. "Oh, so you'll just let him know after he finishes up with work whether his relationship with his only child is over?"

"What I end up telling him is up to you. If you don't want me to have to tell him that you're staying there, then come home. It's as simple as that."

How is she putting this on me? I'm not the one who laid out these ridiculous conditions.

It hits me how unfair the position she's putting me in is. How she's willing to give up a relationship with me if I don't do what she wants. How could a mother do something like that?

I think about Billy, Sam, and Jameson. About the tattoo they all carry. How, no matter what happens, they're always there for each other. They would never make me choose like this.

But it goes beyond them. In the end, this isn't even about them. It's not about my parents, either. It's about me.

I don't like the girl I was before leaving, and there's nothing my mother can hold over me that will make me change my decision. If anything, this phone call has only been a reminder of why I left. A reminder of how quickly I would slip back into the version of myself I'm trying to escape.

"Susan ..." my mother presses.

My heart is racing when I answer, "I haven't changed my mind. I'm not coming home."

"This is your last chance; do you understand me? Your father and I will not be this generous again. If you stay there, you will lose access to your tuition money, your acceptance to Brown—"

She doesn't finish before I add, "And you."

I wait for her to take it back, to tell me I'm wrong, but the other end of the line remains quiet.

This is really happening.

"I understand," I tell her, grateful my voice doesn't sound as shaky as I feel.

"Well," she says, her tone as composed as ever, "I hope you know what you're doing, because as far as I'm concerned, you have just made a choice that will change the rest of your life."

Yes, I did.

"And with that choice," she adds, "you've made raising you the biggest failure of mine."

I slump forward as her words steal the air from my lungs before hearing the other line go dead.

CHAPTER 50

I DROP THE PHONE onto the bed and focus on my breathing, attempting to regain control of myself. I don't know how to process what just happened.

It doesn't feel real.

The mattress dips when Sam sits down beside me. "What happened?"

I shake my head, not wanting to talk about it.

Instead of leaving, like I expect her to, she stays by my side.

"I know she's wrong," I say quietly, "but the words still hurt."

"I know they do," she whispers back.

I startle, hearing the door to the bathroom open and Billy's footsteps approaching.

"Sorry that took so long," he says as he walks over. "I had to shave. It's all yours."

I make my body loose and bring a smile to my face.

Sam's eyebrows raise as she notices the change.

Before Billy makes it to the bed, I say under my breath, "I don't want to upset him." Looking over at her, I add, "He's already worried that I'll leave."

I see the understanding in her eyes before she dips her chin.

When Billy reaches the bed, he glances between us. "Everything all right?"

"Yup," I answer, forcing my voice to be light. Then I jump up from the bed and kiss his cheek. "I'm gonna go shower now."

As I walk away, I hear him ask Sam, "Where's Jameson?"

I didn't even realize he wasn't here.

I don't wait for her answer before I close the bathroom door and try to keep myself from sliding down it and curling into a ball on the floor.

After turning on the faucet, I quickly step out of my clothes and get into the shower. I barely notice how cold the water is as the wall I built up around myself starts to crack. I let go and begin to sob.

My body shakes as I heave in a breath and attempt to empty my mind out. I try to forget all the things my mother said, but they just won't stop playing one after another.

I told your father we spoiled you.

You were always so ungrateful.

You either come home, or you're no longer a part of our lives.

No longer a part of our lives.

No longer a part of our lives.

No longer a part of our lives.

I'm gasping for air, feeling the space around me growing smaller and smaller. Sinking down to the shower floor, I let the water run over the back of my head and grasp for anything that will calm me.

Breathe. I have to breathe.

In.

One, two, three, four, five.

Out.

One, two, three, four, five

I do it again, and again, and again. Until I feel the space around me open up again. Until I feel the weight lift off my chest. Until, finally, I realize I've stopped crying.

Carefully, I stand back up and stare at the tile wall. I don't know what to do. I don't know how to feel. Something like this isn't supposed to happen. How could my parents just walk away from me like that? Like I'm nothing.

The tears start again, and I wrap my arms around my body just to feel like I'm not alone.

I cry until my tears turn into anger. And I realize that I'm done. I'm done letting them have this hold over me. I'm done with all of it.

I run my hands down my face, wiping the last of my tears away. That's all they'll get from me.

At least for today.

I put the words my mother said into a box and shove them into the back of my mind. I know from experience that they'll live there, come out to haunt me when I'm not strong enough to silence them. But today, I am. Today, I refuse to listen to them. I refuse to believe them.

Instead, I mourn what could have been and let go of the hope that my parents cared for me the way parents are supposed to care for their child.

I close my eyes and let the water run over me. Then, silently, I say goodbye to the two people in my life who were supposed to love me no matter what, but instead showed me just how conditional love can be.

CHAPTER 51

IT'S BEEN A FEW weeks since the call with my mother, and I still haven't told Billy.

I don't think I ever will.

I've thought about it, especially when I've wished I had him to lean on, but I ultimately decided it would do more harm than good. I don't want to put doubts in his mind that have no place being there. After hearing the story of how his mom left and him telling me how scared he was that I'd leave him, I know those demons can wreak havoc on him.

So, I keep it to myself.

Billy carries so much for the people he loves, and I don't want this to add to the weight.

I've felt Sam watching me since the phone call, waiting for me to break, but I never do, at least not until I'm alone.

Every night, I cry in the shower. It's nothing like it was right after the phone call, but it's the only time I'm actually alone and allow myself to break down.

I don't even really know what I'm upset about. I don't want to go home. I don't regret my choice. I don't miss my parents or my life. But it's a lot to take in. A lot of change.

Each day that passes, I cry a little less, and the door to my old life closes a little more. Until tonight, when I get in the shower, and nothing comes.

It's become so routine that I expect the tears to start flowing and my thoughts to plunge me into a spiral. Instead, there's just ... nothing.

It's an odd feeling, one that I'm not sure how to work through. I expected that the sting of the conversation would wane and that I would begin to move on, but I didn't expect it to happen so soon. I didn't expect it to feel like such an emptiness. Like a piece of my heart has been cut out and left hollow. But I guess maybe the space in my heart that belonged to my parents has always been hollow, and I just haven't accepted it until now. Maybe that's why I can move on so quickly. Because you can't feel a loss for something that never existed.

A knock at the door snaps me from my thoughts.

"You almost done, babe?" Billy asks. "We're trying to head out soon."

I blink, looking down at my pruning fingers. *How long have I been in here?*

"Two more minutes," I call out.

I speed through my shower routine, realizing all I've done so far is shampoo my hair. Then I get ready as fast as I can, not wanting to make everyone wait any longer than I already have. I really didn't mean to lose track of time like that.

Sam comes in while I'm brushing my teeth, shuts the door behind her, and begins rummaging through the makeup bag she left on the counter. She's staring down at it when she says, "Are you okay?"

My mouth is full of toothpaste, so I simply nod.

She glances at me for a second then fixes her attention back on the bag.

I don't know if she's trying to give me space or if she just isn't used to having conversations like this. Now that I think about it, she's never mentioned having any friends other than Billy and Jameson.

I peer over at her and notice how uncomfortable she seems. *Has she ever had a girlfriend?*

"Look, I know that's bullshit," she replies bluntly.

Her words catch me off guard, making me go still.

She clears her throat, and this time, her voice is softer. "I don't know what she said to you, but from how you answered and what you looked like when the call ended…" She drops her gaze again, focusing intently on the contents of her makeup bag. "I know what those kinds of talks are like. What they can do to you. And I understand why you haven't told Billy. But if you want to talk about it, you can talk to me." Her words come out unsure, and she begins to fidget as she waits for me to respond.

I lean under the tap and rinse the toothpaste out of my mouth before turning to face her. "It means a lot to me that you would offer. I just—"

"I understand," she cuts in.

I don't think she does.

"It's not that I don't want to talk to *you* about it. I just don't want to talk to *anyone* about it. At least, not right now."

She's studying me like she can see right through me, through the walls I've built up and the brave face I've put on, right down to my core. "No, really, I understand," she tells me slowly then begins to walk away. She stops in the doorway and says, "When you're ready though, I'm here."

"Thank you," I answer before she leaves, shutting the door behind her.

I turn back, my eyes landing on her makeup bag. For all that time she spent looking through it, she left empty-handed.

My lips pull up into a smile as I realize why she really came in here. How she gave me something I didn't know I needed. Something maybe she didn't realize she needed, either.

A friend.

CHAPTER 52

I COME OUT TO find everyone waiting for me in the living room. It's Friday night, so we're going to grab a couple pizzas and head over to the garage.

On the way home from the diner, Billy told us that he's really close to getting his motorcycle running and thinks tonight might finally be the night it starts.

We stop for the pizzas, Jameson running into a corner store to grab a case of beer, and then we pull into our usual spot at the garage. I'm surprised to see the lights still on when we step inside. We're almost always the only ones here when we come after hours.

"That you, kid?" Lou yells from the front room.

"Yeah, it's me," Billy shouts back.

Lou rounds the corner, followed by Candi.

Her face lights up when she sees the four of us. "How've y'all been?"

We all mumble some variation of "good."

She looks between me and Sam. "Did you end up getting that job at the diner?"

I nod. "Yeah, thanks for suggesting it. It's been great!"

She smiles one of those smiles that makes you forget all of your problems and says, "Good, I'm glad."

Billy holds up the boxes of pizza. "Have you guys had dinner? We've got plenty."

"I'm starving," Lou grunts. At the same time, Candi replies, "Oh, we don't want to take your food."

Billy laughs. "After everything you guys have done for us, I think we can share a couple slices."

"Well, aren't y'all sweet?" Candi drawls.

We follow them into the break room and fill in around the table.

My mind flashes back to the first night we all sat here, how we had no idea how we'd get by or what was coming next.

"Thank you again for everything you've both done to help us get settled," I say, glancing between Candi and Lou. "Both of you have been more than generous, and I really don't know what we would have done without your kindness."

Billy brushes his hand over mine as Candi answers, "Of course we're gonna help you. You're just kids. You shouldn't have to do it all on your own."

Jameson lets out a bitter laugh. "I haven't been *just a kid* for a long time."

"Well, that's a shame," Candi responds, her voice somehow even more delicate than before. "And just because you didn't have anyone to help you then doesn't mean it has to be like that now."

Jameson rolls his lips like he's trying to keep from saying something, as Billy shoots him a warning look that has him dropping back in his chair.

Lou clears his throat. "So, you close to getting that thing running?" he asks Billy.

They launch into a long conversation about some part Billy's having a problem with. I tune most of it out, but I'm grateful for the change in topic. I'm not sure what would have come out of Jameson's mouth if Billy hadn't stopped him.

I look at him, and my mind catches on what he did say. That one sentence that holds so much.

I haven't been just a kid for a long time.

Have any of them?

Have I?

Sam leans closer to him until she closes the space between them completely and whispers in his ear. He mutters something back to her then pushes away from the table.

"Going out for a smoke," he says, Sam getting up to follow after him.

Candi's face falls as she watches them go. Turning back to me, she asks, "Is it something I said?"

I shake my head.

"Then, what is it?"

I think for a moment, not sure how to explain it to her. "When you've lived one way for so long, and then everything changes, it can be hard to accept the things you've never had, even if they're good for you."

Candi nods tentatively.

I take a breath. "It isn't easy to suddenly believe you deserve the things that were always kept from you. And even if you finally believe you deserve them, there's always that part of you that's waiting for them to be taken away. He's still learning..." I pause. "We're *all* still learning to accept the good that's offered and believe we deserve it, to not question the motives behind it or be afraid that it'll end just as quickly as we got it." I give her a sad smile. "He needed to hear those things you said, though, because even if he still doesn't believe them now, one day, he eventually will."

CHAPTER 53

It's just past midnight when Billy finally gets the bike to start, the roar of the engine echoing through the garage.

"Fuck yes!" he yells over the noise, drumming his hands against the handlebars.

I jump up from the crate I've been sitting on and run over to him. "You did it!" I squeal as he grabs my face and pulls me in for a kiss.

He cuts off the engine and stands.

"You actually fucking did it," Jameson says with a hint of disbelief.

"Told you I was gonna do it!" Billy grins.

Jameson holds out a hand that Billy grabs, and they pull each other into one of those bro hugs, Jameson slapping him on the back. "I knew you would."

Sam snorts. "I didn't. That thing looked like a complete piece of shit when you first showed it to us."

Billy feigns offense, gasping and pressing a hand to his chest. "Don't talk about her like that."

I arch a brow. "*Her*?"

"Yeah, her," he says, tipping his chin toward the motorcycle. "All bikes are a she."

This time, it's me who snorts. "What—do you name it, too?"

"'Course I do."

"What? Really? I was joking." I look between him and the bike. "What's its ...? I mean, what's *her* name?"

"I haven't decided yet."

"Take her for a ride," Sam says.

I thought the "her" Sam was talking about was the bike until Billy looks at me and says, "Well, get on."

"What?" I stammer, watching how easily he settles onto it. "I don't have a helmet or anything. Don't you need a helmet?"

He drops his eyes down my body, and it's only then that I realize I'm anxiously shifting from foot to foot. I can tell he's trying not to laugh.

"I'll stay in the parking lot and be real safe, okay? We'll get you a helmet before we do anything crazy."

"I don't ever want to do anything crazy," I blurt out.

"You sure?" Sam asks, her tone teasing. "All the best ideas are the crazy ones."

Billy laughs. "Of course you'd say that."

She flips him off with a smile on her face before he turns back to me.

"We won't do anything crazy. I promise. Just get on."

I walk over to him, but stop short. "I—"

"If you don't like it at any time, you just tap my thigh, and I'll stop."

I bite my lip, still hesitating.

"But I think you're gonna like it," he adds.

"You do?"

"Mmhmm," he answers, his voice a low rumble. "You trust me?" he asks.

"Of course I do."

"Then get on the back of the bike, baby."

I step forward. "Okay."

A grin spreads across his face. "Okay?"

"Yeah, okay," I tell him, my stomach flipping. Then I swing my leg over the bike, holding onto his shoulder so I don't lose my balance.

"Move closer to me," he says.

I scooch in toward him.

"Closer."

I move until I'm flush against his back, wrapping my arms around his middle.

"Hold on tight ... here," he says, running his hand along my arm. "And here," he adds, pulling my thigh against him. "Got it?"

I nod against his back.

Suddenly, the bike comes to life under us, and I instinctively tighten my grip around his waist.

He pulls out into the parking lot, and I feel the warm wind against my face. We round the back of the garage, which opens into a wide lot where they keep the cars they're working on. He drives up and down the length of it, and with each pass, I relax a little more against him.

We drive for long enough that it feels unfamiliar when the low rumble of the bike is replaced with a still quiet. Billy tells me how to get off the bike, and then he follows after me.

He steps into my space, looking down at me. "So?"

"I get it."

He tips my chin up with his finger. "Yeah?"

"Yeah, I loved it."

His face lights up. "I said you would."

"Another assumption you got right." I pause. "Sometimes it feels like you know me even better than I know myself." I step in closer to him. "Thank you for pushing me."

He brushes a hand down my body, settling on my hip.

"You make me feel like I'm awake, like the world around me is alive," I whisper. "I didn't know it could feel like that."

He closes his eyes, taking in my words, and before they've even opened, his lips are crashing against mine. He pulls me up with the arm that's snaked behind my waist, and my legs find their place around his body. I didn't even realize we were moving until he sets me down on the seat of the bike.

I trail my eyes up and find him staring down, watching me like I'm the most precious thing he's ever seen.

"Loving you has been the best thing that's ever happened to me," he says, his voice full of conviction. "*You're* the best thing that's ever happened to me."

I don't have time to respond because his lips are already back on mine. We fall into that easy rhythm, like we know exactly what to take from each other. Then he breaks away, trailing kisses up my neck, and I feel his breath against my ear as his words wrap around my heart.

"Your love gives me life."

"You—" I start but look over his shoulder when a horn blares in the distance.

Jameson leans out of the truck's driver's side window and yells, "Time to go."

Billy reaches out a hand to help me off the bike. "Seriously, the worst timing," he says under his breath. He throws his arm around my shoulders, pulling me into him. "I'll make it up to you when we get home."

My cheeks warm from his promise as he guides me back to the truck.

Once we've slid into our seats, Sam looks back at me and smirks.

"What?" I ask.

"Nothing," she says, holding back a laugh.

"Come on. What?"

"I was just thinking about what the girl I met at the food bank would have thought about seeing you now, propped up on the back of someone like Billy's bike in the middle of the night, about to be f—"

"Oh my God, stop," I cut her off. "We were not about to—"

Her laugh breaks free, and it comes out louder than it should. It's then that I realize she isn't sober.

She seemed fine when Billy and I left.

He must notice it, too, because his eyes find Jameson's in the rearview mirror, the look on his face holding a question. But Jameson only shakes his head and shifts the car into drive, focusing his attention on the road.

"I'd want to get out of that stuck-up life, too, if I were you," she mutters. "No wonder she had to try so hard to get you to come back."

Billy goes rigid, and I feel him slowly turn toward me. "What's she talking about?" he asks, his voice unnervingly calm.

Sam's hand flies to her mouth. "Oh, shit. Sorry, I forgot." She hunches over and puts her index finger in front of her lips. "Shh," she says, like the two of us are sharing a secret, even though she just blew that secret up in my face.

"Jesus, Sam," Jameson hisses, shaking his head.

"What's your problem?" she snaps back defensively.

Billy's voice drowns her out, his question sounding more frantic this time. "What's she talking about?"

"She ..." I try to think of the right words.

"Just tell me," he says.

I sigh. "My mom called."

"She always calls. You never answer."

"I answered this time."

He runs his fingers through his hair. "Why?"

"Why what?"

"Why'd you answer?"

"I had to at some point."

"When?" he asks.

"Huh?"

"When. Did. She. Call?" He drags out each word, his tone growing harsher.

"Why does that matter?"

He scoffs. "Why are you answering all my questions with questions?"

"I'm not."

"Then tell me when she called."

I throw my hands up. "I don't know, like maybe three weeks ago."

He flinches. "*Three weeks ago?*" He glances between us all. "And what—you all knew?"

Sam and Jameson stay quiet.

"You're making this a way bigger deal than it is, Billy. Sam was in the room when she called, that's it. I didn't tell Jameson, either." I reach out to grab his hand, but he snatches it back.

I stare down at the hand he just pulled away then drag my gaze up to his face. His expression is completely empty.

The truck comes to a stop, and I drift my eyes past him, realizing we're already home.

His voice cracks. "Why didn't you tell me?"

"I didn't want to upset you."

"Right, 'cause it's better for you if you're already gone when I find out. Easier that way."

Without thinking, I shift closer to him. "What are you talking about?"

"I fucking knew this would happen," he says to himself, nodding like he can't control the movement.

It's like he can't figure out how he's supposed to react, what he's supposed to do.

"I fucking knew this would happen," he repeats over and over again, beginning to rock as he pulls at his hair.

He's losing it.

"I'm not leaving, Billy," I tell him, but it's like he doesn't even hear me.

I reach for him, trying to get him to stop, afraid he's going to hurt himself.

"Don't touch me," he says, pulling away from me. "I don't want you to fucking touch me."

I choke out his name, but he keeps going.

"I told you I didn't want you to love me. I told you, and you did it, anyway." He opens the door and staggers out.

Jameson quickly rounds the truck to meet him.

I stare at them, trying to wrap my head around how fast things escalated.

Jameson's saying something to him that I can't hear. He only gets a few words in before Billy is pushing him back and pointing at him.

Billy starts to walk away, and Jameson turns from him, jogging over to the car. He grabs my hand and places the keys in my palm, closing my fist over them. "Go inside, and I'll bring him in soon," he says, his tone leaving no room for argument. But I don't care.

I start to shake my head. "No, I have to talk to him. I have to explain that I'm not leaving. He thinks I'm leaving him."

Jameson looks over his shoulder, checking in on Billy, before looking back at me. He brings his hands down on my shoulders, steadying me. "You will, okay? He just needs a minute to cool down; trust me."

He wipes a tear away from my cheek.

When did I start crying?

"It's all going to be okay," he tells me, sounding entirely sure.

The strength in his voice calms my nerves, but I still ask, "How do you know?"

"Because," Jameson says, "he's just scared."

I shake my head. "How is that a good thing?"

"It means he cares."

Another tear falls down my face.

"You're the first girl he's ever let in," Jameson mutters. "He keeps up a bigger wall than people think. This"—he motions to me—"trusting people doesn't come easy to him."

"I know," I whisper.

"That doubt he has might take a long time to go away."

I look past him, finding Billy pacing down the street. "Then I'll keep reminding him that I'm here until it finally does."

CHAPTER 54

I watch Jameson trail after Billy as I walk to the apartment. I fumble with the key, trying to get it into the lock, Sam stumbling up behind me. Finally, I get the door open and drop down onto the bed, looking across the room to see Sam still standing in the doorway.

"How could you do that?" I ask her, my voice breaking.

She only stares back at me, her eyes glazed.

I hesitate. "Did something happen?"

"I'm not supposed to call anymore," she says.

"What? Who are you not supposed to call?"

"I've been calling Cathleen." She shrugs. "But she never answers." She sits beside me on the bed, twisting the ring she always plays with when she's upset. "She answered tonight."

I begin to put it together.

"He must have found out I've been calling."

"Your dad?"

She nods. "He must have made her say those things. There's …" She gets up and begins pacing. "There's no way she'd say those things unless he made her."

"What'd she say?" I ask, softly.

"Doesn't matter." She shakes her head. "I'm just gonna forget it."

"I don't think—"

"Yeah," she says to herself. "That's what I'm gonna do. I'm just gonna forget it."

"Sam—"

"I'm sorry, though, okay? She turns toward me, cutting me off. "For what I said … I didn't mean to." Her arms are wrapped around her body, and her eyes are pleading, begging me to forgive her. "Please don't hate me," she croaks out. "I really, really don't want you to hate me."

I pull my head back. "I don't hate you."

She stops pacing. "You don't?"

"No," I tell her.

Just then, the door opens, and Jameson walks through.

I stand, looking behind him, searching for Billy. I let go of a breath when I see him walk into the room, his eyes going right to me.

Jameson takes Sam's hand and leads her into the bedroom as Billy comes in and sits on the bed.

"I'm not leaving," I whisper, but it's like he doesn't even hear me.

Instead, he asks, "What'd your mother say to you?"

I shake my head. "It's not important."

"Why won't you tell me?" It doesn't sound accusatory this time, but like a genuine question.

"Because it doesn't change my decision."

"Please, I want to know." He shifts to look at me. "I *need* to know."

I swallow. "She said that was my last chance to come home, and if I said no, then it was over."

"*Over?*"

"Their financial support, college"—I take a breath—"my relationship with them."

His eyes go wide. "They can't make you choose like that."

"Well, they did. And like I said, it doesn't change my decision."

"Maybe it should," he says softly enough that I convince myself I must have heard him wrong.

"What did you say?"

"Maybe it should," he repeats, louder this time.

"Why would you even say that?" Panic starts to spread through me, threatening to swallow me whole. *Does he want me to go home?*

He throws his hands up. "Think about it, Susan. Think about all you're giving up."

"I did think about it," I answer, barely keeping my voice below shouting.

"I don't want to be the reason you lose your family."

"You're not. *My parents* are the reason I'm losing my family."

"What if, years from now, you resent me? I don't want you to look back and feel like you never had an out."

The words sting. "*An out?*"

He stands, dragging his hands down his face. "Fuck, I don't know. I'm just trying to do the right thing. I just want you to be happy."

"Do you want me to stay?"

He stops and looks at me. "It's more complicated—"

"It's a simple yes or no question, Billy," I cut in, throwing the words he always says to me back at him. "Do you want me to stay?" I ask again.

"Yes, of course, yes," he fumbles, like he can't get the response out fast enough.

I catch my breath on a sob, feeling a tear roll down my face. Then I walk over to where he's standing and look up at him. "Now, ask me."

He's quiet for a moment before he says, "Do you really want to stay?"

I don't even hesitate. "Yes. I told you I'm not leaving, Billy, and I mean it. Of course, yes."

"Yes?" he asks, and the word sounds like hope.

I nod right as he pulls me into his arms, twirling me around like a scene in a cheesy movie, peppering kisses all over my face. I giggle as he spins us, relaxing into his hold.

"Yes," he repeats between kisses, like he wants to remind himself that it's real.

Finally, he sets me down. "About what I said—"

"It's okay—"

"No, babe, listen. I know I overreacted, and I know you understand why I did."

I nod.

"But I want you to know one thing. When I said I don't want you to love me"—he runs a hand through his hair—"I didn't mean it. More than anything, I want you to love me."

I bite my lip, holding back the feelings that are swelling inside me.

"And I want to love you." He slides his hand along my cheek. "I want to love you the way you deserve to be loved, and I promise that every day you let me, I'll give you everything I have. I might not ..." He blows out a breath. "I might not always be perfect or know what to do, I can't promise that I won't ever lose it again like I just did, but I'll always try. For you, I will always try."

Another tear falls down my cheek, and he wipes it away.

"So many times in my life, choices have been made for me. Or I did things just because it was what was expected of me," I say. "But now that the choice for what comes next is truly mine, I didn't make the decision lightly. I'll tell you as many times as it takes for you to believe me because this"—I wave my hand around the apartment—"this is what I want. *You* are what I want. And no choice has ever been easier. Nothing has ever felt more clear or more right than saying yes to this life, than saying yes to you." I gaze up at him. "So, I'll try, too. For you, for us, I'll always try."

EPILOGUE

I NEVER ONCE REGRETTED saying yes.

Thank You For Reading!

If you enjoyed the book, please consider leaving a review! They're like gold, especially to indie authors. Your review can help other readers find the book and hopefully connect to these characters.

WANT MORE?

Visit laurenmonicawrites.com and join my newsletter to read a bonus chapter from Billy's POV!

What's Next?

Sam and Jameson's story is coming soon! Join my newsletter or follow me on socials @laurenmonicawrites for updates.

ACKNOWLEDGEMENTS

I've had a version of this story in my head since I was maybe thirteen years old. Now, just over thirteen years later, it's finally out in the world! To say this is a surreal feeling is truly an understatement. These characters have been a part of me for so long that, in a way, it feels like they're mine. But now, I hand them over to you and hope they've given you even a fraction of what they've given me.

To my mom – From the bottom of my heart, thank you. Thank you for always believing in me and making me feel like I can accomplish whatever I set my mind to. Thank you for loving these characters, spending countless hours talking through the plot with me, and eagerly reading every chapter as soon as I finished writing it. This process has been long, and many times I wanted to throw in the towel, but your encouragement kept me going. In life, your encouragement has always kept me going. This book is for you. I love you like one hundred!

To Dave – Thank you for always being there for me and proving that family doesn't have to be blood. Your family is who you choose, and I would choose you to be my dad every day.

To Ashley – One of the biggest gifts in my life is getting you as my sister. I'm forever grateful for the joy and love you bring into my life. Thank you for all of your suggestions about the book. It wouldn't be the story it is without you.

To Tasha – Thank you for showing me what real friendship looks like. Over the last twenty years, you've become more than just my best friend, but truly family. I can't imagine doing life without you.

To Auntie Donna – Thank you for your overwhelming support in my writing. Your kind feedback and enthusiasm has been so wonderful during this experience.

To Kate – Thank you for creating such a beautiful cover illustration and making my vision a reality.

To Angelee – Thank you for helping me design the cover of my dreams.

To Brittani, Alex, and Kristin – Thank you for all of your suggestions, tweaks, and fixes on this story. You helped me create the best version of this book.

To myself – You finally wrote the book! I'm so proud of you! Now, let's go do it again.

ALSO BY LAUREN MONICA

What I Would Have Told You – A Poetry Collection

About the Author

Lauren Monica is a writer and poet who lives in Austin, Texas. When not writing or getting lost in her ever-growing TBR, she loves to spend time with family, cuddle her two kitties, cheer on the Texas Longhorns (Hook 'Em), and go to concerts.

Website: laurenmonicawrites.com
Instagram: @laurenmonicawrites
TikTok: @laurenmonicawrites

www.ingramcontent.com/pod-product-compliance
Lightning Source LLC
Chambersburg PA
CBHW030105310726
48970CB00004B/1156